D0010971

Eason
Eason, Lynette
No place to hide : a novel

WITHDRAWN          $14.99
                  ocn899265758
                  05/27/2015

# NO PLACE TO HIDE

## Books by Lynette Eason

### WOMEN OF JUSTICE

### DEADLY REUNIONS

### HIDDEN IDENTITY

# NO PLACE TO HIDE

A NOVEL

## LYNETTE EASON

Revell

*a division of Baker Publishing Group*
Grand Rapids, Michigan

© 2015 by Lynette Eason

Published by Revell
a division of Baker Publishing Group
P.O. Box 6287, Grand Rapids, MI 49516-6287
www.revellbooks.com

Printed in the United States of America

All rights reserved. No part of this publication may be reproduced, stored in a retrieval system, or transmitted in any form or by any means—for example, electronic, photocopy, recording—without the prior written permission of the publisher. The only exception is brief quotations in printed reviews.

Library of Congress Cataloging-in-Publication Data
Eason, Lynette.
    No place to hide : a novel / Lynette Eason.
        pages ; cm. — (Hidden identity ; book 3)
    ISBN 978-0-8007-2210-4 (softcover)
        1. Terrorism investigation—Fiction. 2. Terrorism—Prevention—Fiction. 3. Man-woman relationships—Fiction. I. Title.
    PS3605.A79N63 2015
    813'.6—dc23                                                    2014049450

Scripture used in this book, whether quoted or paraphrased by the characters, is from the Holy Bible, New International Version®. NIV®. Copyright © 1973, 1978, 1984, 2011 by Biblica, Inc.™ Used by permission of Zondervan. All rights reserved worldwide. www.zondervan.com

This book is a work of fiction. Names, characters, places, and incidents are the product of the author's imagination or are used fictitiously. Any resemblance to actual events, locales, or persons, living or dead, is coincidental.

Published in association with Tamela Hancock Murray, The Steve Laube Agency, 5025 N. Central Ave., #635, Phoenix, AZ 85012

15  16  17  18  19  20  21      7  6  5  4  3  2  1

Dedicated to my family
and to my Lord and Savior Jesus Christ.

# PROLOGUE

"It's time," the voice said. "Remember what we told you."

CDC employee Anwar Goff wanted to rip the small piece from his ear and stomp it into oblivion. But his tormentors had been very clear about what would happen if he did so. "If at any time we can't hear you, they will die. Ask for help, they will die. Write a message, they will die. Use your phone, they will die. Am I clear?" So Anwar left the earpiece alone and slipped from the bathroom. His footsteps echoed on the tile flooring as he walked down the empty hall.

CDC Building 18 had shut down about an hour ago. Anwar moved with slow strides that all too quickly ate up the distance between the bathroom and the Biosafety Level 4 lab. Sweat threatened to drip into his eyes and he drew his left arm across his forehead.

With shaking fingers, he swiped the key card and the first set of doors opened, then closed behind him. For a moment, he just stood there, trembling. "God, help me," he whispered, then moved once again.

"God can't help you. Only I can," the voice whispered, then gave a brusque laugh. Evil clung to the words and Anwar clamped his lips shut.

Once inside the changing area, he set his briefcase on the bench next to the lockers and drew in a deep breath. He couldn't help the stifled sob that slipped from him as he opened the third locker from the left.

*Don't think, just do it.* Within seconds he was in protective clothing complete with mask, gloves, and gown.

Next, he rolled the combination on the briefcase to unlock it. With short, faltering steps, Anwar left the changing room and approached the next set of doors. He swiped his card again. The doors opened with a soft whoosh and he stepped into the BSL-4 lab.

His target lay in the locked freezer just ahead. Muttering another prayer, he crossed the room, opened the freezer door, and found what he'd come for. He paused and swallowed hard as he simply stared, feeling paralyzed. Helpless. For the past seven years, he'd worked his way up the ranks of the CDC, gaining the confidence of his superiors. And now all of his hard work had brought him to this.

"We're waiting. Your family is waiting."

He thought of his wife and two teenage children. With another deep breath, he reached into the freezer. Carefully, he transferred the tray that held the one-inch-long plastic vials topped with the plastic screw caps. The vials sat in seven little white cardboard boxes. One by one, he removed the boxes and placed them in the black case. There they would be kept frozen by the dry ice during transport.

Anwar snapped the briefcase closed and rolled the combination to lock it.

He'd done it. He'd really done it. Tremors raced through him as he glanced at the clock on the wall. He had very few minutes to spare, but he wasn't quite sure his legs would be able to carry him back through the two sets of doors. He didn't move. Couldn't. He simply couldn't do this. "I can't do this," he whispered.

"But you will."

Yes. He would.

So this is how he would go down, how he would be remembered. *Don't do it!* But the faces of his children, his wife rose up before him. He squared his shoulders and tightened his grip on the bag.

He left the lab, not looking back, not thinking about all of the people who would soon die. He was only thinking of the three people he was trying to save. With hurried, erratic movements, he entered the lobby and waved to the security guard who barely looked up from the computer. "Night, Anwar. See you next week."

Anwar didn't answer, just strode through the glass doors and out into the night. He shivered as the wind cut through his heavy coat. Even Atlanta had its fair share of cold weather.

For a moment Anwar hesitated. If he went left—

"Why aren't you moving, Mr. Goff?"

Anwar jerked. They were watching him. He moved to his car and climbed in. He placed the briefcase on the seat beside him. Just earlier that day, his wife had sat in that spot and they'd talked about their plans for Thanksgiving. His parents were coming, but hers couldn't make it. With a tight throat and tears in his eyes, he cranked the car and pulled from the curb.

# 1

SUNDAY, NOVEMBER 22
9:00 P.M.
NORTHEAST ATLANTA SUBURB

One down, one to go. Breaking into houses had never been on her top ten list of things to do with her weekend, so when she found herself picking the deadbolt on Ian Lockwood's two-story home this chilly November evening, Jackie Sellers had a hard time ignoring the adrenaline rushing through her veins.

Finally. The soft snick on lock number two told her she'd done it. A thrill shot through her. Lock-picking had been one skill that she'd worked hard on, but wasn't very good at. Not that she used it that often. But occasionally it came in handy.

Like now.

Shoving aside the self-congratulations, she twisted the knob, placed her fingertips on the wood, and slowly pushed. The door opened inward without a sound.

Apple spice and cinnamon air freshener greeted her. Jackie slipped inside and shut the door behind her carefully. Softly.

The house was quiet. Silent. Yet she could almost feel the tension surrounding her. Which was silly. Houses didn't have

11

tension. Only the people in them. She took note of the layout. Stairs straight ahead. Kitchen to the right.

A cologne she couldn't identify tickled her nose. A sound to her left. She stiffened, turning her head a fraction in order to probe the darkness. With only a sliver of a moon in the sky and the blinds closed on every window, the black in the house was deep, broken only by the small nightlight in the foyer. To her left, she could make out the shadows of the furniture in the den. The rectangular windows on either side of the fireplace.

She listened. Where had the noise come from? Definitely to her left.

Her heart pounded. Should she call out and identify herself? Make the first move in an attack? Or just wait? The air shifted and she moved.

A lamp crashed into the wall where she'd been standing a split second ago.

Movement in front of her.

Coming straight at her.

No time to dodge it. She dove for the dark shape and slammed against a rock solid chest.

A grunt.

They both went to the floor. Her right hip connected with the hard wood. Pain shot through her and she gasped.

She rolled and he lunged after her. His hard breaths came just inches from her face and his hands clamped down on her upper arms.

Instinct, training, and fear combined to give her the strength to break his hold and lash out with the palm of her hand. She aimed for his nose, hoping to drive it into his head. Instead, she thought she caught his chin.

"Ah!" His hold broke and she rolled to her feet. He did the

12

same and moved fast. She caught a blow to the stomach and went back to her knees.

A hard fist landed on her shoulder and she couldn't stop the cry from escaping her lips.

She struggled for breath even as she searched for the front door. He was strong and knew the layout. She was hurting and couldn't see.

Time to run.

She rose to her feet and whirled for the exit as he moved in for another hit. She ducked and spun. His fist whistled past her nose, and she knew if he managed to connect with her face, she was down for the count. She tripped and went down, her knee kissing the floor with a hard thud. She cried out and rolled, scrambled up and to the door. Her fingers wrapped around the knob.

"Oh no you don't," he barked.

A hand grasped her shoulder and gave a hard jerk. She went down again, this time slamming her elbow against the floor. Pain shot through her arm.

But she'd recognized the voice. "Ian? Stop!" she gasped. "Stop."

A low growl to her left. Nails clicked on the hardwoods. Jackie froze.

"Off, Gus." His hand flexed. Released.

Her stomach hurt, her shoulder, knee, and elbow throbbed. She fought to catch her breath. Her weapon still rested in the holster under her left arm.

"Who are you?" he demanded in a low voice.

"Jackie . . . Sellers." She needed a minute. He had a hard punch. Her stomach cramped and nausea swept through her. She thought she could take care of herself just fine, but he had some wicked-good fighting skills.

Silence. "Jackie?"

She heard his shock. "Yes. Can we turn on a light?"

"No." The sharp whisper stilled her movement toward the light switch.

"Why not?"

"Because they're watching the house."

"Who?"

"The people who want to kill me."

---

Ian Lockwood rolled to his feet in one smooth move. He pulled Jackie to hers. "Gus, heel." The dog moved from the shadows and sat at Ian's left side.

"Who wants to kill you?" she asked.

A sound came from the second floor. They both stilled. "Whoever's upstairs." His hand gripped hers and he pulled her toward the kitchen. Gus followed, a silent, obedient shadow.

A dark silhouette at the kitchen door stopped them cold. "Okay, this isn't good," he whispered.

"This way." She gave his fingers a tug and he followed her back into the foyer, then into the den. She went straight to the window next to the fireplace. "Stand on that side of the window." She pointed and he obeyed her instruction, not quite sure what she had planned, but figuring it was better than what he had.

Which was nothing.

She used one finger to nudge aside the curtain and barely part the blind to enable her to look out of the window. For a good ten seconds, she just stood there, silent, watchful. Ian kept his ear tuned toward the kitchen, expecting to hear the door open at any moment.

The floor creaked again, this time closer to the stairs that would lead straight down to them. Ian thought his heart might very well explode.

In one smooth move, she moved to the French doors and pushed one open. Cold air rushed in. She motioned to him and he didn't hesitate. He slid through the opening and she followed.

"Gus, come," he whispered. The dog bolted out and took up position next to him.

Jackie shut the door with a quiet click.

He snagged her fingers and started to lead her, then realized he didn't know where he was going. "What are we doing?" he whispered.

"Getting out of here."

"How? My car's in the garage."

She led him across the street and they slipped behind a large oak tree. Gus nudged up against Ian's knee and he rested a hand on the animal's head.

"There," she said, her voice so low he had to lean close to hear it. "See that car down the street about three houses?"

"Yes. The one with the two guys in the front seat?"

"That's my vehicle."

"Uh oh."

"Exactly." She drew in a deep breath. "How many did you count?"

"At least four."

"That's what I got too. I'm hoping they think we're still in the house."

"They might, but it won't be long before they figure out we're not." The dog shifted and Ian whispered a command. Gus went still.

"So, two inside and two working on my car."

"What are you thinking?"

"That I know where to get a vehicle. Then we're getting out of here and finding a nice safe place to call the cops."

Ian jerked. "No cops."

"We'll talk about it on the way to safety. They've left their car running."

"So you want to take it?"

"We're going to have to. As soon as they notice us gone, they'll be canvassing the neighborhood and the streets leading from it. I don't know what kind of manpower they have."

"A lot. Trust me on that one. They've already tried to kill me once."

"Then I guess that's our answer."

He could feel the tension radiating from her. He placed a hand on her back. Tightly coiled springs rippled under his palm.

"Now," she whispered.

She darted from behind the tree and jogged to the dark sedan parked in front of his next-door neighbor's house. She grabbed the driver's door and flung it open.

A shout reached his ears. They'd been discovered.

Jackie dove into the driver's seat. "Get in!"

He didn't need her urging. Gus went first, then Ian threw himself into the passenger seat as the first shot slammed into the door behind him. She had the car in drive before he had the door shut. "If they hit a tire, we're done for."

She swerved back and forth as two more bullets hit the vehicle. Gus barked from the backseat. "Down!" Ian ordered. He and the dog dropped.

Then they were around the corner and at the subdivision entrance. Jackie didn't bother to stop at the sign, she shot out and into the far right lane of the four-lane road.

Ian kept his eyes on the side mirrors. "If they try to follow us, they'll have to find another vehicle."

"Or radio for one of their buddies to pick us up."

"Oh. Right." He fell silent.

She hooked a left and glanced in the rearview mirror. Seeing nothing so far, she loosened her grip only slightly. "So . . . what have you been up to for the past fifteen years and why is your face splashed all over the news with the words 'Possible Terrorist' written beneath it?"

**2**

Jackie white-knuckled the steering wheel and headed toward the police station. In spite of the light question, dark and grim gripped her. She pulled the black hat from her head and yanked the hair tie from her ponytail.

"Where are we going?" Ian asked.

"I told you. To the cops."

He stiffened. "Then let me out here." He reached for the door handle.

"Are you crazy?" She tapped the brake, then released it. "I'm not letting you out of here, they'll be on you within minutes. Maybe seconds."

"I'd rather take my chances with them than a jail cell. Which is where I'll sit until someone manages to kill me there. If I want to live and prove I'm innocent, I have to run. I didn't steal anything from Wainwright Labs." He shook his head and clenched a fist. "They're saying I'm a terrorist, Jackie."

She glanced at him out of the corner of her eye. "Innocent men don't run."

A muscle jumped in his jaw. "This one does."

"I saw your face on the news and I couldn't believe it."

"Is that why you tried to break into my house tonight?"

"Yes. And please note, I did knock first. I even pounded and called your name."

"I heard the pounding and the calling. Sort of. I couldn't tell what you were saying."

"You thought I was the bad guys?"

"Yes."

"Why didn't Gus bark?"

"I told him not to. I didn't want anyone to know he was inside. They would have shot him without hesitation."

She rubbed her sore belly and stretched her bruised shoulder. "You've picked up some fighting skills since we last saw each other."

"I got tired of being bullied. One day, I said, no more. I signed up to learn how to defend myself. Tae Kwon Do took my mind off of . . . things . . . and gave me self-confidence."

Gave him some muscles too. Yeah, she'd noticed.

"You've picked up a few yourself."

She blinked. "Huh?" Muscles?

"Fighting skills."

"Oh. Yeah. In my line of work they come in handy occasionally."

He turned to scan the area behind him. "I don't see any headlights. At least not any that are too close. What exactly is your line of work? I thought you were a cop."

"I was." She glanced in the rearview mirror and tested her sore elbow. Bruised and battered, but nothing broken, thank goodness. "Doesn't mean they're not back there," she said in response to his statement that he didn't see anything.

"Let me out if you're going to the cops. At least give me a head start."

"What are you going to do on your own? The cops aren't stupid. They'll find you eventually." Jackie made a left turn, then a right. She stayed on the back roads hoping the men they were running from would assume she would hit the highway.

"I don't know what I'm going to do. So far I've just been winging it. I need to be able to slow down and think, but I've been dodging them since I left work yesterday."

"What do you mean?"

"One minute I'm walking to my car after work, and the next thing I know, someone's trying to run me down. I managed to avoid getting hit, got in my car, and took off. I called the cops and they started talking to me like I was a fugitive who needed to turn himself in. So no. No cops. Not until I figure out what's going on and why I'm a wanted man all of a sudden."

"All right, no cops. Yet." She tapped the steering wheel as she thought. She really didn't like the idea of harboring a fugitive. It was stupid and wasn't a place she thought she'd ever find herself in. But this was Ian. "I work for an organization called Operation Refuge." She tightened her fingers around the steering wheel and thought fast. "We'll go there, sit down and talk, and work out a plan."

"Operation Refuge? What is that? How many people are there?"

"At this time of night? No one probably. But we can rest up and jump in with a plan first thing in the morning. And ironically enough, Operation Refuge is an organization that helps people who can't help themselves."

He snorted. "I can help myself." A pause. "But I don't think I'd mind some outside help."

Silence descended for another tense moment as she kept one eye on the road in front of her and one eye on the rear.

"Those guys were going through your car. Is Operation Refuge's address on anything?" he asked.

Jackie snapped her lips together and thought. "No. But my home address is on the registration. If they go there and start searching my house, they may find something related to Operation Refuge."

"I've never heard of it."

"It's not a secret organization, but we don't advertise either except for a website that will show up in your search engine if you type in certain phrases." She sighed and reached for her phone. "I'll call David and tell him what's going on."

He snatched the phone from her fingers and she jerked the wheel. His head smacked the window and he winced.

"What are you doing?" she demanded.

He powered down the phone. "If they know who you are, they can trace you through your phone."

"I realize that," she snapped.

"Then we can't go to your office or contact anyone related to it. Don't you have somewhere else we can go? Please, Jackie, you came looking for me for a reason. Won't you at least help me find a safe place and hear me out?"

Jackie glanced at the man who'd once been her childhood best friend. With the potential to be more. Until her life had fallen apart and she'd had to leave him. She sighed. "Fine. We'll talk. I've just got to figure out where to go to do it."

"What about your grandfather's place in Virginia? Is he still there?"

Jackie jerked, then shot him a look of disbelief. "You remember that place?"

"Of course. It was all you talked about that fall after spending all summer there. Then you went to live there permanently—" He looked away and swallowed hard. "Anyway, I remember it."

She bit her lip. Her parents had been going through one of their many times of "on again–off again." When her father had shoved her mother against the wall and threatened to kill her, Jackie had jumped on his back. He shook her off like a rag doll, then punched her hard enough to break her nose. As a result, she took it upon herself to hitchhike to the Appalachian mountains in western Virginia so she didn't have to listen to them argue—or worry about being beat up.

Her grandfather was stunned when she'd shown up on his doorstep, then welcomed her with a warm hug, buckets of hot chocolate, and a visit to the ER to get her nose set.

He made three phone calls. One to her parents to let them know she wouldn't be coming home. The second one to his lawyer. And the third to Child Protective Services who promptly investigated and placed her in her grandfather's custody.

Her mother took off shortly after that, and Jackie and her father managed to come to a peaceful understanding. As long as he left her alone and let her live with her grandfather, she wouldn't cause him any trouble—or press any charges for the broken nose.

Three years later, her grandfather was dead of a massive heart attack and she was on her own at the age of nineteen. Her uncle, one of the only three people in the world that she loved, had been deployed somewhere overseas, and she was under strict orders not to reveal his identity or that they were related.

The other two were Ian and his cousin, Holly. Jackie wasn't sure about showing back up in their lives after her rather dramatic exit, so she'd focused her attention on building a life for herself. Thank God for the police academy.

She took the next three left turns and headed for the interstate, arguing with herself the entire time. "I *really* should go to the police."

"You know me, Jackie."

"I haven't seen you in fifteen years. The occasional Facebook status update doesn't count." She pulled onto the highway and moved over into the left lane.

"But you *know* me. You know I'd never do what they're accusing me of."

She sighed. "My grandfather's cabin is a six-hour drive, Ian."

"Please. I need to get out of here, go somewhere safe. That's your job, right? To keep people safe?"

Jackie didn't answer at first. Her brain spun with what she should do. Like go to the cops. She was harboring a fugitive. "My job is to uphold the law. But . . ." A sigh slipped out. "Tighten your seat belt and start talking. Looks like we're going to have plenty of time."

Just as Ian opened his mouth, the first bullet shattered the back window.

---

Ian ducked. Glass flew. He felt the sting of the shards hitting the back of his head. Gus whined.

Jackie spun the wheel and did a one-eighty in the middle of the highway. He heard her yell as she punched the gas. The sedan shot forward. Tires screeched, horns blared. Headlights blinded him. "You're going the wrong way!"

"Just for a minute." She moved over as far as she could go without dumping them into the ditch.

He held on and whispered prayers. Then he leaned forward and opened the glove compartment. Nothing. He slammed it shut.

A break opened in the median. A little bridge over the ditch that led to the other side of the highway. She slammed on the brakes and the seat belt cut into Ian's shoulder.

"Give me your gun!" Ian yelled.

Jackie didn't spare him a glance as she shot across the small ramp. She spun the wheel and landed in the left-hand lane going in the right direction this time. She sped up and passed an eighteen-wheeler who laid on his horn. "Are they back there?"

Ian twisted and scanned the highway. His heart sank as he righted himself back in the seat. "Headlights approaching fast."

She reached across her torso and grabbed her weapon. She handed it to him. "Since you asked for it, I'm assuming you know how to use this?"

"I've only shot at paper targets before, but I figure if someone feels like they have the right to shoot at me, I can shoot back."

Approval glinted at him before she swung her attention back to driving. "How are they staying with us like this?" she muttered.

"It's like they came out of nowhere back there."

"Still won't let me call my friends?"

He caught her watching the rearview mirror. "No. How are we going to lose them?"

She tapped her fingers and scooted into the next lane. "Hold on." Then she pressed the brake and slowed.

"What are you doing?"

"Letting them catch up."

"What? Why?"

She didn't have a chance to answer. The headlights from behind illuminated the interior of the sedan like someone flipped on the overhead.

Jackie didn't seem to care. She drove with slow, careful precision. "Hold on tight and be ready to duck if the bullets start flying again."

Just past the off ramp to the next exit, she slammed on the brakes and yanked the wheel to the right. The car behind them shot past as Jackie stomped the gas pedal and roared across the shoulder and up the exit ramp. She slowed for the light. Turned left, then made the first right into the nearest gas station. She pulled around and parked in a dark corner. "Let's go," she said as she unbuckled her seat belt.

He mimicked her actions, but couldn't help wondering if she'd lost her mind. "Why?"

"I don't know this car. They may have some sort of tracker on it."

Understanding clicked. He threw the passenger door open and climbed out. Gus bounded after him. Together, the trio made their way around the side of the gas station to get out of sight of the road. He handed her the weapon and she holstered it, but he noticed she left the safety strap off.

"We need a phone. An untraceable one," she said.

"I have cash. Let's get one."

"We may not have time."

"No sense in standing here wondering." He moved to the door and she followed. Gus stayed at his heels. Inside, he appreciated the warmth that seeped into his chilled bones even while he moved to snag a prepaid cell from the rack.

"Hey, that dog can't come in here." The clerk shoved the cash register shut and eyed Gus.

"See the orange vest? He's a service dog," Ian said and made a motion with his hand. Gus dropped to his hindquarters and his tongue lolled out as he panted and waited.

The clerk lifted a brow. "Oh. Cool."

Jackie pulled a few items from the shelf along with a pair of reading glasses, sunglasses, and two baseball caps. She handed them to him and hung back near the door.

Ian moved to the counter to pay when he looked up and saw the television playing behind the counter. The sound was off, but a ticker tape ran across the bottom of the screen.

And then Ian saw his picture take up the right-hand corner

while Jackie's flashed in the left, identifying them as persons of interest. Ian was wanted for questioning in the theft of vital information from the company he worked for. The company believed the information had been stolen with the intent to sell to enemies of the United States, and Jackie was listed as his accomplice. Somehow they'd already connected her abandoned car to him.

He froze and glanced at the clerk. When the young man showed no sign of recognition, he took a deep breath and slid his gaze over to Jackie only to find her attention locked on the television screen. She finally glanced at him and made a calming motion with her right hand. Ian sucked in a deep breath and gave her a short nod. Keeping his head lowered, he set the items on the counter and fished in his pocket for his wallet.

"That'll be forty-nine eighty-five. You want a bag?"

"Sure, thanks."

The entire transaction took less than five minutes since entering the store. It felt like an eternity.

Ian grabbed the bag and walked to the door. Gus kept pace with him. Jackie pushed open the door just as headlights turned into the parking lot. She let out a little gasp. "Rats," she whispered. She backed up into him and stumbled.

He caught her against him and held her for the split second it took to get her footing. "What now?" he whispered.

"I guess we run."

# 3

Jackie shook off the feeling of being held in Ian's arms for that brief moment. Her mind registered the sensations and she chalked it up to the high tension running through both of them. With the clerk busy with another customer, she and Ian made their way to the back of the store, Gus a silent shadow right behind them.

Within seconds they slipped out the back exit and found themselves outside near the car they'd parked. She shivered as the cold wind blew across her face, but ignored it and gazed at the landscape behind the gas station. Rocky but wooded. *Think, think.*

"They'll find the car and think we took off through the woods," he murmured. His fingers crunched the bag.

"Yeah." She pulled up the edge of her black sweatshirt and jabbed the key through the material of the thin white camisole she wore underneath. The shirt gave way and she ripped off a large chunk. "Come on."

"You've got a plan?"

"For whatever it's worth." They slipped a little ways into the trees, going the opposite direction he thought they should go. "Do you see them?" she asked.

"Not ye—uh, yeah." The car that had been following them pulled into the spot next to the beat-up sedan. She, Ian, and Gus moved further back into the trees until she could no longer see the parking area.

Car doors slammed and a voice rose. "Find them. Fan out."

Jackie hung the white cloth on the tree about waist high. "Now move left," she whispered. "Stay parallel to the parking lot." He must have understood what she had in mind. He started moving. She stayed beside him. "Go slow, as quiet as you can."

Thankfully, their pursuers weren't trying to be very quiet. "Where are they?" She heard one curse. "Hey! Victor, look here."

Victor. She made a mental note of the name. One of the others must have found the piece of cloth. She tried to listen and figure out how many of them there were, but the voices mingled. She thought three, maybe four.

"Go, go, go," another ordered. "Don't lose them."

She and Ian kept moving. If the men had been thinking, they would have realized she hadn't been wearing white when they saw her. Hopefully they wouldn't remember.

Finally, she and Ian reached the edge of the trees that ran along the side of the parking lot. The voices faded. Ian stepped out onto the asphalt and Jackie followed him. Gus stayed right next to Ian, his superb training and absolute trust in Ian clear. She looked back over her shoulder and down toward where the cars were parked. "We need a vehicle."

"Yeah. One they can't track this time."

"I'd have one within minutes if you'd let me call my friends."

"I'd rather not. I'm sorry, I just don't know who I can trust at this point."

"Even trusting me is a stretch, huh?"

He shrugged, regret stamped on his features.

"Right." She nodded toward the next building. "Let's get out of here before they figure out we've doubled back. Stay in the shadows."

He nodded, signaled Gus to follow, and led the way. Together they made their way along the back of the buildings parallel to the road. Gravel, broken glass, and other debris littered the area. Ian knelt and tapped behind his right shoulder.

The dog leapt onto his back and Ian rose with a grunt to carry his four-legged friend. His gentle consideration of the animal grabbed at her heart. There was no way he could be guilty of anything related to a terrorist act, could he? She grimaced. Just because he liked animals didn't mean he wasn't a terrorist.

They stepped gingerly, careful not to make any noise that might draw curiosity from anyone within hearing distance. "Any sign of them?" he asked, his voice low.

"No, I don't think so."

"I think I know where we can get a car."

She glanced at him. "Where?"

"My brother."

"That's not a good idea. They'll be watching him."

"Do you have a better suggestion?"

"Not at the moment." She looked around and shivered. "Does he live near here?"

"About ten miles away." He paused. "If you don't want me to call him, what about catching a cab?"

Jackie thought about that. "That's a pretty big risk. The cab driver might recognize you."

He looked around. "Let's find a place to hole up and get that cell phone working, then we can decide." He set Gus back on the ground and the dog shook himself, then sat, waiting for his next order.

Jackie shivered again. It was already below freezing. Not even her heavy sweatshirt was doing much to protect her from the wind. "Holing up sounds good." Traveling far away from the men after them and figuring out what she'd gotten herself into sounded better. But they had to come up with a plan. She thought about finding a pay phone and simply calling her co-workers. She trusted them with her life, but then Ian would decide she couldn't be trusted and strike out on his own.

And she just couldn't let him do that.

"Where?" he muttered.

"Someplace that doesn't have the news streaming on their television."

He nodded toward a shopping center. "How about the café in that bookstore?"

"All right," she looked back over her shoulder, "let's go."

They hurried down the sidewalk, crossed the street, and went into the warmth of the bookstore. Jackie finally had time to process the vest Gus wore when Ian pulled a leash from his pocket and snapped it onto the dog's collar. She'd heard Ian point out the vest to the clerk in the convenience store and wondered why Ian would have a service dog. Maybe she'd get a chance to ask soon.

The small café nestled in the corner offered a bit of privacy if they could grab the last booth on the right. "Do you see a television anywhere?"

She glanced around. "No. Let's just hope no one's watching the news on their laptops."

He slid in the seat opposite her and pulled his baseball cap lower. He slipped on the low-powered reading glasses. At Ian's signal, Gus took up residence under the table and placed his head on his paws. Ian looked at her over the top of the glasses. "You want some coffee?"

"No, I *need* some coffee." She set her back to the wall and gazed out over the store, processing it from the distance, formulating a plan. "And make it a double."

---

"Where are they?" Gunter shouted, then spewed obscenities as he realized they'd slipped away.

Nick glared. "They don't have a car, it's freezing cold out here. Where are they going to go?"

"To a hotel, where else?" Hector said. "Or maybe friends who would take them in and not call the cops on them."

"Right. To a hotel. Or friends." Gunter snorted. "That's what you idiots would do. Obviously they're smarter than you two."

Victor Stroebel stared at the men who worked for him. They'd failed him and he should shoot them all, leaving their carcasses for the rats that foraged behind the small gas station. He lit his cigarette and flicked the lighter closed. "Shut up." Though his words were quiet, they had greater effect than if he'd shouted. The other three men froze and slowly turned to look at him. If he hadn't been so irritated at the fact that Lockwood was still alive, he might have laughed at the fear he could instill by just being in their presence. They weren't used to seeing him, as he usually called the shots from behind the scenes. But this was too important. And as soon as they'd outlived their usefulness, they would die, but for now, he needed them—and their fear-induced loyalty.

He drew in a deep breath. "Priority number one. Find out everything you can about Ian Lockwood and his pretty companion, Jackie Sellers. I want to know every single teeny tiny detail about their lives. I want family names and numbers, co-workers, friends, everything. And then find me something I can use to lure them out into the open."

"Uh . . . like what, boss?" Gunter asked.

Victor simply looked at the man. "Like a kid or a relative we can snatch and hold for ransom. Or in this case, a trade. Only it won't be a trade, they all have to die."

"Right, right. I got it. Okay. We'll get right on it." The man paused and anxiety had him nearly twitching.

"What is it, Gunter?" Vic asked as though he had all the patience in the world.

"Um . . . well, should we keep looking for them?"

Idiot. Victor lifted his gun, thankful he'd already placed the suppressor on the end, and shot the man in the forehead.

The other two gaped, backing away in terror.

Victor shoved the weapon into the back of his waistband. "Where are you going?" They froze. "Get in the car." They scrambled to obey. Victor climbed in the back. "Now what have you learned tonight, boys?" Neither man volunteered an answer. "I'm waiting."

"I'll tell you what I learned, boss," Hector said, his voice not quite steady.

"What's that, son?"

"Don't ask stupid questions."

Victor smiled.

# 4

Jackie walked over to Ian, who stood in line to order. "I'll be right back."

His gaze bored into hers. "Where are you going?"

"The ladies' room." She handed him the phone still in the package. "While I'm there, could you get this thing working and charging? There's a plug right near the table."

"Okay."

"But don't make any calls yet, all right?"

Confusion knit his brows together. She could see the protest hovering on his lips.

"Just please? You're asking an awful lot of me by not going to the cops and telling them what's going on, so humor me, okay?"

He gave her a long stare. She shifted, but didn't look away. Finally he nodded and lowered his voice. "You're not going to turn me in?"

"Ian, if I was going to do that, we wouldn't be here right now." But she didn't want him making any calls until she had a plan. And while one was in the process of forming, it wasn't fully developed yet.

He sighed. "All right."

"Just don't sit where someone looking in can see you."

"Right."

She pulled her gaze away from him and took note of the layout of the store as she made her way to the ladies' room. Once inside, she kept her eyes down and head averted. One other person stood at the sink washing her hands. Jackie slipped into the nearest stall and hung the backpack on a hook. She took the baseball cap from her head and pulled her hair up into a ponytail, then threaded the mass through the opening of the ball cap.

She heard the other occupant leave. After finishing her business, she stepped out of the stall, washed her hands, then exited the restroom. With a glance around to make sure no one was watching her with any real interest, she strolled down the aisle and slipped into position near the Employees Only door. With careful deliberation, she perused the books on the nearby shelf.

It cost her about a ten-minute wait, but her patience finally paid off. She just hoped Ian was still waiting on her and hadn't decided she'd turned him in. She got the information she needed and made her way back to the booth, pulling off the backpack and sliding in opposite Ian, where he had two cups of coffee and two pizzas waiting. "Okay, I know you want to call your brother, but I don't think it's a good idea."

He stiffened. "Why not?"

"Think about it. The first people law enforcement are going to contact are your relatives, checking anyone who'd be willing to harbor a fugitive."

He went quiet and shoved his wallet back into his pocket, picked up one of the two cups of coffee he'd placed on the table, and took a sip. Jackie took note of the phone charging just like she'd asked.

She reached for the coffee. "Thanks."

"Sure."

After a big sip that burned all the way down, she placed her cup on the table and reached for one of the pizzas. "Smart."

"What?"

"Getting food while we can."

"Oh. I was just hungry and didn't want to eat in front of you."

She nodded to his pizza box. "Didn't want to share either, I take it."

He finished off his second piece in just about as many seconds. "No way."

"You always were stingy when it came to your food."

He snickered, but his mirth didn't reach his eyes. "And you were always a mooch. I learned my lesson early on to get you your own food."

Jackie finished half the pizza and pushed the box away from her. He looked at the remaining half.

"You going to eat that?"

"Now who's the mooch?" she teased. She slid the food in front of him.

He got started on her half and she got up to throw the other box away. All the while, her eyes never rested. She let them slide over the faces of the people nearest her. Then back to Ian.

He had his attention focused on the window while he chewed. His forehead creased and she couldn't help wonder if he was seeing anything other than his internal thoughts.

Standing near the trash can, Jackie stuck her hand into the pocket of her sweatshirt and wrapped her fingers around her personal cell phone. She debated. A quick call or a short text would bring help.

And probably the people tracking them. If her face was already on the evening news, she had no doubt they had the ability to ping her phone.

But that might not be a bad thing, right? Get them out in the open, have backup waiting on them, and grab them. Then again, their actions screamed power. Did she want to blatantly mess with that? Or perhaps be a bit more subtle?

Jackie tugged at the brim of her own cap and bit her lip while she studied Ian. Subtle wasn't exactly her forte. She was trained to help people, trained to fight for the underdog. Was he the underdog? Or was he playing her? Her childhood friend wouldn't, but what about the man he'd become? The man she hadn't seen in fifteen years?

While she pondered those questions, she made a slow three-sixty, thinking, watching, planning.

An idea in mind, she turned to go back to the table when she saw Ian on the phone. Her blood pressure shot up and she marched over to him. "What are you doing?" she hissed.

He turned his back to her and the others in the area and spoke in a low voice. One so low, she almost couldn't hear him. She slid back into the booth and leaned closer.

"Hey man, I know you've seen the news. I've got to keep this short. Basically, I need your car. Can you bring it to me?" He tilted his head and lifted his eyes to meet Jackie's. She saw a guilty apology there with a hint of defiance. "I know it looks bad, but if I turn myself in, I'm toast." More listening. "People are trying to kill me and the cops are trying to arrest me. I need your help." The person on the other end said something else. Ian squeezed his eyes shut and she could see his effort to keep his impatience and frustration in check. "Yes, I think I know why they're trying to kill me, I just haven't had a chance to do anything about it yet. Running for my life has kind of brought everything else to a screeching halt." He paused, then snorted. "No one's going to fight for me, but me." His eyes narrowed and his jaw tightened. "It's been that way all my life, Terry. Why would you think it's going to change now?"

Terry. Ian's brother. She wanted to groan. Instead, she pressed her lips together. He was right. She remembered the skinny, pimply-faced teenager he'd been. He'd definitely had no sense of fashion and he'd been awkward, clumsy, and shy. The bullies had honed in on him like ants on cake at a picnic. And his parents hadn't done much about it that she recalled.

He nodded. "Great. Great. Thanks." He paused and listened and Jackie felt the tension in her belly grow. "I don't want to give the address over the phone, but you remember where we used to go after working out? That's where we are." He sucked in a breath. "Thanks, Terry. And make sure no one follows you, okay?"

"He's coming?" she asked.

"He'll be here in ten."

She had a really bad feeling about this. She leaned forward. "Why did you call him without clearing that with me?"

His jaw tensed. "You're not in charge here, Jackie. You broke into my house, remember? I'm sorry you got caught in the middle, but it's time for us to part ways."

"I don't think you get it, Ian," she murmured. "Whatever *this* is, it's bigger than you. You won't beat it on your own."

He groaned. "I understand this is what you do for a living— help people. But I feel awful you're involved. I want you to go to the cops and tell them everything."

"But, Ian, you're—"

He held up a hand. "I'm serious." He swallowed hard. "I have a feeling this isn't going to end very well and I don't want to take you down with me. Terry's going to bring me his car and I'm going to leave. I'm assuming you'll call someone to pick you up. If you would make sure Terry gets home safe too, I'd appreciate it."

She stared at him, mouth open, disbelief rendering her speechless. Did he really believe it was going to go down like that? She leaned forward. *Be nice, Jackie. Don't say something you'll regret. This isn't his line of work. He doesn't do this every day. Guard your tongue*—"Don't start being stupid," she snapped.

He blinked, then anger glinted. "I'm not being stu—"

"Or a martyr then. There's no playing nice in this game." She slapped a hand to the table and tried to loosen the muscles around her jaw when she saw people stop mid-bite to stare at them. She took a deep breath and leaned back. "These people have messed with me now too. Even if I go to the cops at this point, there's no guarantee they'll believe me. I'm in this for the long haul. This thing won't end well if you don't have some help. Now let me tell you how this is going to work." She reached for the backpack. "We're leaving. Now."

He stared up at her. "Terry will be here shortly."

"No, Ian." Weariness hit her. How could she make him understand? "The cops will be here shortly. They probably listened to every word of that conversation you just had with Terry."

"How? It's an untraceable phone."

"But Terry's isn't. As soon as you became a person of interest in a terrorist plot, every immediate family member who's close by—and probably some who aren't—had their phone tapped. And while you didn't give the address of the café, all they have to do is follow him."

He went silent for a brief second, then stood. "I'm an idiot. Let's go before—"

She looked at him as she slid out of the booth.

Hands curled into fists, he had his eyes on the front door of the store. "Cops," he said.

She turned her head to see the two uniformed officers stroll in. Their body language shouted their tension. One went left, one started toward the café. "And there are probably more on the way." She grabbed his hand. "Walk toward the back of the store and lean into me like you're listening to something I'm saying."

He grabbed the bags from the floor and Gus's leash in one hand, then wrapped his free arm around her shoulder to tuck her up next to him. "And here we go again."

What had he done? He'd been stupid, that's what. He and Gus stayed right with Jackie as she weaved in and out of book aisles. He'd meant well and wound up putting them all in danger again. Not just he and Jackie, but now he'd dragged his brother into it. Ian tightened his jaw.

Time to stop being stupid.

She stopped and punched the code in for the Employees Only door and shut it behind them.

"You went to the bathroom, huh?"

She gave him a tight smile. "Yes. And on a scouting mission. For every one way in, always have two ways out."

"Nice." She was smart. And right. He needed her. He studied her. She didn't look too much different than when they were in high school. Bouncy blonde curls, blue eyes that could frost over when angry or reach into your soul when empathizing. Right now, they were hard and determined. She led him to a back room. A conference table sat in the center, surrounded by plush chairs. Another door was in the corner of the room that would lead them to the parking lot.

He pulled the phone from his pocket and dialed Terry's number.

"I didn't tell them you were here," his brother blurted after half a ring. "I'm in the parking lot. As soon as I turned in, a cruiser did too." Ian heard the man swallow. "And now they're coming toward my car. I've got to go. Get out of here if you can. I won't tell them anything, I promise."

Again Jackie had been right after all. Why wasn't he surprised? "No. Tell them everything. Be honest and hold nothing back. It's the best way to avoid getting in—" Ian realized he was talking to dead air.

He looked at Jackie. "What do you want to do?"

She pinched the bridge of her nose and he felt remorse nearly bring him to his knees.

"You know what?" he said. "I'm going back to my original plan. You shouldn't even be involved in this."

She dropped her hand and looked up. "Well, I am and I'm afraid there's no going back to any original plan. We're going with the whatever-works-do-it plan as of right now. And I need you to start thinking because I don't have one of those at the moment." She moved to the door, opened it, and looked out.

"I'm not a terrorist. I didn't betray my country. These guys set me up fast and good, but there's no reason for me to take you down too. I'll figure something out. I just know I'm not going to jail for something I didn't do."

She shut the door. "It's clear for now. Let's go."

"No. You just tell them I grabbed you and forced you to go with me. Tell them whatever it takes to stay out of trouble, but I'm not involving you anymore."

"Ian, stop being—"

"Where do you need to go? I'll take you." The soft voice to his right sent his heart pounding. Ian jerked around to see a young woman about eighteen years old. She stared at Gus for a moment, then lifted her eyes to meet his.

Jackie moved toward the exit. "Thank you, but we can't

involve you." She paused and glanced at the door behind the young woman. "But if you could hold off on telling anyone we were back here, I'd appreciate it."

The girl stepped in front of Jackie, cutting her off. "I heard what you said. That you were set up. I believe you and I want to help."

"Why?" Ian whispered.

She gave a wry smile. "Because you didn't know I was here and I doubt you'd be arguing about it if you were guilty. My dad was accused of something he didn't do and it was a nightmare. If you want to run, then I'll help you." She rummaged in her purse and pulled out her keys. "I was just leaving. Let's go." She moved to the exit like it was a done deal.

Ian closed his eyes, then opened them to find Jackie and the girl staring at him.

"We can't let her be involved," he said to Jackie.

"I know, but we can't stay here much longer. They're probably already searching the store and may even have the back covered at this point. We need her help, but it has to look like she didn't have a choice," she whispered. "It's too late to call my friends and it's going to be too late to get out of here soon." To the girl, she said, "You can't go with us. They'll arrest you for helping us."

Indecision flitted across her face. Then her jaw hardened. She dumped her purse on the floor, then tossed the keys onto the pile. "I don't think I'm ready to leave yet. I'll just go tell my boss I saw two suspicious people in the 'Employees Only' area. I got scared and dropped my purse."

Jackie snatched the keys. "That'll work. God bless you, hon." She headed for the exit, Ian right behind her. She paused, one hand on the door and turned back. "What's your name?"

"Karly."

Jackie nodded. "Thanks, Karly. The cops will find your car eventually and return it to you, but it could be a couple of days."

"I understand."

"Is there a security camera back here?"

Karly nodded. "Yes, but not in this conference area. If they watch it, they'll see that you walked in here and that I was already here. I'm sure they'll ask me questions, but I can handle it. I'll tell them the truth. That I saw you, you scared me—which you did—and that I dropped my purse—which I did."

"Thank you, Karly," Ian said and pushed the door open. "Any cops out there?"

He glanced the length of the building. "Not yet." He stepped into the back alley parking lot.

"But they will be soon." Jackie clicked the remote and Ian started when the Ford Taurus next to him beeped to life.

"Guess that's it."

"Guess so. Climb in." She opened the door and Gus bounded into the driver's seat and then on into the back.

"Where are we going?" he asked as he shut the door.

"To my grandfather's cabin. It's a good idea and we need to be able to talk without looking over our shoulder every three seconds." She cranked the car, backed up, and drove down the back alley behind the store until she came to the end of the strip. Blue lights flashed behind her and Ian tensed his hand reaching for the car handle. "Relax," she murmured. "He's not following us."

Ian didn't take his eyes from the side mirror. "Yet."

She pressed the gas pedal, pulled out around the side of the building, and flipped the car lights off. Darkness encased them. He looked left. The bookstore parking lot held a dozen law enforcement vehicles. He wondered if the FBI had been called in yet. He might not have been officially named a suspect, but he knew it was only a matter of time.

"They're going to be stopping everyone shortly," Jackie said. "We need to get out of here before that happens."

"I'm surprised it hasn't already happened."

"They were being careful not to tip us off. As soon as they discover we're not in there, the hunt will ramp up." Jackie turned her headlights back on and continued to the right, past other shops in the strip mall, and then circled around. "Okay, I guess it's now or never."

She made it to the edge of the lot.

Ian tensed. "Look." Police cars, a SWAT van, and unmarked cars headed their way.

"They're going for the parking lot of the coffee shop," she said.

"They think we're still in there."

"Which is going to enable us to slip away." She turned right onto the road parallel to the parking lot. The interstate lay just ahead.

Ian thought he might stop breathing before they managed to get on the highway, but somehow, someway, they'd made it. "They'll be looking for this car."

"I know. In about ten minutes, I can get off the highway and take the back roads."

Exhaustion swamped him. He leaned his head against the window and closed his eyes as he tried to figure out how he found himself on the run from the cops and the guys who wanted him dead.

Which may or may not be the same people.

# 5

In the parking lot of the large bookstore, South Carolina Law Enforcement Division Agent Sam Ferguson slammed a fist on the hood of his black Chevy SUV. "How'd they do it? How did they slip away? We had the brother's phone tapped, officers followed him here, and Lockwood and Sellers still got away. How?"

FBI Special Agent Elizabeth Miller simply raised an eyebrow and looked around. Organized chaos reigned, but she knew Jackie and Ian were gone. "They're smart. They didn't panic and they had a plan for when we showed up. And they stole a car." She glanced at her phone, then Sam. "Who's this Jackie Sellers woman?"

"She works for an agency called Operation Refuge. We have someone locating her co-workers."

"Operation Refuge?" Elizabeth pursed her lips. "I've heard of that."

Sam nodded. "It's an organization that was set up by the governor a couple of years ago. Or supported by the governor. Or whatever. However it came about, all of their 'operatives'—

for want of a better word—are highly trained people who've worked in some area of law enforcement before."

"What's Jackie's background?"

"She turned thirty-three two weeks ago. She did four years of college and majored in criminal justice. She joined the police force, then made detective. Had an exemplary record. Then six years ago, she took a leave of absence and never went back. Last year she was hired by Operation Refuge."

"Where was she during the LOA?"

"No idea. It's like she dropped off the face of the earth. No credit card activity during that time, nothing. She resurfaced when she took the job with Operation Refuge."

"Why *did* she take the LOA?" Elizabeth scanned the area, her mind spinning, creating scenario after scenario of how they'd slipped through their fingers.

"Her partner was killed," Sam said.

"Oh no. That's awful."

"He died on a Thursday night and she walked away after his funeral on Saturday afternoon. His death wasn't her fault, but apparently she blames herself."

"Of course she does." Elizabeth shot him a black look. "Any good partner would."

He snorted. "Well, she shouldn't blame herself for this one. It's so cliché it makes me sick. Her partner walked into a convenience store sometime after midnight. Two guys come in with shotguns and blow everyone away. They got two hundred bucks and some change."

"That's terrible." She frowned. "But why blame herself?"

"No one seems to know the answer to that one. They were off duty, she was home in bed . . ." He shrugged.

"Was there something more than just being partners?"

"You mean a romance thing?"

Elizabeth shrugged. "It happens."

"Agreed."

"So why did she blame herself? Survivor's guilt?"

"Probably."

"Did they catch the guys?"

"Yes. After they killed two more people. They're doing life."

She winced. "So how did she get involved with Ian Lockwood?"

He checked his phone. "According to the information that came in about thirty minutes ago, they went to high school together and were good friends."

"Did Lockwood call her when he found himself a person of interest in this case?"

"Phone records don't indicate that he called her. It looks like she tried to call him, but the call lasted only for a couple of seconds."

"Like when it goes to voice mail and you hang up without leaving a message. Then how did they hook up?"

He shrugged. "I can speculate, but that's all it is." He narrowed his eyes. "I don't really care. If Lockwood's guilty—and it sure looks like he is—and she's helping him run from us, I'm going to bring them both down. No matter what I have to do to make that happen."

*GREENVILLE, SC*

David Hackett hung up with a low growl. His wife, Summer, looked up at him. She placed the knife she'd been using to slice an apple on the kitchen counter. She turned the faucet on to wash her hands. "Nothing?"

"Not a word. Jackie's cell phone goes straight to voice mail. Adam's at her house now. I'm just waiting for him to call me."

Adam Buchanan, another Operation Refuge operative. Summer pursed her lips and kept one ear tuned to the baby monitor. Two-year-old Riley had been coughing and sniffling all day and Summer thought she might be coming down with something.

The phone rang and David snatched it.

"Put it on speaker, please," Summer said.

He did.

Adam's deep voice came over the line. "Her apartment's been torn apart. Her car isn't here. There's no sign of her. I'm worried."

David frowned and glanced at Summer. "All right. What about the cops?"

"The cops just pulled up so this isn't their work. I didn't think it was when I saw it. This looks like someone was looking for something—and they didn't find it."

"Keep an eye on the place for tonight. Just in case she decides to come back for some reason."

"Will do."

Summer stepped behind David and massaged his shoulders. He let out a low groan and dropped his forehead into his hands.

"She'll call," Summer said.

"Not if she can't." He stopped and thought about that. "But why wouldn't she be able to?"

"She's in trouble. Deep trouble. You saw the news."

"I saw it, but she has a phone," David said, rubbing his eyes.

"Unless she doesn't?"

"Stop. She can find a phone somewhere. She can stop a stranger and sweet-talk him into letting her use it."

"But she's not doing that."

"I know that, thank you," he mumbled.

"You're welcome." She kissed the top of his ear. "So, what are we going to do?"

David sighed and lifted his head. "Until she gets in touch with us, there's nothing we really *can* do." He glanced at the television on the wall. Jackie and Ian's pictures once again flashed across the national news channel. "We can pray."

Summer's gaze followed his. "Yeah. A lot." Silence surrounded them, broken only by the television reporter giving information about calling "if anyone spots the two fugitives wanted for questioning regarding terrorist acts against the United States." Summer finally broke the quiet. "Think Ron could find her?"

"If anyone can, it'll be him. Maybe she'll call him."

"Yeah. Maybe." She tapped her lip and her frown deepened. "Keep trying. She's bound to turn her phone on at some point."

"Let's hope so."

The baby monitor crackled. "Mama. Come get me. Now." Summer smiled. She slid into David's lap to wrap her arms around his neck. "I'm going to get Riley, but I want to go to Jackie's house and look around."

"What do you think you'll be able to find that Adam couldn't?"

"I don't know," Summer sighed. "But at least I'd feel proactive." She glanced at the quiet baby monitor. She wouldn't have long before Riley would demand her attention again.

"Let's give it awhile longer and let Adam take care of Jackie's house." He studied the television. "I sure hope she knows what she's doing."

Summer nodded and headed for the baby's room. "I hope so too. I really do."

---

Victor looked at the computer. He studied the information his inside man had retrieved and sent just minutes ago. He'd finally given up the chase and decided to let the cops handle it. Once Lockwood and Sellers were in custody, he could get to them as easily as he could cross the street.

Right now, he needed to make sure he conducted as much damage control as possible. He picked up the phone and dialed his contact.

The man answered on the second ring. "Did you get it?" he asked Victor.

"I did. So these are the numbers Lockwood called that day?"

"Yes."

"And you traced all of them."

"I did."

"So who is Holly Kent?" Victor asked.

"Lockwood's cousin. She lives in New York with her daughter, Lucy. Holly and Lockwood are close and they stay in touch. He visits her three to four times a year. Her husband was in the military, but he went missing about a year ago."

"All right. Why is she important?"

"It looks like he faxed several things that day, including something to her. The fax was one page. I'm thinking it must have been the email."

"Why would he fax it to her?" Victor frowned.

"She's a cryptologist."

Victor sucked in a breath. "Well now, that wrinkles the picture a bit, doesn't it?"

"I would say. If she deciphers that code and tells someone . . ."

"Yes. You don't have to tell me what a disaster that would be."

"I'm assuming you want her found."

"Yesterday."

"She'll be taken care of by the end of the night."

---

Special Agent Elizabeth Miller stepped inside Jackie's small cottage-style house and stopped. "Someone beat us here." She reached for her Glock and Sam did the same. She nodded for

Sam to go left and she went right. Elizabeth stepped sideways and moved slow, eyes roaming, senses alert. She absently noted the tasteful if plain décor, the lack of family pictures or plants. Jackie didn't spend much time here.

Her gut said whoever had trashed the place had already left, but she wasn't taking any chances.

"Clear!" Sam's voice came from the kitchen.

She picked up the pace and cleared two bedrooms and a bathroom. All in the same state of upheaval as the den, but no sign of anyone still in the house. "Clear!"

They met back in the foyer. "What do you think they were looking for?"

She shrugged. "Whatever Lockwood stole from Wainwright Labs."

"But why look for it here?"

Sam sighed. And holstered his weapon. "I don't know. All I know is the two of them are together and they're running when they should be turning themselves in. Why run if you're not guilty?"

"You either run if you're guilty . . ."

"Or?" he prodded.

"Or you're innocent, but don't have a hope of proving it."

# 6

Jackie supposed she'd finally snapped. Because driving the back roads, heading for Virginia, with a wanted man lightly snoring in the passenger seat didn't say positive things about her sanity. Then again, she was wanted too, so . . .

On the positive side of things, they were almost to her grandfather's home. The home she'd spent the last two years of high school in. The home she'd had in college. The home her uncle had promised was hers for as long as she wanted it. As she drove, she pushed aside the memories. Even the good ones. She didn't have time to think about those. She had to figure out how to help Ian prove his innocence.

If he was innocent.

Which she thought he was.

But what if she was wrong?

Doubts assailed her. She figured now would be a good time to start praying.

If she was a praying woman.

Which she wasn't.

At least not usually.

51

She'd stopped praying after John was killed. Scenes from their last day together flashed across her mind and she sucked in a deep breath. Six years. It had been six years and the grief could still rip into her if she let it.

She didn't. She'd come to grips with her past and moved on. Still. Some memories wounded more than others.

Gus whined from the backseat. He seemed to sense her inner turmoil. She glanced in the rearview mirror. The dog moved closer and laid his big head on her shoulder. And just stayed there.

Her mind circled back to John, a good man, a good cop, and a partner in more ways than one. She just didn't understand a God who let good people die while evil people seemed to live and flourish.

God. She snorted.

She and God had a complicated relationship and she had a feeling that was her fault. No. Correction. She *knew* it was her fault. She believed *in* God, she just wasn't sure she *believed* him. Two very different things. It would almost be easier if she just didn't believe in him, if she could just convince herself that he didn't even exist. But she couldn't. She'd felt his presence too many times in the past. At least up until six years ago. No, the problem wasn't trying to figure out if he was real, the problem was, she just didn't trust him anymore. He'd thrown so many curve balls at her in her lifetime that she'd finally gotten tired of trying to dodge them. She'd given up on love and she'd given up on God.

She climbed the winding road until she reached the gravel strip that led to the parking area of the cabin—a three-bedroom, two-bath ranch-style log cabin home. Not what most people thought of when picturing a mountain cabin.

The home sat tucked into the mountain on one side. Her favorite part of the house was the rambling deck off the back that overlooked the mountains. When inside, she felt like no one could see her or the house. Private and secure. Jackie instantly felt better. She cut the car off and Ian jerked awake. Gus moved over to Ian's side of the car and snuffled his ear. Ian gave the dog's snout a gentle push away and yawned.

"We're here," she said.

Remorse flashed across his face. "I can't believe I didn't help you drive."

"You were exhausted. I'm better off with you sleeping so you can be alert when I need to rest."

He shot her a tender look. "You always did try to save my pride."

She swallowed hard and hoped the darkness hid the flush she felt crawling up her neck. She shrugged. She wasn't just blowing smoke and trying to make him feel better. "Come on, I know where the key is and I bet Gus is ready to take care of business."

Ian climbed out and motioned for Gus to find a tree. The dog raced off.

"He'll come back, won't he?" she asked.

"Yes. He'll do his thing, run off some steam, then be begging to come inside where it's warm."

He followed her to the door. "Some cabin. The only thing resembling a cabin is the logs. This place is big."

She smiled. "I know. Cabin makes it sound so humble, doesn't it?" Jackie punched in the code and the lockbox opened. She snagged the key and opened the door. "Come on in."

Ian stepped into the foyer. "Nice."

"Yeah, but it's freezing in here."

"I'll find the thermostat."

He disappeared around the corner while she went to the gas logs and turned them on, then walked into the kitchen and went straight to the coffeepot. After measuring the grounds, she turned to find Ian looking around and tried to see the place with his eyes. A large open area with two couches, a flat screen television mounted above the fireplace, and the dining area just off the kitchen—the open-concept living area was attractive and well laid out. And large.

"I understand why you like this place so much," he said. He set the bag from the gas station on the kitchen table.

"I love it. Not just because it's a comfortable home, but because of the memories I have here. Good memories." She ran a hand across the countertop. "Needs dusting." She wiped her palm on her jeans and frowned.

Ian eyed her. "What is it?"

"Just wondering if anyone will put two and two together and come looking for us here."

"Who would put it together?"

She gave a low laugh. "My team at Operation Refuge, for one. The FBI, the counterterrorism unit that's probably investigating, SLED." She shrugged. "You name it."

"Is the place in your name?"

"No. My aunt's." She tilted her head. "And it's in her maiden name, so maybe we'll be all right for at least a night here." She glanced at the clock on the wall. "Or a few hours anyway. Night has come and is almost gone."

He dropped into a chair at the table.

"I have a question," Jackie said as she poured the coffee and set a mug in front of him.

"Just one?"

She grimaced and slid into a chair. "Touché. How about one for now?"

"Sure."

She took a sip of her coffee, then studied him for a moment. "Why do you have a very highly trained service dog?"

He blinked. "That wasn't the question I thought you were

going to ask." He glanced toward the door, then back at her. "He was Gina's."

"Oh." Enough said. His sister Gina had stepped on an IED while serving in Afghanistan and had lost most of her left leg and part of her right. She'd been in a wheelchair for the last three years of her life and had died a little over six months ago of kidney failure. Jackie had seen the announcement in the paper.

"I wanted to come to her funeral."

"Why didn't you?"

"I was working an assignment and couldn't get away at the last minute. I would have if I could have."

"I understand."

"So you took in Gus."

"Yeah. He and I have always gotten along." He sipped his coffee and cleared his throat. "He listens well and doesn't tell anyone my secrets."

"You have secrets?"

"Don't we all?" he murmured.

She met his gaze and for a brief moment was transported back into the past, to those lazy summer days when she and Ian were the best of friends, escaping the stress of their troubled home lives. Spending time with him and his cousin Holly. She blinked. "Yes, I suppose we do. What are yours?"

He gave her a slow smile. "Maybe I'll tell you one day."

"So if you're not going to share your deepest secrets, tell me what all this is about," Jackie said. "Who wants to kill you and why do they feel it's necessary to accuse me of being an accessory?"

Ian took another sip of his coffee and grimaced. "It started with an email meant for another person." He rubbed his chin. "I think."

"You think?"

He ran his hands through his short-cropped reddish-blond

hair and took a deep breath. Jackie nursed her coffee while she kept one eye on him and one on the parking area. She wanted to hear his story, but she didn't need any surprises.

"As you know from my Facebook page, I'm in research and development. I'm also a professor at the University of South Carolina Upstate. To put it simply, I spend my days playing with germs and other yucky stuff."

"Right."

"There are two Ians with Wainwright Research and Development. Ian Peterson, who's the grandson of the founder of the company, and me. I was in the lab the day before yesterday and got an email. It was password protected." He flushed but continued. "I closed it out without reading it, then opened it back up. I was tired, I'd been up all night working on what I thought was a breakthrough on a vaccine for malaria."

"Malaria?"

"It's a huge third-world problem. A vaccine would do wonders."

"I thought there was already a vaccine."

"No, there's medication you can take that may or may not help if you go into a high-risk country, but there's no vaccine. But that's beside the point. As I was saying, I was exhausted. I needed a break. So," he gave a self-deprecating shrug, "I hacked into the email and read it."

"What did it say?"

He dug into his pocket and handed her a sheet of paper. She read:

NYonSTBY.
d,s;;[pcfr;obrtrf.
H4W9
aasjl;;

/fg'g[.jl]]u
Cnt:T8R sas1sjg2hjha3

She looked up. "It's gobbledy gook. Or code. You know what it means?"

"No idea. I think the first line may mean 'New York on standby,' but the rest of it I don't have a clue."

"New York." She shook her head. "And you've been accused of conspiring with enemies of the United States."

He rubbed his chin. "I think I'm still just a person of interest. But they're leaning that way. They've all but said I'm a bioterrorist. It's just a matter of time before it's an all-out accusation, and if they catch me, they arrest me." He shook his head. "I can't figure it out. I've wracked my brain trying to decide if I stumbled across something in the lab, saw someone do something and didn't realize it. Trust me, the loop is endless. The only thing that I can come up with that makes any sense is the hacked email."

She nodded. "As soon as you entered the password, it would have notified the sender if he put a read receipt on it."

"I'm sure he did. And when he saw the name, he would have realized his mistake. Unfortunately, he decided it was worth killing me over."

"Who knows you saw this email?"

"A co-worker. Daniel Armstrong. He came in while I was reading it. I told him what happened and read it to him. He just shrugged and said it was weird, then asked if I was ready to get back to work. I almost closed the screen without another thought, then paused and hit Print." He gave her a sheepish smile. "You know how I am about riddles and puzzles."

She did know. He couldn't resist them. "And then what?"

"I left late afternoon because I had to pick up my dry-cleaning."

He looked around the room. "But they must have been watching because someone tried to kill me in the parking lot by running me over. I managed to get out of the way, though. When they came back for a second try, I ran. I guess they're not happy they failed."

"You think?" She couldn't help the sarcasm.

He stared at the email. "I need to figure out what this means. This is the ticket. There's something that I saw in this that has people scared to death."

Jackie grabbed the remote from the mantel and clicked the power button for the large screen television mounted on the wall above the fireplace. She turned it to Fox News. "We're still the top story," she muttered. She turned the volume down low and joined Ian at the table.

Jackie felt a sudden wave of exhaustion sweep over her. Her adrenaline had been pumping for so long, now that she was still and feeling relatively safe for the moment, she was ready to crash. But she needed some answers before that could happen. The clock pushed close to five in the morning. Jackie stood and went back to the coffeepot. While she poured another cup, she thought out loud. "That email. It didn't have a header or a footer. No names."

"No. The printer had been acting up. The service guy was supposed to come Friday afternoon and fix it. Anyway, when I printed the email, it printed on two pages. The first page had the email's information. The second page had the body. I threw the first page in the trash and just kept what I thought was a puzzle to be solved in my spare time." He pursed his lips in disgust.

"Do you remember who the email came from? Were there any other names on there?"

He nodded. "It came from my boss. Any other names were blind copied."

"So we know he's involved in whatever is going on. What's his name?"

"Cedric Wainwright, CEO of Wainwright Labs."

"How well do you know him?"

"Obviously not as well as I thought I did." He shrugged. "I never had much contact with him except when he gave a company speech or made the rounds at Christmastime. His main office is in New York, but around the holidays, he visits each branch to meet with employees on an individual basis. I thought he was a pretty decent guy."

"Until now."

"Until now."

The television caught her eye. She stood and walked closer to it. "Look." She picked up the remote and upped the volume.

A dark-headed female reporter spoke solemnly into the microphone. "Here in Atlanta, state police and the FBI are working together to figure out who would have cause to kill this family. Anwar and Meredith Goff were found murdered this morning. Executed with a single shot to the back of the head. Their two children, ages sixteen and nineteen, were also killed in the same manner. It's suspected that they were killed sometime either late Friday night or early Saturday morning. Anwar worked for the CDC here in Atlanta. Stay tuned for more information as we follow this developing story."

Ian swallowed. "That's awful. Who are they?"

"No idea. You're right it's awful, but that's not what caught my interest. Look at the scrolling tape. It's getting ready to come back around, but you know your co-worker? Daniel Armstrong?"

"Yes," he said, his eyes wary like he didn't want to hear why she was asking him about his friend.

"He's dead."

# 7

Ian gaped. "What?"

"He was found in his home earlier tonight." She glanced at the clock. "I mean yesterday evening. He was murdered and they just announced that you're a person of interest in that too."

Ian sank onto the love seat. The lack of color in his face worried her. "It's definitely the email then," he said.

"Looks like it."

"But how did they know he saw it?"

She shrugged. "I don't know. Maybe he asked someone about it. Or someone overheard you talking about it."

"So first they try to kill me. When they fail, they set me up as a terrorist, and now I'm going to be the fall guy for Daniel's murder too." She wouldn't have thought it possible, but he paled even more. "Holly," he whispered.

"Holly?"

"Holly, my cousin. She used to visit during the holidays and summers, remember?"

"Of course I remember. She was one of my best friends. Still is. What about her?" Tension corded the muscles along the base of her neck.

"You asked me who else knew about the email. She does. I faxed her a copy." He swallowed. "She's as crazy as I am about puzzles."

Jackie bit her lip. Holly. Ian's sweet cousin who'd been like a sister to Jackie before she'd moved away. "Do they know you sent it to her?"

He ran a hand through his hair. "I have no idea what they know, but I faxed it from my office, so if they check the phone lines . . ."

"They won't know what you faxed, but they'll see her number on there and probably check it out."

"Yeah." He stood and paced to the French doors that led to the deck. "It could take them a little while, but still . . . We're always faxing stuff, but if they're determined—and it looks like they are—they'll find her eventually. I need to call her." She handed him the phone and he dialed the number. After a few moments, he looked up. "Voice mail." Jackie heard the beep. "Holly, call me when you get this," Ian said. "It's important. And use this number, not my cell. If you've been watching the news, I'm sure you know why at this point." He hung up and tried again. Punched in another number and tried again. He gave a low growl. "She's not answering." He paced from one end of the room to the other, then stopped. "I have one more possibility." He dialed the number and still no answer.

Jackie was just as worried as he was. She tried to think about anyone she knew who he could call. A friend of Holly's, someone. She came up blank. "Is there another number you could try?"

"I called her home number, her cell number, and her work number." He shook his head. "Nothing."

"Okay, it's a little after five in the morning. Maybe she just has her phone on silent." Please let it be that.

"Maybe," he said, but the frustration on his face said that he doubted it.

"Lucy. What about Lucy?"

He shot her a funny look and Jackie lifted a brow. "Like I said, she was one of my best friends. We still keep in touch. Occasionally. She told me she'd adopted a little girl."

Ian nodded. "Lucy's great."

"Do you see her often?"

"I try to. We talk on the phone a lot. She has my number on speed dial and I'm the one person she knows she can call without asking permission." His frown deepened. "But I'm worried that Holly didn't pick up. She usually answers when I call no matter what she's doing, even sleeping. And if she thought I was in trouble, she'd be waiting for me to call." A muscle in his jaw jumped and she was afraid if she touched him, he'd come apart.

"I remember the puzzle competitions you guys used to have." She smiled at the memory and ignored all the emotions sweeping through her. The past held so much. A Pandora's box of memories. She sighed. "The truth is, I haven't spoken to Holly in probably two years." Her fault, not Holly's. "Is she still working as a cryptologist?"

He looked at her. "Yes. In New York. She's with an encryption company there. She's one of the best." She could hear the pride in his voice. "She does a lot of training and teaching too."

"So she has to travel?"

"Sometimes."

"Maybe that's why she's not answering."

He rubbed his eyes. "Maybe. It's never stopped her before, though."

"So she works with an encryption company?"

He nodded. "She's the one who creates the algorithms that

are used to disguise the information we enter into search engines on the internet. You know, like online banking websites or other payment sites like PayPal." He sighed and dropped his head. "After I deleted the email, I decided to go back and forward it to her. But when I went to retrieve it from my trash folder, it was gone, I couldn't find it." He shrugged. "I didn't think much about it, stuff like that happens occasionally. So I faxed it to her. I thought she'd find it intriguing. Just like I did."

"They must have removed it from the server," she murmured. Jackie rubbed her face and slapped her cheeks. She needed sleep. How long had she been awake anyway? "This is serious stuff, Ian. We're going to need help. Holly and Lucy might be in serious danger." The thought terrified her.

Ian swallowed hard and turned to stare at the television. Finally, he looked at her. "Not the cops, not yet. I may not have a choice soon, but I want to find out who's setting me up like this and get as much evidence as I can before I have to turn myself in—or get caught. But you're right. I need to know that Holly and Lucy are okay."

"Then let me call my friends," she pleaded.

He sighed and palmed his eyes before his shoulders drooped and he gave a hesitant nod. "Is there one person you trust above all else? Someone who would keep his mouth shut while helping?"

She thought for a moment, then gave a small nod. "Ron."

"Why him?"

"Because he has a passion for helping the underdog and he's not afraid to do whatever it takes to do so." She shook her head. "And I'd say you're—we're—definitely the underdogs here."

Ian drew in a deep breath and closed his eyes. Was he praying?

"Ian, think about Holly, think about if these people know who and where she is. There's no telling what they'll do." She tried to keep the rising panic at bay. Unsuspecting Holly. Whose sunny disposition and trusting attitude meant anyone would be able to take advantage of her. Trick her. Deceive her. Kill her. And her daughter. "Ian?"

A full sixty seconds later, he looked at her and nodded. "Okay. Call him."

A sound at the door made them both jump. Jackie reached for her weapon, but Ian waved her down. "It's probably just Gus."

She didn't let herself relax until she peered out the window to see the dog sitting at the door, waiting. She opened the door and he walked inside like he owned the place. He went straight to the kitchen and sat in front of the sink.

"He's thirsty," Ian said and went to rummage for a bowl.

"Probably hungry too. Check the deep freeze and see if there's some deer meat. My uncle is a hunter and keeps the place stocked, so I'm sure there's something."

While Ian readied the food for the dog, she took the phone they'd purchased at the gas station and dialed Ron's number. He answered on the second ring. "Hello?"

"It's Jackie."

"Jackie," Ron's deep voice rumbled in her ear. She caught the relief in the sigh that filtered through the line. "Thank goodness. Are you okay?"

"For now."

"Where are you?"

"At a little place in the mountains." She didn't want to be too specific in case someone was listening in. But Ron would know where she meant.

"The mountains, huh? Glad you made it there. Everyone's worried about you. Care to explain why your face is on the news and why people are saying you're associating with a terrorist? The media's camped out at the office and the feds are questioning David and Summer and everyone else they can get their hands on."

She winced. "I'm so sorry. I didn't plan on that happening."

"I'm guessing you didn't plan on any of this happening."

He had that right. "I don't have time to go into the whole story right now, but we need your help."

"We?"

"I have a friend with me."

"Is he guilty?"

She sighed and studied the man she'd known so well once upon a time. "I don't think so."

"You don't think?"

"Yeah."

"You're giving him the benefit of the doubt."

"Right."

A slight pause. "Did you have anything to do with the man who was shot and killed at a little gas station off 85?"

"What? No. Who was killed?"

"He hasn't been identified yet. Clean your gun if you used it."

"Ron, come on." She frowned as though he could see her. "I'm telling you I didn't. I don't know anything about anyone getting killed. We've been too busy dodging death ourselves."

"Okay, good. That's good to know. So why won't your friend go to the cops?"

"He says even the cops can't help him. They'll just lock him up and the people he's running from will have him knocked off in prison."

Ron paused and she knew he was thinking. "He might be right," he said. "Even if the cops do happen to believe him, the proof against him is pretty tight. They'll still put him behind bars until it's proven he's innocent."

"I know. Which is why I'm still helping him." She sucked in

a deep breath and forced her tired brain to produce a coherent thought. "Okay. Can you get us to New York?"

"New York?"

"I have my reasons and will share them with you as soon as I have permission." She shot a glance at Ian who rubbed his eyes and continued to frown as he listened.

"Fine. I'm going to make a few phone calls," Ron said. "Give me ten minutes and I'll call you back."

Jackie hung up and filled Ian in on what was going on. Ian paced, his agitation clear.

"Don't worry, Ron's not going to turn us in. He's going to help us."

"How?"

"I want to share the email with him. And the FBI and whoever else needs to know about it." She tapped a hand against her thigh as she thought. "If you're being accused of terrorism and that accusation is tied to that email, then it stands to reason that the email may be part of a plan related to a terrorist act. And if it's code, then it needs to be deciphered as soon as possible."

The air left Ian's lungs and he buried his face in his hands. "This is crazy. This kind of stuff doesn't happen to people like me." He shook his head. "I'm going to try Holly again." Jackie handed him the phone and waited while he dialed. When she didn't answer once again, frustration and fear for his cousin glinted in his eyes. He hung up. "I'm going to call the cops and have them go check on her."

She nodded. "Yes, please do."

He hesitated. "No, they'll know it's me and might not take me seriously—or try to bargain with me."

"Bargain with you?"

"Like they'll check on her if I'll just turn myself in."

She raised an eyebrow, proud of him for thinking of that. "That's true. Good point."

"I'll call her dad."

"That might be a bad idea. The FBI have no doubt contacted him. You know he'll cooperate with them. They may be listening."

He paused and frowned. Then he finally drew in a deep breath. "I have to try. Holly could be in danger because of me. I have to at least try. Can you at least understand that?"

"Yeah," she said softly. "I can."

He dialed and Jackie listened via speakerphone. The phone clicked on the third ring. "Uncle Dean, it's me. Don't hang up."

A slight pause as though the man were debating whether to do exactly what his nephew had asked him not to. "Turn yourself in, kid," he finally said. "What goes around comes around, eh? Not so high and mighty now, are you?"

Jackie wanted to be snarky right back, but Ian ignored the jab. He waved a hand as though to say it wasn't important. He was right, so she bit her lip.

"I need you to check on Holly and Lucy," Ian said.

"They're fine. You leave those girls alone."

"You don't understand, Uncle Dean. I sent Holly something. She could be in danger. Lucy too."

Silence. Then swearing. Ian flinched. "What did you do, you moron?"

Ian closed his eyes. "I didn't know—never mind. Please check on them and make sure they're all right."

"I will."

*Click.*

Jackie lifted a brow. "That was harsh."

"He has his reasons, I suppose."

"Will he really check on them?"

"Yes. He will. He and Holly don't get along, but he'll track her down." He cleared his throat. "The only thing is, I won't know if she's okay because he won't tell me and she won't know to call me until she listens to my voice mails." He nearly growled. "Why won't she answer her phone?"

"Sounds like we need to find that out ourselves." He handed her the phone and it vibrated. Ron. "Hey."

"I've got you bus tickets. You need to be on it first thing this morning. I'll text you the information."

"To New York?"

"To New York." Ron paused. She heard the clicks on the keyboard of a computer. "When do we get to bring in the team on this?"

"I'll let you know. Thanks, Ron."

"Check in with me, Jackie. I'll keep quiet until you say I can share."

A small measure of tension released in her shoulders. She'd made the right decision to call Ron. "I know. Thank you." She disconnected the call and turned to look at Ian. "We're going to New York." Her phone buzzed with the promised travel information from Ron.

He shivered. "Okay, I think that's what we need to do. But it's cold up there."

She snorted. "It's cold here. And if that 'NY' in the email stands for New York, then we might find some answers there."

"And we can check on Holly and Lucy."

"And we can definitely check on Holly and Lucy."

"But that 'NY' could stand for anything."

"True. It could be code for something else entirely. But everything seems to be pointing to New York." She pursed her lips. "Hopping on a bus may be the best thing we can do. I want to get away from these guys who are accusing you of being a terrorist and trying to kill you."

"Us."

"What?"

"They're accusing—and trying to kill—us."

"Okay." She lifted her head and met his gaze. "When you're right, you're right. *Us* if that makes you feel better."

"It does. I've never liked being in trouble by myself." She snorted and he shrugged. "Sorry. When I get scared, I crack stupid jokes."

She softened. "Yeah, I seem to remember that about you." She gave him a small smile. "I suppose that's better than freaking out."

"Don't worry. I'm doing that on the inside."

**8**

Maria Fox stood on the float platform and ran her hands over the belly of the framed-out and burlap-covered dragon. One of the five first-year clients for Hands Down Parade Company, Manguson's Toy Factory had chosen a dinosaur toy–themed float for the upcoming parade.

The fire-breathing dragon attached to the belly stood twelve feet tall. His jaw was permanently open and his jagged teeth were fearsome. She smiled. The kids would love him. Bubbles would spill from his mouth, taking the place of flames. Maria could already envision the children's delight in popping them as they drifted over their heads. "Looks great."

"All that's left is the painting," Henry Franklin said. "You'll work your magic and make it come alive."

Maria smiled. She took great pleasure in her job. Painting floats for parades was a dream come true. She'd gotten her degree in portraiture from Pacific Northwest College of Art. She had the responsibility for the details such as carving heads, painting faces, and making signs. Henry was the organizer. He handled the larger aspects of the floats, like overseeing the initial decoration that included covering the structure with burlap and constructing decorative pieces. All of which Maria would paint. "The countdown is on."

"It's going to be long days and nights."

A flicker of apprehension darted through her. "I know."

"Leo's been working quite a bit too, hasn't he?"

"Yes. A lot." She frowned. They'd argued about that just a few days ago. She knew she shouldn't badger him about staying home more, but when poor Lewis constantly nagged her about why his father had to be gone so much, she almost couldn't help it.

"You have someone to watch Lewis?"

Lewis, her five-year-old son. A little boy who needed his parents to be there for him. "My mother's moved in with us for the next few weeks."

"You're fortunate to have her."

"I know." Maria's heart ached at the schedule she and her husband were required to keep. He worked for the Bureau of Alcohol, Tobacco and Firearms as an explosives expert and had just been assigned an extremely complex case. Unfortunately, his hours were even worse than hers lately.

And all they seemed to do was argue when they were together. It was killing her. Killing their marriage.

But he'd promised to try harder and she wanted to give him the opportunity to do so.

"What about your father? Is he still living?"

"No." She breathed in. "He died when I was twelve. He was murdered, actually. Along with my brother and younger sister."

Henry's jaw dropped and he gaped at her. "I—I didn't know. I'm so sorry."

71

"Yes. Me too. We were living in Russia at the time. Thieves broke into our house and I'm sure my father fought back. My brother was sixteen, my sister was seven." Maria had escaped because she and her mother had decided to go shopping at the last minute. When her mother had gotten a phone call from her father, they rushed home to find the carnage. The police tried to keep them from entering, but her mother pushed her way through and Maria had followed. She blinked against the memories and blew out a slow breath. It had been almost fifteen years ago, but she could still see her father, brother, and sister lying on the floor, their blood black beneath them. Nausea swirled. Why had she told him all of that?

The door to the studio opened and Maria turned to see three men enter. Grateful for the distraction, she studied them, curious. She glanced at Henry, who caught her silent question. He shrugged.

She walked toward the visitors. "Hello." She held out a hand. "I'm Maria Fox. May I help you?"

The older, gray-headed man stepped forward and grasped her fingers. "Drew Manguson. We're here to see the progress on the float."

"Of course. Mr. Manguson of Manguson Toys, I presume." She turned to look at the float, and as always, pride and awe filled her that she had a hand in creating it. "This is a magnificent piece. I'm looking forward to getting it finished."

"Excellent." Maria noted the other two men flanking the gentleman she'd spoken with. For some reason, an icy warning slithered up her spine and she shivered. She frowned at her reaction and told herself not to be silly. Mr. Manguson approached the masterpiece he'd paid well over a hundred thousand dollars for.

The man examined every inch, including the platform the

float was built on. He turned to his two associates and nodded. To Maria, he said, "Everything looks great. You're doing a wonderful job."

She flushed. "Well, thank you, Mr. Manguson. I appreciate that."

"We'll be by early the morning of the parade to examine it one more time."

"Of course. We'll have a full house that day and it will seem very chaotic."

"Organized chaos, I'm sure."

"Exactly. Yes sir."

He tilted his head and gave a small smile. "Until then." He turned on his heel and nodded once more. His friends fell into step beside him and followed him from the building. Maria frowned. Something—

"What is it, Maria?"

"Something about him bothered me."

"What?"

"Well, for one thing, why bring two other men with you when all they're going to do is stand around and watch? What was their purpose?"

"He's rich, right?"

"Of course."

"Bodyguards."

Maria shrugged, but couldn't stop frowning. "I guess."

"What else is bothering you?"

"His eyes."

"His eyes?" Henry frowned at her.

"Didn't you notice?"

"Notice what?"

She heard his exasperation and sighed. "Nothing."

But it wasn't nothing. While Mr. Manguson had smiled

and seemed kind enough, his eyes had been empty pools of black tar.

And that sent more uncomfortable shivers dancing up her spine.

---

7:00 A.M.
VIRGINIA

By seven o'clock, Ian had let Gus out and proceeded to raid the pantry. He'd managed to find several bags of chips, every kind of canned bean known to man, a tin of crackers, a jar of Cheez Whiz, and a box of chocolate Pop-Tarts still within the expiration date.

Jackie emerged from the back bedroom, freshly showered, dressed in the clothes she had worn yesterday—and looking entirely *not* like herself. He blinked. "Wow." Jet black hair cut about three inches shorter had turned her into another person. "You did a good job."

"Your turn." She handed him a box of hair dye.

He grimaced. "Gray?"

"The older you look, the better off you are. If you could develop a few wrinkles and lose *a lot* of muscles over the next little bit, we'd be in good shape."

A grin tugged the corners of his lips. "I'll do my best." She'd noticed his muscles. He felt downright silly at the pleasure he took in that. He gripped the box. "I was thinking."

"About?" She grabbed a Pop-Tart and took a bite of it. Cold.

He grimaced. "Don't you want to toast that?"

She stopped chewing and looked at the pastry, then back at him. "And ruin a perfectly good Pop-Tart? Are you nuts?"

"Definitely." He sighed and dropped his chocolate rectangle into the toaster. Then he let Gus in and fed the dog the leftover meat from the night before. With a full tummy, the animal seemed content and stretched out on the kitchen floor to watch them.

"He's really smart, isn't he?" Jackie asked.

"Scary smart."

Jackie leaned over and scratched Gus's ears. The dog's eyes dropped to half-mast. "So what were you thinking about?" she asked.

"New York. And not just because I'm worried about Holly and Lucy, although they're the top priority."

"Okay." She finished the first pastry, grabbed a bag of chips, and hoisted herself up onto the counter. "And?"

"Cedric Wainwright is in New York where his father started the company. But, Wainwright Labs has facilities in South Carolina, Atlanta, Chicago, Los Angeles, Montana, and Honolulu too."

She crunched a handful of chips. "But that might mean something. It might be a place to start."

"Maybe. Or NY could stand for nuclear yield or . . . or—"

She held up a hand. "I get it. But unless you're willing to take this to the cops, we're kind of on our own here."

He stiffened. "No. No cops. I just can't take that chance yet." He hefted the box of hair color and nodded to her handful of chips. "Since when did you become such a junk foodie?"

She frowned. "How dare you insult such yumminess?" He rolled his eyes and she smirked, then shrugged. "I'm not usually into junk food, just when I'm super stressed." Her hand went back in the bag. "And if this situation lasts for more than a day or two, I'll have to find something else to battle the stress." She held up a chip and studied it. "Like running marathons." She sighed and munched the chip, then closed the bag and brushed her hands on her jeans. "It's all about control. I can quit any time."

"Promises the addict," he said.

She slid from the counter and made a shooing motion. "Go. I don't know how much time we have before we'll have to bolt. I don't know how they would track us here, but we're going to assume they can and be ready."

He shook his head, took the box of hair color, and slipped into the bathroom.

Twenty minutes later, when he came out, Jackie gave a nod of approval. She had two bags packed and Gus's leash snapped to his collar. The dog looked at him with mournful eyes. "He hates the leash."

Jackie reached down and scratched Gus's ears. Ian interpreted the sudden blissful expression on the dog's face to mean as long as Jackie kept scratching, the leash could stay on.

"He'll be all right," she said, then frowned. "You know, we may have to leave him somewhere. He stands out in a big way."

Ian shook his head. "I don't want to do that if I can help it."

"There hasn't been anything on the news yet about him traveling with us, so we may be all right for a bit."

Ian rubbed Gus's head. His hand collided with Jackie's and he let his fingers wrap around hers. Their eyes met. "I promised my sister I'd take care of him."

She breathed in and he appreciated the fact that she didn't pull away. "Well, at least it won't be a problem getting him on the bus."

"No, it won't be a problem, not if he has his service animal vest on." He released her fingers and mourned the loss.

A light went on in her eyes. She stared at the dog, then him. "He's a service animal. Then his disguise will be . . . a service animal. Let me rummage in my grandfather's shed for just a minute, then we'll go."

7:30 A.M.
ATLANTA

"Can you picture the widespread panic that's going to happen if this gets out?" Center for Disease Control director Tobias Freeman ran a hand through his short-cropped Afro, then tightened his tie and studied his face in his bathroom mirror. His dark eyes reflected his keen intelligence—and infinite worry. Stress had pressed new lines alongside his mouth and he thought he might have developed a few more gray hairs. He could only pray that by the time this was over he wasn't completely white-headed.

Kara, his wife of twenty-two years, lifted herself on her tiptoes to kiss his cheek. "Now, Toby, you'll get this settled today and all will be fine."

He shook his head and pulled her close, burying his face for one brief moment of comfort in her silky black strands. "They're going to blame me, you know," he murmured against her neck.

She pushed him back and cupped his chin. "It's not your fault, Tobias. I'll be praying."

He kissed her and breathed his own prayer. One of thanks for his wife, one for wisdom for the moments to come, and one of pleading for the Lord to intervene and keep innocent people safe. "I've got to go. They're waiting on me. Just pray. Pray like you've never prayed before."

Thirty minutes later, he stepped into the CDC conference room and took in the solemn faces seated at the long table. Faces that consisted of FBI, the Georgia Bureau of Investigation, the Georgia Highway Patrol representative, the mayor, and Chief of Police Harvey Parker.

Tobias loosened his tie and cleared his throat. "Folks, we

have a potential disaster on our hands. Let's make some wise decisions."

The chief leaned forward, dark eyes intense. "I say we keep this as quiet as possible. It will give us a better chance of catching the people who've done this. If we release the fact that we let someone steal the smallpox virus, we'll have chaos."

Nods all around the table.

"This is considered a terrorist act," stated Rebecca Wilson, FBI Special Agent in Charge in Atlanta. Her head bobbed with emphasis. "As such, we've formed this additional Joint Terrorism Task Force. We will continue to add people to it as it becomes necessary."

Tobias nodded. He'd expected nothing less. "We'll want to encourage the public to get the smallpox vaccination." He paused and blew out a slow breath. "I'm not one for lies. I never could have imagined I'd condone lying to the public, but this . . ." He shook his head. "We'll have to find a way to protect the people without causing a panic."

Special Agent Elizabeth Miller pursed her lips, then offered a quiet sigh. "Unfortunately, you're right. We can't tell the truth just yet. What do you think about saying there was an outbreak on a remote island in the Philippines or something?"

"And as a result of that outbreak, there've been several cases reported here in the States," Special Agent Wilson said.

Tobias cleared his throat, not at all sure he liked the idea of concocting a lie, but knowing the truth had to be withheld for now. He would get on his knees and ask forgiveness when the time came. *Lord, tell me what to do.* "Protect the people. That's the priority."

"How did Anwar Goff manage to steal the smallpox virus without any alarms going off? That's what I want to know."

Tobias shook his head. "Goff had top security clearance.

He was a long-term trusted employee and often worked late. There was no reason to suspect he'd ever do anything like this." Tobias paused and met each eye in the room. "And he wouldn't have if his family hadn't been threatened."

"Now we don't know for sure his family was threatened," Rebecca said. "There's no concrete evidence of that."

Tobias lifted a brow. "You mean other than the fact that they're all dead?"

Rebecca cleared her throat.

Tobias honed in on the chief. "You may not know it, but I do. Whoever's behind this held his family hostage and threatened to kill them if he didn't get the virus for them. I don't need any investigation or concrete evidence to tell me that. His actions, his dead family, and the missing virus are all the proof I need."

The chief nodded. "I think you're right, but we still want to prove it without a shadow of a doubt."

"Now," Tobias looked at Rebecca, "you have the lead on this. Who else do we need to bring into this circle of confidence?"

Rebecca pursed her lips, then leaned forward. "We'll have all the manpower we need. All of our resources will be going toward finding that virus and getting it back where it belongs. I'll keep you updated if I think of something."

Tobias nodded. "FBI media coordinator Mark Hughes will handle the media. We'll give him our statement and let him fend off the sharks." He looked over the top of his glasses. "I think our best defense is a good offense at this point."

"You think they'll connect the murder of the Goff family, one of whom worked for the CDC, to the sudden encouragement for citizens to take the smallpox vaccine?" Rebecca asked.

"They'll speculate, but won't be able to prove anything."

Rebecca narrowed her eyes and leaned forward. "What about a connection between Ian Lockwood and the CDC?"

Tobias nodded. "I've thought about that. The timing is just too much to be a coincidence. The smallpox virus goes missing on Thursday and Lockwood, a trusted employee of Wainwright Labs, is accused of working with enemies of the United States to sell a mutated malaria virus?" He steepled his fingers and rested his chin on them. "I'm going with the assumption the two are related." He looked at Rebecca. "What do you think?"

"I'm inclined to agree. We'll work it like it's the same case—or at least related. I'll fill in my agents and headquarters. I'll assign as many as needed to this task force." She tapped her chin. "As well as the agents from South Carolina where Lockwood started this chase. We may even need to swear in other law enforcement officers as federal marshals at some point if Lockwood and Sellers cross state lines."

Tobias narrowed his eyes and once again looked at each individual person. "Right now, we are the only ones aware of what's going on. If something gets leaked to the media that didn't come from Hughes, the consequences won't be pretty. I hope you understand what I'm saying."

Rebecca stood. "Indeed. No leaks of any kind, no talking to prosecutors, nothing. I want complete silence on this. Because if this gets out, we'll all go down. And I don't plan on being one of the casualties." She sounded confident, ready to take on this disaster of mammoth proportions and walk away a hero. Tobias could only pray that's the way the scenario would play out.

# 9

At the bus station, Jackie left Ian sitting in one of the chairs with Gus at his feet. She'd picked a spot as distant from other people as possible. Ian's newly dyed hair looked more salt and pepper than the gray color the box promised, but it gave him a distinguished appearance.

The dark sunglasses and the white piece of PVC pipe with red electrical tape wrapped on both ends gave the impression that he was blind. The orange vest Gus wore completed the disguise.

Jackie just prayed it was good enough. She hadn't had time to get as creative with her own looks as she would have liked, but she thought the large glasses and the black hair did the trick. The station attendant didn't look at her twice as he passed their tickets to her through the slot. "You have about thirty minutes before boarding."

"Thank you."

"Yes ma'am."

She turned and nearly ran over a man in his early sixties.

He had silver hair, a grey Fedora, and thick glasses. Behind the lenses, his bright blue eyes blinked a rapid beat as he caught her by the forearm.

Jackie regained her footing. "Excuse me, I'm sorry. I need to watch where I'm going."

He tipped his hat and winked. "I never mind running into a pretty young woman."

Jackie gave a short laugh and stepped around him. "Excuse me."

"Of course."

She made her way back to Ian and settled in the seat beside him. "Thirty minutes."

"I haven't noticed any suspicious looks, have you?"

"Not yet."

He shifted. "I feel like scum impersonating a blind person."

"You're not scum. You're trying to stay alive. I think anyone would understand that."

"Let's hope so."

Jackie leaned back in her seat and closed her eyes. "Why do you carry Gus's service vest with you when you don't need it anymore?"

He didn't answer right away and she peeked at him from beneath the dark glasses. His focus was on the dog at his feet. "I don't know. I suppose because it reminds me of Gina. She took such pride in Gus and all he could do." He gave her a slight smile. "She trained him herself, you know."

"I didn't realize."

He nodded. "I suppose I should let him go to someone who could use his special skills, but—" he gave a micro-shrug—"I just can't do it yet. He's a little part of her."

Jackie squeezed his hand. "Thanks for sharing that."

"Sure."

"And now, I'm going to continue my little catnap if that's all right with you."

"Perfectly all right. I'm sorry I zonked out on you last night. I'd been up almost thirty-six hours." At her frown, he shook his head. "Not all related to our current situation. I was working on something at the lab and I didn't want to leave until I was finished. By the time I left work and those guys tried to kill me, I was pretty much a zombie. When we got in the car—" He shrugged.

"No need to apologize."

"Thanks. I'll keep my eyes open. You get some rest."

A slight smile curved her lips just before she allowed her muscles to relax and sleep to claim her.

Ian watched Jackie doze. The lines in her face smoothed and she looked peaceful. Young. He was amazed that she could just fall asleep like that. Like she'd flipped a switch. Old feelings rose to the surface as his gaze skimmed her lips. When he'd been a senior in high school, he'd dared to try to kiss her. She'd rebuffed him gently, saving his pride by claiming that she wasn't in the market for romance at the time, but if she was, he'd be her first pick.

A slight smile curved his lips at the memory. He wondered what she'd do if he tried to kiss her now?

Probably knock him senseless.

Which is what she should do. The reason for their frantic flight to New York swept over him and he turned from her deceptively fragile beauty to stare through the dark lenses at the crowd around them. *God, I don't know what your plan is in this, but just keep us safe so we can see it through.*

What if God's plan was for him and Jackie to wind up in jail?

He felt silly even thinking that, but he was mature enough to admit God worked in weird ways. His mind went to the Bible.

Innocence hadn't helped John or Peter, or Paul and Silas—or Jesus. It had happened in biblical times—innocent people going to jail—even dying because they were wrongly accused.

And it for sure happened in present times.

But God had used those situations in miraculous ways. What if Ian was just making things worse for the both of them by insisting on running? What if—

"Bus 591 departing for New York is now boarding."

Ian shut off the what-ifs. If God wanted him in jail, he'd put him there one way or another. In the meantime, Ian planned on running and searching for a way to prove his innocence.

He tapped Jackie on the shoulder. Her eyes opened, clear and aware as though she'd just had a good eight hours of sleep.

"Ready?"

"Definitely." She sat up and grabbed the bags.

Ian stood. "I bought a new phone at the little store over there and tried Holly again. Still no answer. I'm really worried. I even tried my uncle again."

She frowned and he shrugged. "What did he say?" she asked. "Was he able to say if she was all right? Did he say where Lucy was?"

"He was a bit more kind. He said he hadn't heard from Holly yet, but expected to soon. He didn't say anything about Lucy." He grimaced. "Then he tried to get me to tell him where I was and to turn myself in."

Jackie bit her lip. "The feds convinced him to cooperate with them and were probably listening. What about her friends?"

"I don't have their numbers and he wouldn't give them to me. Said he wouldn't be responsible for letting me get anywhere near them." He shifted the cane to his other hand.

"Ouch."

"I don't really care what he thinks of me, I just wish he'd told me where Holly was."

"You think he knows?"

"No. Holly doesn't have much to do with him since I busted him on his affair with his secretary." He snorted. "So cliché, it's stupid."

"What about your aunt, Holly's mother?"

"She finally took off about three years ago to get away from my uncle. We haven't heard from her since. At least I haven't. Holly hasn't said whether she's been in touch with her or not." He paused. "I'm sure my uncle blames me for my aunt's leaving too."

"Wow." She rubbed her eyes. "Okay, let's ditch the phone, they'll have that number now."

He tossed it in the trash, then reached for one of the bags.

She took his hand and gave it a gentle push aside. "You can't see, remember?"

"Right, but that doesn't mean I can't carry a bag."

"Today it does. Just look straight ahead. Hold your cane and Gus's leash in your left hand. With your right, take my arm just above my elbow. You need to look like you've been doing this for a while. Otherwise people are going to stare." Ian followed her instructions and together they merged with the crowd. He kept his head straight, but let his gaze roam. People were staring anyway. Mostly at Gus.

"I don't see anyone that rings alarm bells, do you?"

"Not yet."

Ian kept his hand wrapped securely around her arm. They made their way onto the bus and found their seats. They'd been given priority seating and Ian felt lower than scum. "I can't take up this seat. Let's move back."

"And draw attention to ourselves?" Jackie asked as Gus settled himself at their feet.

Ian sighed and settled back in his handicapped seat and turned to look at her. "Fine, but if someone gets on this bus who really needs it, you're going to have to move us."

"Deal." She glanced at the driver. "And stay in character a little better," she muttered. "Don't look directly at me. Look straight ahead. The bus driver's watching us in the mirror."

Ian stiffened. "Sorry, I never was one for the drama department." He blinked and made his eyes as blank as possible behind the dark glasses, doing his best to stare at nothing and pretend he didn't see the man watching them.

The driver shook his head and shut the door.

Five minutes later, with no one needing the seat Ian occupied, they rolled out of the terminal.

# 10

Jackie leaned her head against the window and allowed the past to flood in. Ian's cousin, Holly, was a redheaded, green-eyed little firecracker whose zest for life and fun infected everyone who came in contact with her. Probably one reason Ian enjoyed spending so much time with her.

Jackie had often escaped her home and found the two of them in his backyard, heads bent over a puzzle book or the newspaper's daily cryptogram—or creating one of their own. She looked at Ian. "I knew Holly was living in New York. She called me and told me when she and Brant decided it was a great career move for her."

"Yes. That was about three years ago. She was super excited about it. It was going to be a big change from that job she had right after college."

"The one with the Navy. Yeah, I knew about that."

"She served about five years with them, then went civilian and outsourced her skills to the highest bidder. That happened to be a large financial banking institution in New York. She now lives near Central Park. Did she tell you that?"

Jackie let out a low whistle. "No, she didn't. That's not cheap. Good for her."

"She's been there a little over two years. She does well with her job, but she married an Army man who came from money, remember?"

"I remember. How is Brant?"

Ian blinked and turned to stare at her, then seemed to remember her admonition not to look at her. Shifting his gaze straight ahead again, he cleared his throat. "He disappeared while on tour last year. You didn't know?"

Jackie sucked in a deep breath. "What? No. No, I didn't know. I'm so sorry. Obviously, I . . . I haven't talked to Holly in a while."

"Why not? You two used to talk every day."

She looked away. "Things change, Ian. People change." She gave a light shrug.

"Lucy misses him."

Jackie felt his hand on her arm and turned back toward him. He still stared through the front window. "How is Lucy?"

"She's a great kid."

"Yeah," Jackie whispered. "She is."

"You've met her?"

Jackie smiled. "A couple of times."

The driver caught her gaze for a moment, then looked back at the road. A sliver of unease slipped up her spine. The driver spoke into his headpiece. She knew he was in constant contact with dispatch and wondered what he was saying. She couldn't hear over the chatter of the other passengers and the baby crying in the seat behind her.

"What is it?" Ian asked, his voice low.

He must have noticed her sudden tension. It amazed her that he was so in tune with her emotions even now. "The driver keeps looking back here at me. Us." She drew in a deep breath. "Okay, so he may just think you're faking it to get the good seat on the bus. It doesn't mean he recognizes you from the news."

"Probably not."

"So let's not overreact."

"Right." Jackie saw him take a deep breath. "Right."

Jackie curled her fingers around the cell phone in her pocket. Should she call Ron and ask him about a backup plan? She knew he'd have one. He always had one.

---

10:45 A.M.

"A person I care about is in trouble and you've waited this long to tell me you knew about it and were helping her?" David asked.

Ron could feel the man's anger pulsing through the radio. "It couldn't be helped, David. I'm sorry. She wouldn't tell me anything until I promised I'd keep my mouth shut."

"I get it but I don't like it. If I had known sooner, I could be doing more than scrambling to help."

Ron stayed silent. There was nothing he could do about it now.

David's sigh reverberated through the line. "All right, I'm done whining. What did you find out?" he asked.

"The feds are waiting on them at the bus stop," Ron said into the headset. He shifted in his seat and felt the seat belt tighten around him. It mirrored the conflict gripping him, like a noose around his neck. The pilot gave him the thumbs up. They were almost ready to land. "The bus driver called it in. As soon as they get off the bus, they'll be arrested. I'm ahead of them and I've arranged for an escape if they can pull it off."

"Won't the FBI stop the bus?"

"No, they want to let the bus get to the original destination. Because of the explosive evidence found at Ian's home, the feds are too scared to make them feel trapped. They're worried if Ian or Jackie have explosives on them and they feel like they're backed into a corner, they'd simply blow the bus up."

"The good news is that we know they don't have any explosives."

"Exactly, but the feds don't know that, and in their minds, just because Jackie and Ian got through bus security doesn't mean they're clean. We're going to use that belief to our advantage."

Ron heard footsteps and could picture David pacing in front of the large window of the Operation Refuge conference room. The slight echo said he was on speakerphone. "I can't believe you're just now bringing us in on this."

"That horse is dead, David. You've gotten to know Jackie well enough by now to know how she thinks. If she's going down, she's going to do it alone. She won't want to take anyone with her. She's going to be mad as a wet hen that I told you." He shook his head and guilt flooded him at the broken confidence. Then he stiffened his spine. "But sometimes you have to make an executive decision for those you love and want to help."

"In spite of the fact that she's with Ian Lockwood."

"Yes."

"Helping him run from the authorities."

Ron didn't like David's calm, flat tone.

"Yes."

David went silent and Ron let him think. "All right then," he finally said. "She trusts you, but she can trust us too. What can we do to help?"

Ron pulled his phone from his pocket. "I have an idea. Give me an hour to put something together. I'll call you."

Ron left without a backward glance and fifteen minutes later found himself pacing District Attorney Kenneth Thompson's spacious office. "What are the charges against them?"

Kenneth steepled his fingers in front of him and studied Ron. "Terrorism charges."

"So you have evidence?"

"Emails on his computer at work, emails at home. Detailed notes about his work at the lab." The DA paused. "Names of potential buyers for what he was working on."

"Which was?"

"A way to take the malaria virus and turn it into a fine powder that could be spread over a large area."

"A fine powder? Seriously?"

"Yes. But that's not all. He was actually enhancing the virus."

"Enhancing it?"

"Strengthening it, mutating it, whatever. He was making it impervious to antibiotic treatment. He'd made a batch and was getting ready to sell it to the highest bidder. Wainwright found out about it and called in the authorities. Unfortunately word got back to Lockwood that he'd been discovered."

"Bioterrorism at its finest." Ron sighed and rubbed his chin. "That makes no sense. Not only is malaria a stupid choice of bio-weapon, but he's never been connected to anyone even remotely suspected of terrorism."

"Stupid weapon?"

"Come on. Think about it. Lockwood had access to everything from anthrax to Ebola, for crying out loud. Why choose malaria? He may have been working on something with malaria, but it wasn't to turn it into a bio-weapon. It's a bunch of fabricated hooey and you know it."

Kenneth held his hands up in a gesture of surrender. "I don't know. And I don't know what to tell you, Ron. The FBI has done a thorough job of collecting the evidence and bringing the charges. We'll be notifying the media in about one hour, upgrading Lockwood from person of interest to one of the FBI's most wanted."

Ron dropped onto the love seat opposite the man's desk. "What about Jackie?"

"Same thing. Looks like she's helping him." Kenneth narrowed his eyes. "You know as well as I do, anyone aiding a terrorist is not a friend of the US. And anyone aiding and abetting a terrorist will face charges and prison time."

"Of course I know that."

"Anything you want to tell me, Ron?"

Ron stood and walked to the window, hands shoved deep into his front pockets. "No. Nothing." He turned and walked to the door and pulled it open. "I'll be in touch."

---

*12:10 P.M.*

Three hours into the trip, Jackie knew the bus driver was up to something. Or suspected something. His gaze had been constantly shifting between her and Ian and the road.

She elbowed Ian. "We have a rest stop coming up in about an hour. We're going to have to get off the bus before then."

"How do you propose to do that?"

"I'm not sure, but I'm thinking." She really only had one choice. She called Ron. Heard the background noise. "Where are you?"

"In a chopper coming after you."

"What? Why? How did you know I needed you?"

He barked a short laugh. "You're in trouble, Jackie. I'm calling in every favor ever owed in order to stay one step ahead.

92

Now listen up, I've got a plan. They're going to arrest you as soon as you show your faces at the next stop, so here's—"

"No, Ron." Jackie's stomach tensed and she lowered her voice further. "You'll get in major trouble."

"I said I've got a plan."

"You always have a plan."

"Of course. Now quit interrupting and start listening. I won't be able to get to you in the helicopter, there's no place to land that the cops aren't covering. You won't be able to get through. So we're going to get creative. Remember this address and directions to get there." He rattled it off and Jackie closed her eyes, concentrating on his words. "You got it?"

"I've got it."

"Now David, Summer, Adam, and everyone are working around the clock to help figure this out. But it's bad, Jackie, very bad. Someone has a lot of power, influence, equipment, and everything. I've talked to the DA, and he told me the evidence against Ian and you is overwhelming. They've started an all-out nationwide manhunt. You're fugitives and terrorists and are now on the FBI's most wanted list."

Jackie closed her eyes, doing her best to ignore the fear shooting through her. What had Ian stumbled onto? "I promise I'll never pick a lock again," she muttered.

"What?"

"Nothing. What kind of evidence?"

"You have emails in your account that I'm working on tracing because I know they're bogus. Ian does too. They found explosive devices in Ian's house along with a detailed plan to blow up several churches in the area. They also have detailed notes about his work with malaria and even some written scribbles that look like formulas that may be ways to enhance the malaria virus and turn it into a bio-weapon. The FBI is examining everything."

Jackie pressed her forefinger and thumb to her eyes. "Okay, let's start with the emails. What emails? What did they say they had?"

"They're mostly between you and Ian, plotting to sell the information he stole, including a bio-weapon—probably the malaria thing—from Wainwright Labs to enemies of the United States, most specifically the highest bidder."

"But that's crazy—what—how—?"

"We're working on figuring that out, but whoever set all this up is good. Very good and very powerful."

Jackie pulled in a calming breath. "Ian wouldn't do anything to hurt this country. His sister gave her life for it and he wouldn't sell it out."

"You sound a hundred percent."

She looked at Ian and knew by his absolute stillness that he was listening and following the one-sided conversation. "A hundred and ten."

"Then that's good enough for me."

"All right. So we keep going?"

"Absolutely. If you turn yourselves in now, you're going to prison. And once you're in prison, it'll be a lot harder for me to protect you." He paused. "Which is what I think the people after you may have in mind. Getting the cops after you and getting you in prison will allow easy access. Not too hard to find someone on the inside who's willing to carry out a hit."

"Right."

"So they can only charge you if they catch you. Make sure they don't before you have evidence to back up what you know."

"Okay, I'll keep that in mind," she muttered. "What about the explosive devices and the plans?"

"Same thing. Evidence that's going to make them search for you and Ian and search hard."

"All right. Thanks, Ron. I'll be in touch."

Jackie hung up and powered the phone down, stunned at the direction her life had taken in less than twenty-four hours.

Ian's hand covered hers, jerking her from her thoughts. "I'm sorry, Jac—"

She cut him off with a finger to his lips and a glance at the bus driver. She reached for his hand and squeezed. "It's okay. I'm here for a reason."

"I don't know what God's doing, but I'm glad he sent you to help me through this." He frowned. "Although I'm sorry it's gotten you into such a mess."

Jackie snorted. "God? I don't think he's involved in this."

Ian shot her a sad smile. "Still the skeptic?"

She sighed and caught the driver watching them again. "You know the saying that there are no atheists in foxholes?"

"Yes."

"That's true to some extent. I've found myself in some pretty extreme situations and tried to pray my way out of them, but . . ." She shrugged and swallowed, the nightmare coming back full force. "God seems to have abandoned me. If he doesn't want anything to do with me, why should I force myself on him by praying?"

Jackie found herself wrapped in a hug tighter than she'd ever experienced. "My word, that's one of the saddest things I've ever heard."

Tears surfaced for the first time in a long time. She shut them off and broke out of Ian's embrace. "Sorry. I didn't mean to get sappy." She sniffed and looked at her watch. "We've got to get off this bus."

---

ATF Explosives Enforcement Officer Leo Fox glanced at his watch. He'd been called in to assist in the arrest of Ian Lockwood and Jackie Sellers.

And to ensure that there weren't any explosives on the bus. He'd sat in on the rundown of the type of explosives found in Lockwood's home. He knew what to look for and he knew how to take care of it. He'd been with the ATF for twelve years. He loved his job, but . . .

"How's it going, Leo?"

He looked up to find Chris Hall dressed in full gear. "Just waiting. You?"

Chris sat beside him. "Good." He pulled out a piece of beef jerky and bit off a hunk. "You think there's a bomb on that bus?" he asked around the bite.

"Dunno. Guess we'll find out."

"You think the dude's guilty of this terrorist stuff?"

"Probably."

"Yeah." Chris shook his head. "Man, this country's just going from bad to worse."

"Which is why we do what we do."

Chris snorted. "Well, it sure ain't for the pay."

Leo thought about his wife and son. Everything he did was for them. It was why he took precautions and made sure he didn't get himself blown up. It was why he was so careful with every penny he made. He had to secure a future for his family.

Just in case.

"Hey, your mother-in-law making any of her famous pound cake?"

Leo barked a laugh. "She's got you hooked on that stuff."

"Provides a better high than any drug out there."

"I'll ask her."

"No, you married her daughter. She doesn't like you. I'll call her."

"I helped give her a grandson. She loves me. You got her number?"

"She gave it to me the last time she came to the office with her pound cake. She told me to call anytime to make a request."

And no doubt Chris would. Naomi Hunter loved to bake almost as much as she loved her daughter and grandson. And the agents in the Alcohol, Tobacco and Firearms New York office loved her. Most specifically her pound cake. And anything else she made. The way the guys hounded him to bring something in, one would think he didn't have anything better to do.

But he did.

Leo reached into his pocket and pulled out a picture. Maria, Lewis, and himself. Smiling. He shoved the photo back into his pocket and vowed to make sure they kept on smiling.

## 11

Maria held the heavy-duty paint sprayer and went over the dinosaur one more time, careful to get every crease, every spot covered. She wanted to enjoy the work, but she kept picturing her son's face. Lewis had cried when she'd sent him off to school this morning, but at least she'd been there to put him on the bus. She hadn't seen her husband in almost three days. Then again, Lewis's tears had dried quickly when his friend, Lucy, had taken his hand and told him she would sit with him on the bus.

It broke her heart that Lewis missed her so much, but she and her husband had come into the marriage with a pile of debt that had only worsened after Lewis was born early and spent three months in NICU.

Lewis would have to adjust. And besides, once the parade was over, her hours would settle back into something resembling a more normal schedule.

At least until the next parade.

She eyed her work and felt a surge of pride. Lewis would love the final result. She'd have to bring him by and show it to him.

She turned the sprayer off. Henry had called in sick today,

so Maria had taken it upon herself to do the body of the dinosaur. Now she would let it dry for a bit before tackling the head and face.

"Need any help?"

Maria turned to see Christine Bridges, another talented artist, coming from the office. "Just trying to get some of this painting done."

"Let me grab a sprayer and I'll do this area."

"Thanks."

Christine returned and they got to work. "It's hard to believe it's already time for the parade. It seems like this year just flew by."

"I know." Maria smiled. This was her first year to work the parade. To her surprise, Leo had finagled the job for her and she loved it. She loved the steady income and the easing of some of the financial stress. They were actually getting some debt paid. "I'm eager to see it all come together."

"It's a sight, that's for sure."

Soon volunteers and other workers would swarm the float, covering every last piece of metal and burlap with greenery. They would help add the fine details to make the float a work of perfection. Maria couldn't wait to see it roll down the street.

"Leo's coming," she said.

"Really?" Christine paused in her painting and looked up. "Are you two working things out between you?"

"Trying to. He promised to come so we could enjoy the parade as a family." Once the painting was finished, her job was basically done. "We're keeping it as a surprise for Lewis."

"He'll be so excited, you'll have to sit on him to keep him still."

Maria laughed. "I know." But a wave of sadness hit her. She knew they'd agreed on the surprise aspect because they both wondered if it would really happen.

"What about your mother?"

Maria shrugged. "I asked her, but she just talks about how she's an old woman and doesn't have any business being in a crowd of people standing in the cold for hours." She sighed. "I guess I don't blame her, but it would be fun to have her here." An idea hit her. "Hey, Christine?"

"Yes?"

"This float is all about attracting kids to the client's toy store, right?"

"Sure. Dinosaurs, airplanes, toy soldiers—they're all on here. Why?"

"What if we had real children ride in the float, playing with some of the toys, screaming their delight, et cetera?"

Christine raised a brow and her eyes lit up. "What a fabulous idea."

"You think I should talk to the boss about it?"

"Absolutely."

Maria nodded. "Okay. I'll do that." She played it cool on the outside, but on the inside she was dancing. She didn't think it would be a stretch to go from having children on the float to having Lewis's class be the lucky kids to actually ride on it.

And this could be one thing that she could do to surprise Leo. She'd keep it a secret until the morning of the parade. He'd be so proud.

———

Jackie heard the *whomp-whomp-whomp* of the law enforcement helicopter above and knew it was time. "Get ready."

"What are you going to do?"

"Not sure, just go with it."

"Ah! Oh no! Help . . ."

Jackie swiveled in her seat to find the man who'd tipped his

100

hat to her in the bus station gripping his left arm and leaning forward in his seat. She jumped up and slid into the aisle.

"Sir, what is it?" She reached for him, but another man pushed her aside.

"I'm a doctor. Let me see him."

Sweat dripped from the passenger's brow, his breathing sounded labored.

"Is it a heart attack?" she asked.

"Driver! Stop this bus immediately!"

Jackie blinked at the doctor's order.

But knew what the plan was now. She started to back up when the heart attack victim caught her eye. And winked.

She dropped to her knees beside him, nudging the doctor aside. The aisle didn't make for much room, but she grabbed his hand when he lifted it toward her.

"Be careful," he whispered. His palm scraped hers and she curled her fingers around a paper he'd left behind.

She scooted back as the driver slowed the bus to a stop on the shoulder of the highway. The driver was on his microphone and the other passengers muttered amongst themselves.

"Driver! Where's the AED device?"

"I'll get it, I'm coming." The driver grabbed it from the console at the front of the bus and shoved his way past Jackie and Ian.

"Open the door and get the man some air. You people move back!" The doctor shouted orders and people obeyed.

Jackie opened the door. She grabbed Ian's hand and together, they slipped off the bus, Gus at their heels.

"Where are we going?"

"Wherever we can find shelter and regroup."

The helicopter roared overhead. Sirens sounded, getting closer by the second. "Stay under cover of the trees," she panted.

Ian didn't let go of her hand or Gus's leash. They leapt over the guardrail and headed down the sloping hill. Jackie swept her gaze left. Then to the right and up above. Had the chopper spotted them racing from the stopped bus?

Once in the midst of a copse of trees that backed up to a field she could see just beyond, she stopped to assess the situation. Ian and Gus came to a halt beside her.

"Did we really just do that?" he asked.

"Yeah."

"So now what?" He glanced around. "They'll be coming. We need to find some shelter and figure out our next step."

Jackie nudged him. "That barn over there. Let's get inside and hope no one's there."

He looked up at the clouds hovering above them. "It looks like it's going to snow." He breathed deep. "Smells like it too."

"That would just be our luck right now," she muttered.

They headed for the barn and Ian opened the door for her. She slipped inside, relieved to be out of the wind. "It's still cold, but at least we can sit and think for a minute."

"Maybe there's an office with some heat."

"Good idea." She inhaled the scent of hay and horses. "Hello? Anyone here?" Her only answer came in the form of a nicker from the nearest stall. "Hello?"

"I think we're good," Ian said.

It took only a minute to scope out the barn and find what they were looking for. The office was dusty, but one flick of the heater on the wall had warmth pouring through the vents. Jackie sat in the cracked vinyl chair behind the desk and pulled out the piece of paper the "heart attack victim" had slipped into her hand.

Ian sat across from her in the wooden straight-backed chair. Gus settled on the floor at his feet and put his head on his paws.

"What is it?" Ian asked.

"The man on the bus who faked the heart attack gave me this."

"Faked?"

"He winked at me. The doctor was probably bogus too. Ron set it all up, I'm sure. Just in case."

Ian blinked. "Wow. That was sharp thinking."

She gave him a thin smile. "See why I wanted to call in reinforcements?"

"Yes," he said, his voice soft. "I see."

"Ron's coming for us, we've just got to get there."

"Where?"

"To an abandoned gas station not too far away. He gave me the address."

"All right, then. Let's get going."

"Are you forgetting that everyone is looking for us?"

He shot her a sour look. "Not likely. In fact they're going to be looking for us around here, probably going house to house to make sure we haven't holed up somewhere." He looked around, then let his eyes come back to meet hers. "Like in a barn."

She wrinkled her nose at him. "I know. And we need to get moving before they get here, but we also need to take a moment to plan."

Gus's head lifted and he turned his attention to the door. Jackie stiffened. A loud screech disturbed the air. Ian slapped the off button of the heater and pulled Gus with him to press his back against the wall. Jackie joined him. Whoever opened the door wouldn't see them at first, leaving them with the element of surprise.

Footsteps sounded just outside the office. Jackie kept herself pressed against Ian's side and his warmth wrapped itself around her, making her wish for different circumstances. Gus shifted and sat.

She swallowed and focused on listening. The footsteps stopped, followed by a thud.

"Hey, Jojo boy, you ready for a ride?" The voice sounded like it belonged to a young girl. Jackie relaxed a fraction. Maybe she was just going to take the horse for a ride and wouldn't come into the office. After several tense moments, the doorknob turned, dashing Jackie's short-lived hope.

The door opened and the girl stepped into the office and walked over to the heater. Jackie held her breath and could sense Ian doing the same.

Because when the girl turned, there was no way she would miss them.

# 12

"They couldn't have just dropped off the face of the earth." Victor Stroebel stood from behind his desk and walked to the coffeepot. He poured himself a cup, then splashed a generous amount of whiskey in it.

A long sip later, he set the cup down and stared at his hired help. Owning one of South Carolina's largest construction companies gave him access to all kinds of people. Some good, some not so good. Today he needed the not so good. Nick Stafford had proven useful in the past, and Victor had hopes the man would once again earn his pay. "Wainwright's an idiot," he mumbled.

"Sir?"

"Nothing. I just don't like it when people mess up and I have to clean up behind them. He should never have gone to the cops with his accusation. We could have taken care of the problem without broadcasting—" Victor cursed and shook his head. "Forget it."

Stafford clasped his hands in front of him and lifted his chin. "The cops are crawling all over the area where the bus stopped.

It's on every news channel available. All we have to do is follow them and they'll lead us straight to Lockwood and Sellers."

"Then why aren't you doing that?"

Nick swallowed, his attempt at growing a spine failing miserably. "Right, we'll do that right now." He slapped Hector's head. "Come on. Let's move."

Hector shoved Nick and curled his fingers into a fist. Victor cleared his throat and Hector tightened his jaw, shot another glare at Nick, and strode toward the door. A small smile curved Victor's lips. He liked that Hector kid.

He turned back to the flat screen television mounted on the wall over his desk.

One thing Nick was right about was the fact that Jackie and Ian were one of the top stories. If not *the* top story.

His phone rang. With one last look at the screen, he snatched the handset. "Yes."

"Why do we still have loose ends running around?"

"Because Ian's got help. Specialized help. If he didn't, he would be dead by now."

"Where did he get this help?"

"It looks like a childhood friend came to his rescue. From what I could pull on her, Jackie Sellers used to be a cop. She now works for Operation Refuge—an organization that specializes in making people disappear."

The curses that blistered the line didn't even make Victor blink. He might work for Cedric Wainwright, but he wasn't afraid of him. "Calm down. We're not finished yet."

"I hope not."

"You blew it when you accused Ian of stealing company secrets."

"How do you figure that?"

"Because if the cops get to him first, he'll talk, tell them everything he knows. Which might not be much and they might not actually believe everything he says, but it might be enough to launch an investigation into Wainwright Labs. And while I won't have any trouble getting to Lockwood once he's in prison, I'd rather take him out before he has a chance to cast suspicion."

Wainwright's long pause made Victor frown. Then he heard the man sigh. "Should I retract the charge? Get the cops to back off? Make them feel like it's safe to stop running?"

Victor blinked back his surprise. Wainwright didn't often swallow his pride. He considered the questions. "No. I don't think that would work. As soon as they stop running, they'll still talk. I think our original plan to get Lockwood arrested then knocked off in jail isn't going to work now. He's got help. He's been talking. At this point, we need to get to them before law enforcement. We'll stay on it. I may have a lead on where they're headed anyway."

"Where?"

"Holly Kent, Lockwood's cousin, is an encryption expert. The story is she's been out of the country doing some kind of seminar for cryptologists on the latest protection software, but I can't find a record of her flight. She's not answering her phone either. We're still looking for her."

"So why is she still alive?"

"She never got the fax. My guy walked into her office and pulled it off her machine."

"Good. Then we don't have to worry about her."

"No, we have to worry about her. Lockwood is heading toward New York. All the major networks are broadcasting the hunt for them live. If you turn it on, you'll see the news teams doing helicopter sweeps. Law enforcement's in the air too. You need to have people nearby who can take them out if they get caught."

Another pause. When Wainwright spoke, he sounded nervous. "I'll get someone on it. We can't have them talking to the cops."

"I'm guessing he's going to be looking for Mrs. Kent to help him with the code."

"Then your people will be waiting."

"Waiting and watching. You take care of them if the feds catch them first. I've got people ready in New York. As soon as Lockwood, Sellers, and Kent are in the same place, we'll grab them." He paused. "We'll have to be careful, though. She lives in a very populated area near Central Park. It'll be hard to either grab them or kill them without attracting a lot of attention."

"I want him—them—dead—or in jail. If they're in jail, they'll be dead within hours of darkening the door. But if they're roaming around and figure out what that email means . . ."

"Or if they show it to the wrong person like Kent . . ."

"Five years of planning is circling the drain, Victor. Five years. We finally found our inside person, one willing to sell out his country for a few million dollars. This goes down as planned or we're done."

"We?"

"Yeah. We. And now I'll have to report this failure."

"Report—what? Report to whom?"

"None of your business. Now get this done."

"I hope it'll all be wrapped up before nightfall."

"Hope? Hope?"

"I'll be in touch." Victor hung up, not caring that Wainwright was most likely turning all shades of red and purple. He had bigger things to worry about. Like whether or not he was going to lose ten million dollars if the plan didn't go off as promised. He frowned, though. Wainwright seemed to be the one calling the shots, but apparently there was someone else. Someone even more powerful and more invested in making sure this plan went off as designed. Someone Wainwright didn't want to inform of Victor's failure to kill Ian Lockwood. He leaned back in his chair and rubbed his chin as he pondered how to go about finding out exactly who the mastermind was behind the plan. Because once he knew who it was, he could then figure out how to blackmail him for more money.

---

Ian met the scared brown eyes of the pretty teenager. "Don't scream."

Her face bleached white and she brought her hands up to cover her mouth as though to hold back the scream he warned her against.

"We're not going to hurt you, we were just cold and found your barn and thought we'd warm up."

"That's trespassing," she whispered. But at least she didn't scream. "Who are you? Why are you here?" She moved, her back pressing against the wall as though wishing it would suck her through to the other side. Her gaze landed on Gus and then moved to Jackie.

"Like he said, we were cold and came looking for a place to warm up." Jackie rubbed her hands together. "We're warm now. We didn't mean to scare you. We'll leave and you can pretend you never saw us, okay?" She started backing toward the door and the teen seemed to relax a fraction, her fear fading slightly.

"You're really not going to hurt me?"

"We're really not," Jackie said.

"Okay. Um . . . thanks?" Her eyes bounced back and forth between Jackie and Ian and Gus.

The helicopter buzzed overhead and Jackie hesitated. The girl looked at Ian. Then back to Jackie.

Ian rubbed a hand down his face.

The teen's eyes narrowed and she swallowed, recognition hitting her gaze. "Wait a minute, you're the two they're looking for, aren't you?" She bit her lip, every ounce of her previous tension returning full force. "Never mind, I never saw you. Just leave. Please."

"We're leaving, don't worry," Jackie said.

They stepped out of the office, the girl following behind, skittish as one of her colts in the stall. Gus's ears laid back against his head, his body rigid with tension. The dog was special—highly trained and he'd been great up to this point— but he wasn't oblivious to the stress and was confused about why his world had suddenly changed.

Ian opened the door of the barn, looked out, then shut it. "I don't think we're going to be leaving right away after all."

"They're out there?" Jackie asked.

"Not yet, but they're getting close. The helicopter is right overhead. If we step out there, we're done for."

She closed her eyes. "I heard the chopper, but hoped it was further away. All right, let's think."

"Why don't you just turn yourselves in?" the girl asked.

"Because that's not an option right now. What's your name?" Ian asked.

"Leigh." Leigh backed up, away from the two of them, her fear returning.

Ian wanted to pace, but he wasn't about to let Leigh out of his sight. He figured there was a back door somewhere and he couldn't let her slip through it and tip off law enforcement.

"All right, Leigh. You're not stupid, so I'm not going to treat you as though you are. I didn't do what I'm being accused of doing, I just can't prove it. And I definitely can't prove it sitting in a prison cell. We need a way out of here. Have you got any suggestions?"

He didn't really expect her to just jump on the question and provide a ready answer. Instead, he watched her eyes. They flicked to the left, then back to him. "No."

"Right. Jackie?"

"Yes?"

He nodded. "This way."

She took another peek out the window and walked over to him. "Okay, where?"

"Show us, Leigh."

She jutted her chin. "No."

Ian stepped forward. "Yes."

Tears welled in the girl's eyes. She spun and bolted. Jackie made to chase her, but Ian caught her arm. "Let her go. She's terrified."

"And we're going to be toast as soon as she reports us."

"Maybe not. When I asked her about a way out of here, she looked to her left." He walked over to the first door and pulled it open. "Supplies." He shut it.

Jackie opened the next one. "Ah ha."

Ian stepped to look over her shoulder. "Ah ha." Two ATVs sat with keys in the ignition.

"I have a real problem with theft, but we don't have a choice, I suppose."

"I've got a thousand dollars in cash."

"Fine, leave it. The machine is older and probably only worth about half that. Ron will have more cash waiting on us when we get to the vehicle, so we can give yours up. We'll be there within minutes if we can dodge law enforcement long enough. The owner will have his ATV back within the hour."

Ian set the cash on the shelf and climbed into the driver's seat.

Jackie peeked out the window. "No one there that I can see."

"Open the doors. We can't waste any more time around here. Leigh probably squealed on us as fast as she could."

Jackie complied and Ian sent up prayers that they hadn't stayed in the barn too long. He cleared the doors and Jackie shut them, then bolted into the passenger seat. "See that trail?"

"Yes."

"Don't take it."

He understood. "Right." He could still hear the helicopter up above, looking for them. "You think they got our pictures from the bus station cameras?"

"No doubt. Or from the bus camera itself."

He took a deep breath. "All right. We need to stay under some cover."

"We can try to blaze our own trail through the woods or we can head back toward the highway and hope for the best."

He pressed the gas pedal. "We don't have a prayer of escape, do we?"

# 13

Sam glanced at his phone. "They've stopped. The ATV is idle."

Elizabeth pressed the gas. "Does the chopper have it spotted?"

"No, it disappeared into some trees."

Last night, as part of a federal task force, Sam had been sworn in as a federal US marshal. Now he had federal arrest authority along with Elizabeth, and they'd taken off in pursuit of their suspects with the full intention of using that authority. Minutes before, a teen girl had found Lockwood and Sellers in her barn. They hadn't hurt her, but they'd taken one of the ATVs—and left around a thousand dollars on a shelf as payment for the machine. An ATV the owner had installed with a GPS chip in case it should ever be stolen. "Guide me."

"Turn here. Go straight for a mile, then right into the property's drive."

Elizabeth followed his directions only to find other law enforcement officers had beat them there. She and Sam flashed their badges and pulled close to the edge of the woods. Elizabeth climbed from the vehicle and raced toward the stopped ATV, hand on her weapon. Officers surrounded it.

She spotted an agent she'd worked with one other time. "Gayle, fill me in."

Sam stepped up beside her. Gayle shook her head and pursed her lips. "It was empty when we got here. They took off on foot. We've got the K-9's on the way."

"Should have had the K-9's already here," she snapped.

"Yeah, I know. There was a hold-up somewhere. Traffic accident slowed them down."

Elizabeth bit her tongue. It wasn't Gayle's fault. "Sorry. Which way did they take off?"

"We're not sure. There were some tracks that make us think they're heading north."

"What's north?"

Gayle lifted her iPad and touched the button at the bottom of the screen. A full-color map appeared. "Here. This area is still pretty remote. An abandoned gas station along this road, a small church, a neighborhood, and two schools. Agents are searching door to door as we speak. The schools are on lockdown."

Elizabeth nodded. The team was efficient and experienced. Things didn't always go as planned, but it was going as well as possible. Now if it would just continue to go that way, they would have Lockwood and Sellers in custody before nightfall.

---

"Are they behind us?" Ian looked back over his shoulder.

"They're behind us," Jackie said, dodging a branch. "Just keep going. I'm surprised they don't have the dogs on us."

"Thank you, I hadn't thought of that."

She ignored his sarcasm. "Just about another mile, I think."

"How can you tell where we are?"

"I don't know, it's a gift." She really didn't know how to explain it. She never had any problems with directions or knowing where she was. She could look at a map and know how to get from point A to point B without bothering to look again. She stopped to listen.

Nothing. Had they lost them?

Maybe. For now.

"Like doing three-digit multiplication problems in your head?"

She huffed. "You remember that?"

"Of course. You freaked everyone out at the spelling bee when you refused to spell 'pontification' and asked for a math problem."

She snorted and motioned for him to follow her. "My English teacher blackmailed me into doing that spelling bee. It was either that or detention."

"So you decided to do math instead."

"Yep."

"And you answered it right. And the next one. And the next one."

"Uh huh."

"Never did figure out how you did that."

"It's like a puzzle. Simply take the numbers apart and put them back together again in a way that they make sense."

She noticed that while she wasn't winded from their dash through the woods, neither was Ian. Satisfied that he wouldn't physically hold them back, she pressed on harder, knowing their luck wouldn't hold out forever.

They exited the woods and found themselves on the edge of the highway. Jackie didn't stop, just continued her jog. Ian stayed with her.

"We're almost there." She pulled out her phone, turned it on, and dropped it back in her pocket. "We're going to be pretty exposed for the next two or three tenths of a mile, though."

"Where's the helicopter?" he asked.

"It'll be back."

Just as they hit the tree cover again, the phone rang and she snagged it, never breaking her stride. "Yeah?"

"Where are you?" Ron said.

"Trying to get to the rendezvous point."

"Look for a blue Ford king cab truck with a horse logo on the side."

Relief spilled through her. They might have a chance after all. "Thanks, Ron. I'll call later. I'm ditching the phone." She hung up, deleted Ron's number, and turned it off. She stopped for a second, reared back, and gave the phone a hard toss to the right of her. She immediately took off again, Ian beside her. She looked at him. "We've got a vehicle."

"How?"

"You'll see." Jackie started to feel the effects of the run. She ran every other day, but not this fast—and not for her life. She heard sirens in the distance and thought the helicopter might be coming back. Law enforcement was closing the circle and she had no idea how they were going to slip through it.

Finally, the small abandoned shop came into sight. They darted across the street. Jackie heard the helicopter getting closer. "Under the awning, quick." She ducked under and Ian threw himself up beside her with Gus at his side. A few seconds later, the chopper roared overhead. "You think they saw us?"

"Maybe. I don't know. If they did, the cops will be here fast. They definitely know we're in the area so are most likely setting up roadblocks as we speak."

"Then how are we going to get away?"

She didn't bother to answer as they circled the building to find the blue truck Ron promised. With a horse logo on the side and a trailer full of manure hooked to the back.

And Ron sitting in the driver's seat.

Jackie threw herself into the passenger seat, Ian and Gus jumped into the back.

Ron grinned at her. "You're not staying in here."

Jackie groaned. "How did you get here so fast? You're like Houdini." She nodded toward the backseat. "Meet Ian and Gus."

He spared the two a glance. "Nice to meet you fellows." He turned his attention back on Jackie. "Told you I had a chopper. Landed on a friend's farm about a mile out, borrowed his truck, some of his reprocessed hay, and drove in. Now get out."

"Reprocess—what?" Ian asked.

Ron motioned them out of the truck and around to the back where he had the manure piled in the bed. "Reprocessed hay. Get the dog in the cab. You two get under that long wooden box. Might be a tight fit, but it's big enough for the two of you. I'm going to throw that tarp over it while you two hook up to the tanks. Get the masks on good. Then I'm going to shovel this load over you. The wood will keep it from pressing down on you, the tarp will keep it from pushing through the cracks. Get Gus's vest off of him and keep it with you under the manure. I don't want them finding any evidence that I've got a service dog with me. Gus is simply my pet, got it?"

Ian's eyes went wide, but Jackie couldn't miss the determination even if it was mixed with a bit of consternation. He went to the door and opened it. "Ride, Gus." The dog hopped into the passenger seat.

When Ian returned, Jackie hesitated and gripped Ron's arm. "You can't put yourself on the line like this, Ron. I feel horrible even asking you to."

"You didn't ask." Ron pulled at the well-worn cowboy hat on his head and wiped his gloved hands on his mud-spattered jeans. "Been listening to the police scanner. There's a roadblock three miles away. They figured out you were heading north and have taken quick action to shut you down. We're going to get you through that." He handed her a small wireless device. "Put this in your ear so you can hear what's going on." He handed one to Ian too.

Jackie still didn't move. "I'm serious, Ron, you can't do this."

She looked at the three-sided wooden box. The open side faced her, a dark hole waiting for her slide into. "I can't do this. I think I'd rather take my chances with jail." Just the thought of climbing in it made her throat want to close up. "You know how I feel about closed spaces. I really don't think I can do this without panicking and giving you away." She swallowed.

"I *can* do this and I am. And you are too." Ron squeezed her shoulder. "You can dig out with no trouble, Jackie. You won't be trapped. I made sure of that."

He pressed a small shovel into her hand and her fingers tightened around it. She could get out. The thought helped.

Ron turned to Ian. "The cops are everywhere, going door to door, stopping people on the streets, flashing your pictures. They're going to be searching this building pretty soon."

"Exactly. Which means we need to go," Ian urged.

"So how are you going to get through the roadblock if I don't help you? If you don't get in that truck?" Ron asked.

Jackie sighed and thought. And came up empty. "You're right. We need you." She looked at the wooden box, the plastic tarp. The pile of manure that would be shoveled over her. She couldn't do it. Couldn't—

"Now that we've got that settled, we've got about sixty seconds to get going. You're going to get in the back like I instructed and I'm going to shovel this manure over you and drive you through the roadblock. Simple as that."

"Simple as that," she muttered. She eyed Ron, barely keeping her panic under control. "This was your only solution?"

Regret flashed in Ron's eyes. "It's the only way, Jackie. You're stronger than you think. You always have been. You *can* do this."

Her heart fluttered in her chest like a trapped bird. Her fingers spasmed over the handle of the shovel. "Right." She heard the faint sound of the helicopter approaching. She looked at Ian. "You ready?"

His fingers flexed into a fist. "I'm ready." He stared at Ron. "You'll be an accessory. Why are you doing this?"

"Because Jackie believes in you." Ron held Ian's gaze for a brief moment before nodding to the back of the truck. "No time to gab. Hurry up. And take this with you. Can't let them find this in the truck if they decide to search." He shoved a black backpack into Jackie's arms. "I'll explain later."

Jackie wanted to scream, to run. But she couldn't. Ian was counting on her. Ron was risking everything to help them. So . . . she was going to do this. She was going to let Ron bury her alive.

---

Elizabeth watched the live video feed coming from the helicopter. "Where'd they go? They didn't just walk off the earth."

Sam pinched the bridge of his nose. "Why are they so hard to catch?"

"They have help." She slapped her hand against the hood of the car.

"Who?"

"You've got the number Lockwood called his brother from."

"Right." Sam paced, his mind racing, wondering where she was going with this.

"And we have a record of all calls made to that phone and from it?"

"Yes."

"So who did they call?"

"No one."

"That doesn't even make sense. There's a record of several calls. Who did they call?"

"Prepaid cells. No names attached to the phones."

"They're all definitely professionals."

"Sellers is and the organization she works with. She's the one telling him how to stay under the radar."

"I want background checks on everyone connected to Operation Refuge." She typed a text and waited for the response. "Sweeny's on it. We'll have that information shortly." She thought and typed another text. "All information related to any phones in their names. Landline calls, cell calls. Any calls from pay phones. I want a list of everything for the past two days."

Sam nodded. "The chopper's over the roadblock on I-95."

"Backing up traffic pretty bad there, people are going to be fuming."

"It's already on the news. Massive manhunt for suspected terrorist and his accomplice."

Her phone dinged. She swiped the screen and shook her head. "I don't understand why a woman with an outstanding law enforcement background would allow herself to be dragged into this."

Sam shrugged. "Maybe she was just trying to help a friend and it exploded in her face." He paused. "What if he's forcing her to help him?"

Elizabeth shook her head. "She's too well trained. She'd find a way out. A way to call for help. Something."

"Yeah." He fell silent.

Elizabeth turned her attention to the next roadblock. "They're not seeing anything suspicious."

Sam snorted. "That's because there's no way they'd risk going through a roadblock."

"I don't know."

"Come on. Think about it. They're probably running through the woods or hiding out in a deserted shack waiting for us to give up and go home."

"That's why we have the dogs in the woods."

Sam groaned. He slapped the computer shut as a king cab Ford with a horse logo on the side pulled up to the roadblock.

# 14

Ian discovered he didn't like tight spaces. Most especially being buried alive. No, he didn't like it at all. At least the mask on his face blocked the odor. He breathed deep from the rebreather and felt the purified air fill his lungs. Jackie's death grip on his fingers kept him from panicking. His mind clicked with trivia he'd learned from a scuba diving class years ago. The air he was breathing wasn't really oxygen, it was atmospheric air that had been through a compression cycle which thoroughly filtered—

"Officer, what can I do ya fer?"

Ian blinked as Ron's voice came through the wire. He'd affected a country bumpkin accent to near perfection.

"We're looking for two people." A rustle sounded. The officer showing Ron the picture? "Have you seen them?"

"Hmm . . . yep. I seen 'em."

"Where?" Tension threaded the officer's word.

"On the television just afore I left home. You find 'em yet?"

A disgusted sigh. "No sir, that's why we're stopping people and asking if they've seen them."

"Oh right. Gotcha."

"You mind if I take a look?"

121

"Not a'tall." Gus barked and Ian flinched. Jackie's fingers convulsed around his. "Eh, don't mind Mike here," Ron said. "He's harmless. Unless he thinks you're invadin' his space. Or mine."

"Right. Right."

"You want me to get out?"

"No sir, I want you to stay put. Hey Ned, get over here a sec."

Low chatter sounded. "Hold tight, boys and girls," Ron's whisper came through the earpiece. "We might be doing this the hard way."

Ian's stomach twisted and Jackie's fingers tightened.

"All right, sir, do we have your permission to search the back of your truck?"

"A'course. You wantin' me to shovel that manure so you don't get them pretty uniforms dirty?"

Ian heard a low chuckle. "No sir, just let us take a quick look."

"All righty then."

Ian's heart pounded. He could feel Jackie's tension in the way she gripped his hand. It was all he could do to be still, to refrain from ripping the mask from his face and begin to dig his way out. His muscles convulsed. His breathing quickened.

Jackie's warm palm fell gently on his face. She rubbed in slow circles, avoiding the mask over his nose and the rebreather in his mouth. Her hand traveled from his cheek to his shoulder where she dug her fingers into his hard muscles. Ian swallowed, realizing what she was doing. He could almost hear her saying, "You're not alone. I'm here. It's going to be all right."

He flashed to one of the summer days they'd escaped to the lake together.

"Your mom's going to have a cow if you don't let her know where you are," Jackie had said.

Ian had shrugged as only a seventeen-year-old with the weight of the world on his shoulders could. "She probably won't even know I'm gone."

"She'll know."

"Yeah."

They lay there on the warm sand, the sun soaking into their young bones. Jackie broke the silence. "She won't notice, will she?"

Ian sighed. "No. Probably not."

Ian pulled himself from the past. His mother hadn't noticed. No one had noticed that he'd spent the night at the lake on the sand under the stars. He'd come home covered in mosquito bites, but it had been worth it. Jackie had stayed with him just holding his hand and talking to him.

He remembered wanting to kiss her, but he hadn't been able to work up the nerve.

Now with the feel of her strong fingers massaging his tense muscles, his pulse slowed, his breathing evened off. Ian closed his eyes and saw exactly the same thing as when he'd had them open. Pitch black.

He tuned back in to Ron. "Y'all about done? I got to git that there load delivered and get back to the missus."

A grunt. Then the bed of the truck shook. Ian felt something above him, like the manure shifting. Something. An officer's quiet voice came through. "Ned, you want to dig through that load of manure?"

"Not me."

"Yeah. I poked around and didn't see anything."

"Wave him on."

Ian felt his tension lessen by several degrees. The truck started to move.

"Hey, wait a minute." The truck stopped again. "I just got a report there's a dog with them. Some kind of service animal."

Ian's tension ratcheted back up to stroke levels. Jackie's squeeze on his fingers cut his circulation off.

James Walden stood and held out a hand. "Welcome to Walden's Mortuary. You must be the Bateses." He studied the couple, the man's drawn face, the woman's red-rimmed eyes. The faint purple bruise on her right cheekbone. The yellow bruise over her left eye. "I'm so sorry for your loss."

The young man in his early thirties nodded. "I'm Frank and this is my wife, Karla. I'm sorry to just drop in on you, but I don't have many free moments during the workweek. I was able to get away and thought I would take advantage of you being here. So, sorry for just popping in and not giving you any notice."

"There's never very much notice in this business, I'm afraid." James didn't smile when he said it. He wasn't trying to be funny. He glanced at the clock. "We weren't scheduled to meet until tomorrow and I do have another appointment. Do you think we could take care of this later today or even tomorrow?"

"No. I'm sorry. We can't." Mr. Bates dropped his keys onto the desk, settled himself into the nearest chair, and crossed his arms. His wife bit her lip and shot a look toward the door.

James gripped the edge of his desk, anger firing through him. He should grab the little worm by his throat and toss him out on his rear. Instead, he lowered himself into his chair and opened the drawer next to him. He pulled a paper from one of the yellow tabbed files. "Very well. We can see what we can get done until my appointment arrives." He looked at Mrs. Bates, who still stood, uncertain and uncomfortable. Her eyes were on the keys her husband had tossed onto the desk. "Ma'am?"

She flinched and met his gaze for a split second before dropping hers back to the desk.

"Would you like to sit?"

She hesitated a fraction longer, then slid into the chair next to her husband. Her fingers wove the strap of her purse around and around her hand.

James adjusted the glasses on his nose. "Now, your father had everything in order. He expressed his wishes to make his passing as, uh—*easy* just doesn't sound right, but that was the word he used—as possible for your mother and you."

Mr. Bates nodded. "Right, right. He said the same thing at our last visit, just before he died."

James handed Mr. Bates a folded piece of paper. "Now here is a sample of our most popular program. Your father said he didn't need that, but I would recommend it. It lets the attendees know who the people are who are leading the service and what they meant to your father."

Mr. Bates frowned and studied the sample brochure, then placed it back on James's desk. "Fine. We'll take that one. I'll provide the information you need by tonight."

"Excellent." James gave his much-practiced sympathetic smile. "Now, your father also requested to be cremated and he has already paid for it."

"Right, he told me. He didn't want a viewing. Said if people didn't come to see him while he was alive, they sure weren't going to see him dead." The young man cleared his throat. "I . . . um . . . would like to see him before you . . . you know."

"Of course, but, uh . . ."

"What?"

"Well, he's already been prepared for the cremation and is down in the . . . ah . . . crematorium."

Mr. Bates flinched.

The door opened. "Mr. Walden, we've got a prob—" Red Peters came to a halt, his mouth snapping shut as he noticed the Bateses' presence.

James stood. "If you'll excuse me just a moment?"

"No." Mr. Bates stood too. "Let's get this done, then you'll have all the time in the world for your next appointment." He looked at Red. "You don't mind, do you?"

Red's gaze bounced between James and Mr. Bates. He finally shot a narrow-eyed look at James.

James made sure the couple saw only his comforting smile and none of the rage boiling just beneath the surface at the intrusion. "Very well. Mr. Peters, if you'll just have a seat outside, I'll be with you shortly."

Red hesitated. "But this is really import—"

James drew in a deep breath.

Red stopped. "I'll, uh, just be, uh, right outside whenever you're ready, Mr. Walden." To the couple, Red held up a hand in apology. "Please excuse me."

"Of course." Mrs. Bates spoke for the first time.

James waited until Red left the office. He took a deep breath and turned back to the couple. "Would you like to come back tomorrow to do the viewing? I can have him brought up and presentable?"

"No. I'll see him now." Mr. Bates crossed his arms and stared down at James.

Mrs. Bates rose and laid a hand on his arm. "Honey, he said he had an appointment. We're interrupting. Maybe—"

"I said I'd see him now." Mr. Bates cut his wife a sharp glance and she dropped her head and settled back into her seat.

James motioned for the couple to follow him. "Most people don't find it a pleasant place to be."

"I can handle it. I want to see him."

"All right. I understand." James hoped he had his annoyance with the man well hidden.

Mrs. Bates hung back. "I'll wait here if that's all right."

"Of course. We won't be long," James said.

"She's coming with me."

James lifted a brow. Mrs. Bates didn't move from her seat.

"Really," James said. "We need to do this now if you want to see him today."

"Fine," Frank snapped. "Stay here," he told his wife. "I'll deal with you later."

She paled but didn't move to follow.

James frowned. The man really should treat his wife better. Wasn't his business, but still . . . He led the way to the back of the mortuary, down the set of steps, and into the crematorium.

Mr. Bates stopped at the bottom and James turned to look at him. "Is there a problem?"

"It looks different than I thought it would."

James scanned the white tiles, the stainless steel rollers, the green plants on either side of the entrance to the retort.

The cremation chamber.

"Were you expecting something dark and dreary?"

Frank gave a nervous chuckle. "Something like that. You said it wasn't a pleasant place."

"I simply meant what goes on down here. It's not for family members."

"Right."

"He's this way." James stepped over to the refrigerated vaults. "We have some of the same equipment as a morgue, we're just not quite as big."

"I see."

James hesitated, his hand on the handle. "You have to understand, he's not been embalmed, he's not going to look like you remember."

Mr. Bates swallowed. "I know."

James opened the third vault from the bottom. Cold air blew out as he slid the elder Bates from the interior. He glanced at the son, who looked a few shades whiter. "Are you certain?"

The man licked his lips. "I am."

The side door opened and two men entered carrying a black

127

case. They came to an abrupt halt when they saw they weren't alone.

James straightened. "What are you doing here? You're early."

"Red was supposed to give you the message."

"What message?"

"That we're early."

James sighed. "I'm in the middle of something right now. You'll have to wait outside please."

"We're taking care of this now. You'll have to deal with him later."

"Excuse me," Mr. Bates said. "My father died. I'm trying to view his body. Could you just give us a minute and I'll be gone?"

"No, you can't have a minute. Now get. We have business to attend to."

Mr. Bates gaped. Then turned his gaze to James. "I believe we'll take our business elsewhere." His eyes bounced from one man to the next. "Something's not right here." He turned to go.

The *whap whap* made James flinch.

Mr. Bates's body hit the floor with a thud. James looked at Mitch Conlan, who stuck his weapon back into the shoulder holster under his arm. "Are you kidding me?"

"Put him in the chamber and flush the remains. No one will ever know where he went. We couldn't have him complaining about 'something not right,' could we? And plus, I don't like the fact that he saw my face."

James shut his eyes, trying to rein in his temper. This day had gone from bad to worse in seconds. "His wife is upstairs, you idiot."

Mitch raised a brow and handed the black case to the silent man beside him. He withdrew his weapon once more. "Then we have some business to take care of upstairs, don't we?"

# 15

Jackie stayed still, keeping her breathing even.

In. Out. In. Out.

Panic wanted to consume her, so she let her mind drift. Went back to the game she'd played as a young child, locked in the closet.

*You're not here, you're at the beach.*

The place her grandfather had taken her the summer she'd turned seventeen. She pictured the waves flowing up against the sand, the screech of the seagulls as they flew overhead. She'd held crackers up and they swooped in to feast. She drew in a breath and imagined the unique smell that one could only find near the ocean. She heard the crunch of the shells beneath the tires of her bike.

The truck jolted, tumbling her back into the present. The darkness, the inability to move. Or breathe. Fear roared and she fought it, moved the shovel.

She could get out.

She could breathe.

She wasn't trapped.

The dirt shifted.

She focused on the movement of the truck. Had someone climbed onto the bed again? Were they getting ready to dig?

Her hand tingled from her contact with Ian's five o'clock shadow. Touching Ian, feeling his familiar face, his warm skin under her fingers, was the only thing keeping her still, keeping her from screaming and clawing her way out from beneath the weight pressing against the wooden box.

Her coffin.

Buried alive.

The thought made her shudder. The panic rose hot and swift.

Think about the beach.

The waves.

The cool breeze at night and the moon shining down.

The fact that Ian was right beside her. She could feel his warmth, his closeness. She breathed. She *could* breathe. She wasn't suffocating.

The officer spoke again. "There's no reason to keep them. Let them through."

The truck lurched forward, then continued without hesitation. For several seconds, Ian's fingers squeezed and she realized he was waiting too. Waiting to be stopped, to be searched. To be found.

They moved smoothly down the highway and Jackie lost track of time, focusing on breathing, feeling Ian's fingers in hers, knowing he was beside her and she wasn't alone. As soon as she knew they were safely away from the roadblock, she closed her eyes. With her hand held in Ian's, her fingers clamped around his, she let herself drift back to the sand and the waves.

And then they stopped. She opened her eyes to the blackness, felt the panic swarming back, and snapped her lids shut.

"Jackie, girl, you there?"

She let go of the shovel's handle and tapped her earpiece twice. *Yes.*

"Good. Ian, I know you can hear me too. We're away from the

roadblock with only the occasional cop in sight. It's going to take me about thirty more minutes to get to the rendezvous point."

Jackie's fingers convulsed and Ian's tightened in response. Panic roared through her. She tapped the earpiece once for a big fat *no*.

"You can do this, Jackie. You have to, you understand?"

She tapped again. No. No she couldn't. She didn't have to. She wanted out.

"Jackie . . ."

She tapped twice. *Yes.*

"Good girl."

She moved her hand back down beside her and curled her fingers back around the shovel's handle. She kept up an internal dialogue. *You can dig your way out. You can. You're not trapped. You can get out. God? Are you there? If you're there* . . . No, she wouldn't go there. What she'd told Ian was true. God had given up on her, abandoned her when she'd needed him most, she wouldn't bother him now.

She spun her mind back to her previous mantra: *You can dig your way out. You can. You're not trapped. You can get out.* Sweat slid down her back and she wiggled. Ian's hand tightened.

The litany of mental reassurances was the only thing that kept her calm. That, and the shovel in her hand. She *knew* she could start digging her way out and be out from under the manure within minutes.

And Ian's fingers wrapped around hers calmed her in ways she couldn't begin to explain.

Still, she was ready to see daylight. She tapped her earpiece again. Three times. *Talk to me.*

Ron's voice came again. "I like this Gus fellow. Seems he would keep a man from getting too lonely."

Ian's fingers relaxed a fraction.

Time passed at a crawl while Ron kept up a running mono-logue. He seemed to understand that it helped to hear his voice. Finally, the truck slowed to a stop.

Jackie waited. She could *feel* Ian waiting, his impatience. She wondered if she emanated the same vibes.

The truck bed shifted. "I'm going to start digging you out, okay?" She heard the shovel, then Ron again. "Almost there, people."

Light started to filter through.

She blinked against the brightness, squinted and tried to let her eyes adjust even as her hands pushed against the wooden box as though that would help move the manure. It didn't, but it made her feel better.

More shoveling. More light. Then the plastic was pulled away, taking the rest of the manure with it. She yanked the rebreather mouthpiece out. Ron held out a hand and helped her out from the wooden box and off the bed of the truck. Her knees almost buckled. She sucked in several gulps of sweet oxygen and rel-ished the open air while she held on to Ron a moment longer. Ian landed beside her.

He looked at Ron and cleared his throat. "I don't know how to say thanks."

Ron studied him. "You don't have to. But we're in deep now. If we get caught, the only way you and Jackie and I won't serve jail time is if we get a pardon from the president—or find evidence on the people who are setting you up." He shook his head. "I'll be working on that angle while you two figure out what your next step is."

Jackie's eyes finally adjusted, her tremors eased, and she drew in another deep breath as she looked around. "A used car lot?"

Ron shrugged. "Figured it was as good a place as any to hide

132

a car." He smirked. "And they're never very busy, according to my source, so not a lot of people around to see what's going on or ask questions." He motioned for them to follow him. At the truck's passenger door, he opened it and Gus hopped to the ground at Ian's feet. Ian scratched his ears.

"You have that backpack?"

Jackie held it up. "What's in it?"

"IDs, keys to that big black SUV right there. Nine thousand in cash—would have given you ten, but didn't want to have to let the IRS in on anything—a laptop, two new throw phones, and a few other odds and ends to help you change your appearance again. You can't go around looking like that."

Jackie threw her arms around Ron. "Thank you."

Ron gave her a hard squeeze and cleared his throat. "Get this mess cleared up and get yourself back home."

"We will. We've got to find Holly and figure out what that email means."

Ron frowned and nodded. "We'll be working on deciphering that too."

"What about trying to solve the murder of Daniel Armstrong?" Ian asked. "Because I didn't do it."

Ron gave a slow nod. "We can look into that too."

Jackie squeezed the keys. "There's something big happening, Ron. And Ian and I have been drop-kicked into the middle of it."

"The key is the email," Ian said. "Somebody doesn't want us figuring out the code."

"Let's pass it on to the FBI. If anyone can figure it out, they can."

"Who's the agent in charge of the case?" Jackie asked.

Ron pursed his lips. "Rebecca Wilson is the Special Agent in Charge in Atlanta, Cole Maxwell is in South Carolina, and Scott Mitchell is the ADIC, Assistant Director in Charge, in

New York. According to my source, he's handling this person-
ally and working with the Special Agent in Charge over the
counterterrorism unit. The ADIC heads several divisions, each
run by a Special Agent in Charge. But David said two agents
came by to talk to them. FBI Special Agent Elizabeth Miller
and SLED agent Sam Ferguson."

"Fine. Let me get it to her then. They'd want to know how
you came across it and I don't want them to be able to connect
you to us at all," Ian said.

Ron smirked. "I'm in it up to my eyeballs at this point, really
doesn't matter what I do after this."

"They'll figure it out," Jackie said, her voice soft. "They already know I'm with Operation Refuge, they'll do a background
check on all of the employees there—if they haven't already—
question them, and come up with you. And our connection."

Ron nodded. "Maybe."

"They'll question you."

He winked. "They have to find me first."

---

"Holly's not answering." Ian shut the phone off and stared
out the window.

Jackie drove. Ian remembered she liked to drive even as a
teenager. She'd once confessed it was the feeling of being in
control. He could understand that. He couldn't help glancing
out the window to see if anyone followed. It was fast becoming
a habit. "What have you been doing since you left? How did
you get involved in Operation Refuge and rescuing people?"

Her fingers flexed around the wheel and she didn't answer
for a long moment. "My life has been quite the series of ups
and downs since we last saw each other."

"How so?"

"I was married." She blinked and bit her lip.

*Was?* Ian figured she hadn't intended to let those words slip out. "I didn't know that."

She nodded. "That's because no one knew. At least not until much later. And only a handful at that point."

"What? I'm sorry, I'm confused. Why would you not tell anyone you were married?"

"My husband and I were partners on the police force."

"Isn't that against cop rules or something?"

She gave a low laugh. "No, it's not common and it's not encouraged, but there's no rule against it. At least in normal precincts."

"Yours was different?"

"My captain was different. If he thought there was any kind of romantic relationship between partners—or anyone in the precinct—he'd find a way to break it up. And I don't just mean put you with a different partner, he would find a way to get rid of you."

"How? Couldn't you just transfer to another precinct?"

"Not with this guy. It's like he made it a mission to make your life as miserable as possible until you were willing to give up being a cop. I know one officer who was dating another cop in the precinct. They weren't partners, but they worked the same shift a lot of times. The captain gave them both lousy performance reviews. They both quit. John and I had no desire to go through that. Which is why we went to Mexico to do the deed." She shot him a glance and gave him a slight smile before she turned her eyes back to the road. "While we were working together, we were partners. No sneaking kisses, no hand holding. Nothing to give the captain or anyone working for him any ammunition. There's not even a record of our marriage in the United States."

"Wow. That was a bit extreme, wasn't it?"

"Maybe. But it was fun too in some ways."

"Couldn't you report the captain? There are laws against that kind of stuff, aren't there?"

"Sure. And some people did, but his uncle was the mayor."

"Ah. 'Nuff said. So where is he now? Your husband, not the captain."

"He died."

He sucked in a quick breath and searched for the right words. He couldn't find them.

"He was killed in a random convenience store shooting." Her fingers flexed on the wheel. "He was there at one o'clock in the morning when he should have been at home in bed asleep, but . . ." She swallowed hard. "He wasn't."

"Oh—wow—I'm—I—don't know what to say. I'm so sorry."

"I am too. And you don't have to say anything. There's nothing you *can* say. Nothing anyone can say . . ."

"Is that why you're mad at God?"

"Oh yeah."

She fell silent and so did Ian. He wished he had words to offer comfort, make things right, but knew he didn't so he just kept his mouth shut. But his brain kept spinning and worry for his cousin ate at him. He decided to change the subject. "They got to Holly, didn't they? They figured out I faxed that email to her, didn't they?"

"I don't know, Ian. We'll go straight to her apartment and see what we can find."

"I'm sorry I dragged you into this."

"You didn't. I broke into your house, remember?"

"Well. True." He raised a brow. "What's up with that anyway? Why not just knock?"

"I did. Several times."

"Yeah. So why didn't you leave then?"

"I'd seen your face on national news. When you wouldn't answer your phone or your door, I was worried."

"So you picked the lock."

"Yes."

"So back to you being dragged into this."

"Nobody dragged me."

"Regardless . . . I won't go to the cops. And now you've gotten your friends into it. I'm probably going to jail when this is all over. And because of me, you will too."

"Let's just focus on our goals right now."

"What are those?"

"Find Holly and make sure she's safe, get that code to the FBI so they can be working on it, and figuring out what's going to happen in New York."

"If anything."

"And prove your innocence. If we can do that, no one goes to jail except the people who deserve to."

He pulled out the email again and studied it.

NYonSTBY.
d,s;;[pcfr;obrtrf.
H4W9
aasjl;;
/fg'g[.jl]]u
Cnt:T8R sas1sjg2hjha3

He looked up. "Something's going to happen. Don't ask me how I know, I just do."

She reached out to cover his hand. The warmth of her fingers wrapped its way around his heart and he cleared his throat.

She nodded. "Okay. We'll go with that." Her lips tightened. "I sure hope you're right because we're running on borrowed time."

## 16

"Cedric Wainwright is dirtier and stinkier than my daddy's two-day-old socks," Ron said. Four hours earlier he'd stripped the truck of the horse emblems, switched the license plate back to the original, and driven it to a friend's house where it would be parked until this was all over.

And it would be over. Soon.

His buddy had choppered him back to South Carolina thirty minutes ago. David had picked him up at the airport and now they were on their way to the Operation Refuge office.

David lifted a brow and shot him a sideways glance. "Stinkier? Is that a word?"

Ron snorted. "Probably not, but you get my drift." He paused, then gave a slow smile. "No pun intended. Get it? Stinkier and drift—"

David barked a short laugh. "I get it. It's bad, but I get it." He sighed. "We need to dig up every last detail on the man."

The brief flash of humor was gone. "I've dug up enough with a little help from a buddy at the Bureau. I've heard of Wainwright before, of course. He's in the papers all the time for his philanthropic work and all the advances his labs have been responsible for in medicine." Ron scrolled through his phone and held it up. "Makes for some interesting reading. My contact with the FBI is digging deeper, of course."

"He ask you any questions about why you wanted to know this stuff?"

"No. We have an understanding."

"You were in the Army together?"

Ron let a smile play on his lips. "Nothing gets past you, huh?"

"I've come to learn something about you."

"What's that?" Ron asked.

"You have contacts everywhere and an unlimited amount of resources at your fingertips."

"True."

"How did you manage that?"

Ron sighed. "You've never asked before."

David shrugged. "I figured you were entitled to your privacy and if you wanted me to know it, you'd tell me."

"So what's different about now?"

"Now Jackie's involved."

"Yes. She is."

They fell silent for a brief moment. Ron debated whether to share his story or not. He didn't suppose it mattered. And besides, he trusted David. "I was in the Army."

"Right."

"I had some pretty specialized skills and did a few favors for some of the higher-ups in government at the time."

"Higher-ups?"

"All the way to the Oval Office," Ron said.

David blinked. "Okay."

"That made me a few friends."

"And a few enemies, I would hazard to guess."

"A few." He rubbed his chin. "I was also in the Secret Service for a while. When one of those enemies found me and almost took out the president because he was gunning for me, I decided it was time to disappear."

"And keep a low profile."

"Yep."

"I've got to ask one more question while we're reminiscing."

"Sure. Why not?"

"Where'd all your money come from? You seem to have an endless supply of it."

Ron laughed. "That's bugged you from day one, hasn't it? Well, I have to say, all of that money came from hard work. I was in the Army. But I also did some work for a private organization who funded some missions. When my buddies and I were doing missions, sometimes we'd come across a drug lord's stash. We divided up the loot and vowed to do something good with it."

David nodded and Ron knew he was thinking about the time Ron had saved David's life. "I'm glad." He paused. "I'm assuming you never got caught since you're sitting here and not rotting in prison somewhere." Ron knew what David was thinking. As a government employee, Ron's actions were illegal. If he'd been caught, he would have been tried and convicted and sent to prison. Working in the private sector, he had more flexibility.

"No. We weren't caught. And those weren't Army-mandated missions so . . ." He shrugged. "Anyway, as far as my enemies know, I'm dead."

David nodded. "And if they found out you weren't?"

"They'd come after me and everything associated with me."

"I see."

They pulled up to the office and David let the car idle as he looked out the window. Ron let him think.

Finally, David turned back to him. "So Wainwright. He sent that email to his employees, making a huge mistake when he clicked on Ian Lockwood's name instead of Ian Peterson."

"Which means we know at least two people who are involved in this. Cedric Wainwright and Ian Peterson."

"Right."

"Or not."

David narrowed his eyes. "What do you mean?"

"What if someone else sent the emails from Wainwright's computer?"

"You really believe that?"

"I don't have a clue. We know Jackie and Ian didn't send the emails that were found on their computers, so I guess the same thing could have happened to Wainwright. Someone could have hacked his account."

"I don't believe that."

"I'm not saying I do, I'm simply throwing out possibilities."

"Yeah," David muttered. "Lots of possibilities. What did your friend find on Wainwright? Anything tangible?"

"He said he had to peel back layers and layers to get to the core, but it looks like Wainwright has ties to organized crime."

"Ugh."

"Ugh?"

"Organized crime. I've had enough of that to last me a lifetime."

Ron nodded in agreement. David had been in the Witness Protection Program and the mob boss Alessandro Raimondi had targeted him and Summer. They'd barely escaped to live to tell about it. "Something else is bothering me," Ron said.

"What's that?"

Ron pursed his lips. "I heard on the radio this morning that the Department of Health and Environmental Control is encouraging citizens to get vaccinated for smallpox, and vaccines were being made available wherever you could find a flu vaccine."

"What? Smallpox?" David glanced at him.

"An outbreak has been reported."

"Where? What country?"

"Here."

David fell silent and Ron pondered what the announcement meant. His buddy with the FBI hadn't been able to give him any additional information, but the whole thing bothered him.

"An outbreak of smallpox in the United States." David shook his head. "That doesn't make sense. The disease was eradicated years ago."

"In 1979. But there have been a few isolated cases since then."

"So what are you thinking?"

"I'm thinking something's going on and no one's talking about it. Instead they're trying to do damage control."

David nodded. "You know all those resources you have?"

"Yes."

"Any of them with the CDC?"

"No, but I bet the governor can help us out there."

---

*7:45 P.M.*
*NEW YORK CITY*

Jackie breathed a sigh of relief as she drove past the apartment building for the fifth time and saw nothing out of the ordinary. At least nothing apart from what looked like normal night-time busyness near Central Park. No surveillance vans that she could see, but who knew? She itched to get up to Holly's apartment. Her heart thudded at the thought of Holly or her daughter in danger.

Couples huddled on the benches outside while owners walked their dogs. Any of them could be agents, but it just looked like a quiet, clear, cold night and they were going to have to go with that. If those were agents, they'd find out soon enough.

"I can't park in the underground garage, I don't have a card or the code," Ian said.

"We'll find something on the street. We'll just have to be a bit patient." Easier said than done, Jackie decided when she circled again. And again. Impatience bit at her, but she refused to let her emotions make her careless at this point.

Ian pointed. "There. Someone's pulling out. Grab it."

She did, sliding smoothly into the spot. "All right, the FBI is going to be watching her place most likely."

"Why?"

"They'll want to talk to her, interview her about your favorite people, places, et cetera."

"So they're here?"

"Yes. Probably."

"But where?"

She looked around, trying to be subtle, but not wanting to miss something. "They're not going to be obvious, but because I'm looking for them, I should be able to spot them. They'll have her building in view, maybe even her unit."

In front of her, a mother pulled her sleeping toddler from the back of a van and hurried toward the building. Could be an agent. Probably not.

Across the street a young woman with a briefcase climbed out and slammed the door. Jackie finally put the car in park. "I can't believe we made it," she murmured.

"I know."

"Which apartment is hers?" She unbuckled her seat belt.

"2A. Second floor."

"All right. When's the last time you called her?"

"About twenty minutes ago and still no answer."

Jackie pulled a baseball hat down over the strawberry blonde wig she'd donned. Thankfully the night was clear even though it was cold and snow was likely. Ian jammed a hat on his head. He slipped black-framed glasses with clear lenses over his eyes and blinked.

"I don't want to announce that we're here, so no questioning the neighbors." She bit her lip. "Looks like we're going to have to break in and see what we can find."

"Why not just use the key?"

"You have one?"

He shook his head. "But I know where she hides one."

"All right, let's go."

"You see any feds?"

"No. And I'm hoping they don't see us."

They climbed from the car and Ian glanced at the building, then at Gus, who shook himself from head to toe, glad to be out of the car. Ian looked torn. "I need to let him do his business. I don't suppose another couple of minutes will make a difference in finding Holly, will it?"

"Probably not." She shifted. "I'll go up and knock."

"No, I don't want us separated. Just give me three minutes. There's a small area around back that the apartment keeps stocked with supplies and a special trash can."

"Nice." Jackie glanced in the direction of Holly's apartment. *God, please let them be all right . . .*

She shut off the prayer and followed Ian as he took the lead, Gus trotting along beside him. They headed for the back of the building and found the grassy spot for the dog. "It's in the association dues, I'm sure." He smiled, but she saw the tension in it. He wasn't concerned about association dues or how he was going to clean up after Gus. But the small talk was a slice of normal in a world gone crazy. "We'll hurry."

Jackie followed at a slower pace, taking the opportunity to examine the area. Ian's need to walk the dog was actually a blessing. It slowed her down, gave her a moment to think and not act too fast. She kept an eye on the people nearby, carefully studying each person she passed. She breathed a relieved sigh when no one set her inner alarm bells off. She couldn't spot anyone who shouted "FBI agent," but that didn't mean they weren't there. She had spotted a homeless man sitting in front of the building sipping on a bottle out of his paper bag. An agent? Possible. Hopefully not. She sighed. They'd just have to take their chances.

She stayed on the edge of the green area, thinking, her mind spinning, processing what she knew and wondering what she didn't know, satisfied no one knew they were there. Yet.

Ian and Gus approached. "We're ready." Jackie followed him to the back door of the building. He punched in the code and the lock clicked open.

"You come here often."

"A few times. I come to see her and Lucy a few times a year. Enough times to remember the code." He nodded to the short hallway she found herself in. "This is the pass-through. If you keep going straight, you'll find yourself at the front of the building. We want to go about halfway to the staircase on the left and go up."

They walked down the hall to the stairs that would lead them to the second floor. Jackie automatically noted the steps to the left and to the right.

She followed behind Ian and Gus as they ascended and waited for them to stop in front of 2A. Ian went to the locker bolted against the wall next to the door and spun the combination lock. He reached in and lifted a key off one of the silver hooks. "Glad she's a creature of habit."

"So she's in the habit of not answering her phone?"

"No." He frowned. "And that's why I'm freaking with worry." He jammed the key into the lock and twisted.

Jackie stepped in behind him and gasped. "Someone beat us here."

---

Ian stepped forward. "Holly? Lucy? It's Ian." He heard the panic in his voice as he took in the trashed apartment. He vaguely registered Gus coming inside the open door behind him. Ian let go of the dog's leash and raced to the bedroom. Chaos. Drawers pulled out and dumped, the bedclothes ripped off and on the floor. A picture of Lucy and Holly smiled up at him, their expression contorted by the broken glass.

"They've destroyed the whole place," Jackie muttered.

"She's not here," Ian called.

"Yes, I am. What in the world?"

Ian and Jackie turned as one.

"Holly!" Ian bolted to her and grabbed her in a bear hug. "When I saw this place, I thought the worst."

Holly yanked away from him, sputtering as she stared at her apartment, her gaze dazed, afraid. She pulled her stunned gaze away from the disaster and stared at Ian. "Who are you?"

"It's me, Holly. Ian."

"Ian?" Her eyes narrowed, then widened. "Ian? Is that really you?" She threw herself into his arms and hugged him. "I'm so glad you're okay. The news—"

"I know. I know." Ian ran his hands over his cousin's red hair and scanned every inch of her pretty heart-shaped face.

She had lost weight and looked extremely fragile, but she was alive. They hadn't gotten to her.

"We need to go," Jackie said softly. "If the FBI is watching, they know she's here. They'll be up here shortly."

Ian shot a brief look at Jackie and noted her tension, her worry. "Right. Right," he agreed. He looked back at his cousin. Confusion stared back at him, her light green eyes taking in the disaster behind him. Belatedly, he noticed the rolling carry-on sitting in the hallway and the computer bag still looped over her shoulder. "You were traveling."

"Yes." She cleared her throat, her gaze bouncing between him and Jackie. "My . . . uh . . . plane landed about an hour ago." She pulled away from Ian and stepped further inside. "My apartment—what happened here?"

"Why aren't you answering your phone? Where's Lucy?"

She blinked and reached into her coat pocket, her eyes still on the disaster before her. "I had it turned off and just forgot to turn it back on. Lucy's staying with a friend of mine."

"Ian . . ." Jackie nudged him, her jaw tense.

He nodded and moved toward the door. "What about yesterday? Why didn't you answer yesterday?"

"I was . . . um . . . busy yesterday and didn't check my messages until late. I needed some personal time." Her eyes began to spark. "Is there some law against that?"

Ian's shoulders slumped. She was okay. She wasn't lying in a pool of blood in her apartment, dead because of him. And Lucy was safe with a friend. "No, it's fine. Of course it's okay. I'm sorry." He breathed a sigh. "Thank you, Lord," he whispered. "We need to go, though. You'll have to come with us."

"Go with you? Are you insane? I'm not going anywhere. You're in some big trouble, mister." Her brief moment of spunk fled, replaced by concern as she seemed to recall that he was a wanted man.

His laugh held no humor. "Yes, I'm aware." He moved closer to the door. Jackie continued her vigilance at the window, but he could see the impatience vibrating through her.

"I did try to call you, but you didn't answer."

"I had to ditch my phone. I couldn't chance having it traced." Ian grabbed her suitcase and tried to herd her toward the door.

"Stop it. I'm not going anywhere. At least not until I understand what's going on. What happened, Ian? Why are you being accused of terrorism and murder? I don't believe a bit of it."

Jackie's impatience was starting to wear off on him. "Thank you for that. It's not true, of course." He raked a hand through his hair. "I called your father looking for you."

"He finally got me last night and told me." She flushed, the bit of color in her cheeks making her look a little more like his cousin rather than the pale, washed-out waif she'd become since he'd last seen her. "I'd been ignoring him, but when he persisted in calling every thirty minutes, I figured it was important. He told me what was going on. And then ordered me to stay away from you." Her jaw hardened. "Which is why I came home immediately. I figured if you were trying to get in touch with me, you needed me."

"He wouldn't tell me where you were." He paced three steps, then spun on his heel and paced back. "I was imagining all kinds of—" He shuddered. "I'm just glad you're all right. We can talk later. Now we need to go."

She swept a hand toward her belongings. "But I need to call the cops, report this."

"Uh . . . no." Ian nodded to Jackie who stood by the window, her shoulders stiff, a vein pulsing in her forehead.

She turned her gaze on him and Holly, offering a tight smile.

"Holly, we don't have time to explain everything, just that there are people after us who know we might come here. Not to mention the FBI. So we really need to get somewhere safe. Then we can talk."

Holly blinked. And blinked again. Recognition finally hit her. "Jackie? Oh Jackie!" Holly crossed the room, stepping over strewn items including an end table. The two women embraced. "It's so good to see you. Are you all right? What are you doing here?"

"Helping Ian—and on the run myself."

Holly looked around and she shuddered. "This is crazy. What they're accusing him of is too."

"I know. That's why I'm helping him."

"At great risk to herself," Ian said.

Holly's gaze turned back to her cousin. "And you think this break-in has something to do with you? That someone has made the connection between us and came here looking for . . . me?"

"I'm sure it does."

"But why?"

"I sent you a fax. I'm assuming you didn't get it."

His cousin lifted a brow. "No. What fax?"

"A fax with a code on it." Ian started to reach for it, but Jackie shook her head. "Enough. We need to move. Now. Let's go." She walked to the window. "I'm not so worried about the FBI at this point. If they haven't put in an appearance by now, they're probably not here. But we just can't stay here any longer." She looked at Holly. "You'll have to come with us."

"What?" Holly blinked. "Um. No, I can't."

"They'll kill you if you don't."

Her blunt statement made Holly blink. "Wha—why?"

Ian felt his heart break at his cousin's confusion. He'd done this.

"They're here." Jackie moved from the window toward the

door. "Let's go before we're trapped." She looked at Holly. "I'm sorry. Grab the carry-on and move fast."

"Is it the cops or the bad guys?" Ian asked as he grabbed the carry-on and shoved his cousin in front of him.

"Not sure and I'm not stopping to ask." She looked at the dog.

"Doesn't matter anyway," Ian agreed. "Let's go, Gus."

Gus rose and came to Ian's left knee. Holly resisted, her sputtering protests slowing them down.

Ian grabbed her arm and looked her in the eyes. "Do you trust me?"

"Of course." She didn't hesitate.

"Then come with me. Now."

Holly snapped her lips together and followed them out the door. Gus trotted alongside Ian, ears pricked, hackles raised. They clattered down the stairs. "I don't think this is necessary, Ian. If they come back, I'll just tell them I don't know anything."

"Are you really that naïve?"

They reached the bottom of the stairs, walked through the small pass-through, and pushed through the front door that would lead outside.

As the door opened, bullets riddled the sidewalk in front of them.

Holly's scream echoed those in the area. This time there were several people out back and they moved fast, hitting the ground or running. Jackie aimed her weapon, then lowered it. Ian figured she wanted to fire back, but was probably too afraid of hitting an innocent person.

"Run!" she hollered. "Back through the building, then around to the truck!"

"Who is it?" Ian yelled.

"Not the cops."

The police would have identified themselves. And wouldn't

have shot without doing so. His heart thudded and fear for the two women raced like wildfire through his veins.

Holly clutched his hand. Gus followed after Jackie, nearly yanking the leash from Ian's grasp.

More shots followed. His left arm stung and he gasped, but kept going. Horror and fury filled him. These people didn't care who they killed, had no thought for the innocent ones caught in the crossfire. Ian bolted out the back door that led to the grassy area where Gus had taken care of business only a little while earlier. Jackie didn't pause. She hit the line of hedges and forced her way through. She looked back. "This way."

Holly's fingers trembled in his, but she didn't hesitate to follow him and Gus through the bushes.

Jackie led them around the side of the building. Ian pressed his back against it and waited while she peered around the corner. "Come on."

Within seconds, they were in the truck.

"Did they see us?" Ian asked.

"No, I don't think so," Jackie said. "After they shot at us, they took off. I saw two cars blend in with traffic and turn off on a side road." She glanced at Ian. "Are you all right?"

He looked down at his left bicep and remembered the sting he'd felt when they were running. He'd forgotten about it, but now seeing the blood, the pain hit him. "It stings, but I'll be fine. It's just a graze."

"You're sure?"

"I'm sure."

She shook her head. "We were awfully lucky tonight."

"Luck had nothing to do with it. I'm thanking God."

"Then we're safe?" Holly asked.

"For now," Jackie muttered.

Ian didn't like the grim tone, but knew she was right. While they might be safe at this moment, he wasn't going to get too comfortable.

Holly held out her hand. "Let me see the code."

Gus shifted and laid his head on Holly's knee. He gazed up at her and flicked his ears. Holly scratched his head and the dog closed his eyes. Ian shoved a hand into his coat pocket and pulled out the paper and handed it to Holly.

She took it with a frown. "New York on standby?"

"Yes, we got that one. Unless it's code for something else."

"And you want me to figure out the rest?"

"That was the idea, but now I wish I'd never involved you."

She shook her head. "I'll have to study it. It's not a code I recognize right off and I'm sure the underlining means something."

"They probably made up their own code," Jackie said.

"Of course." She looked up. "And you think this email has something to do with—" she looked back in the direction of her trashed home with a hard swallow—"that?"

"Yes."

# 17

Ron climbed the steps to the state house in Columbia, South Carolina. Security greeted him at the door and opened it. He stepped inside and headed for the west wing where he had an appointment with Governor Nancy Harkins. The stately building boasted white Georgian marble walls. His footsteps echoed on the pink-and-white marble floors. On this Monday evening, the place was empty, a vacuum, everyone ready to get home to their families or head to the gym just as soon as the clock had struck five.

Which was perfect. Ron didn't want an audience.

He approached the governor's office and knocked.

"Come in, Ron."

He entered to find the governor sitting behind her desk, glasses perched on the tip of her aristocratic nose, typing something on her keyboard. Her fingers stilled and she looked over the rims of her glasses, smiled, and stood to shake his hand.

"Thank you for seeing me, Nancy."

"Of course. You have me curious. What can I do for you?"

She came around the edge of the desk and motioned for him to take a seat in one of the two wing-backed chairs. He sat and crossed his legs, praying for the right words. She sat next to him.

"I'm involved in the Ian Lockwood case and I need to run some things by you."

Her gaze sharpened and her shoulders straightened. She leaned forward and placed her linked hands on her lap. "Now I understand why you didn't want to meet at the house."

"I didn't want Paul to overhear and I didn't want him to feel left out if I had to ask him to leave the room." Ron liked her husband, but this wasn't a social call.

"All right." She narrowed her intent green eyes. "Tell me."

"As you know, I've been helping with Operation Refuge."

The governor nodded. "I know. That's one pie I keep my finger in."

"Making sure it doesn't come back to bite you?"

Her lips tilted. "Something like that. But they're all professionals and they've done some amazing work."

"I'll be straight with you. I'm concerned about the whole Ian Lockwood thing."

"Ian Lockwood. The terrorist on the run. And Jackie's joined up with him. I never thought I'd see the day."

Ron scoffed. "You don't believe it any more than I do."

Nancy eyed him, studying him. "How do you know? How do Ian Lockwood and Operation Refuge fit together?"

"Jackie's not only one of Operation Refuge's operatives."

"Okay . . . "

He pulled in a deep breath and rubbed his lips. "She's also my niece."

"Ah." She leaned back. "So this case is a bit personal."

"To say the least."

"In all the years we've known each other, worked together, had meals together, you've never mentioned her."

He cleared his throat. "No. You know I like to keep my personal life separate from my business."

"I see."

"No you don't." He sighed. He was messing this up. "You're a good friend, Nancy, but talking about family has never been something either of us has had time for."

"But we do now?"

"I have a reason."

"Go on."

Ron rubbed his chin. "I was overseas for a long time. My father took Jackie in when her parents split up. I came home after he died to take care of his affairs and pick up where he left off."

"Looking after Jackie."

"Right."

"How does she know Ian?"

"He's a childhood friend."

"And now she's on the run with him. I see your dilemma." No, she didn't, but Ron kept his mouth shut. He wasn't ready to let her know exactly how involved he was in this case. Not yet. "So what do you want to know?" She leaned back and clasped her hands loosely in her lap.

"What's going on with the CDC? Why is the government encouraging citizens to get the smallpox vaccine shortly after a high-level employee and his family are murdered? Did he steal the virus? Is that virus out there and the government is covering it up?"

Nancy's expression didn't change. "What makes you think there's a connection?"

Ron simply stared at her. She sighed and rose to pace to the window.

"Just a simple yes or no is all I need, Nancy. I need to know what we're up against. Did someone steal the virus?"

She turned, her face grim. "Yes, and we don't know what they're going to do with it."

# 18

They couldn't keep doing this. Jackie knew that their chances of escape were lessening each time they ran. They'd driven to a hotel and checked in. With part of the cash Ron had given them, Holly had gotten the room so they didn't have to take a chance on someone recognizing Ian or Jackie.

Jackie had familiarized herself with the layout of the hotel, following her unwritten rule of always having a way out. When she'd returned to the suite, they'd snagged a few hours of sleep, and now Holly sat on the bed, rubbing her temples and studying the code. Every once in a while, she'd lower her right hand, grab the pen, and write on the tablet she'd taken from the end table.

"Ron hasn't called me yet," Jackie said. "I need that number for the FBI special agent he mentioned."

Ian turned from the coffeepot he'd made a beeline for. "Why?"

"We've got to get this email to them. They can probably figure out what it means a lot faster than we can."

"Not with Holly on our side."

Holly looked up. "But I don't have access to the software I need to run it through." She gave a tired sigh. "The FBI will. I can work with it manually and see what I can come up with, see if there's a pattern or something. But you really should give it to the FBI."

Ian paced and sipped his coffee.

Jackie gave him a few minutes to think it through while she studied Holly. "Are you all right?"

"Just a headache. I'll be okay."

Ian turned. "Fine. I trust Ron, but how are you going to make the call without them tracing it?"

"I'll have to figure that out."

Holly rose and went to her overnight case. She pulled out a plastic bag filled with medicine bottles. Jackie blinked, but before she could say anything, Holly opened one of the bottles and popped a pill. She stuffed the bag back into the case and turned to Jackie.

"Why didn't you just give Ron the email and let him take it to the authorities?" Holly asked.

Ian shook his head. "Because then the authorities would know Ron had been in contact with us and we don't want to get him in trouble."

"Oh. Then email it."

Jackie stood. "I can't email it to them unless I'm ready to leave the location I send it from. They'll track the IP address." She gave the still befuddled woman a soft smile. "We'll get it to them." She laid a hand on Holly's arm. "There's a drugstore up the street."

"Right. I know which one you're talking about," Holly said.

"It's a good walk from here, but we need you to do it. Just like when you checked us in to the hotel room. Your face hasn't been splashed across the news yet. You came home early from your business trip and no one should easily recognize you."

"What about the bad guys?" Ian asked. "They know she's with us."

Jackie pursed her lips. "I know."

"We can't send her out there."

Jackie sighed. "You're right. I'll have to chance it and just go myself."

Holly placed a hand on her arm. "It's all right. I'll wear my hood and glasses. What do you need me to do?"

Ian didn't look so sure. Jackie hesitated.

"Just tell me what I need to do," Holly pressed. "I'm less recognizable than you two and I really want to help."

Jackie finally nodded. "All right. Go buy three phones. Activate one before you leave the store and call the hotel and ask for the room. That way the new cell phone number isn't connected to this one that the cops already know about. Let us know when you're on the way back." She wrote the hotel number down and handed it to Holly. "I'll keep this one active until you get back, just in case, but call the hotel if you need us." She glanced at Ian. "Also get a first-aid kit. I need to patch up the slow one."

"Slow?" Ian huffed.

Jackie lifted a brow. "I'm not the one that got winged."

He rolled his eyes and pulled out several large bills from his wallet and passed them to Holly. She stuffed the money into her coat pocket and chewed on her bottom lip. "How can you joke about this?"

Jackie sighed. "It's a coping tactic. Don't worry, we're both as scared as you are."

"That doesn't make me feel better. Are you sure you shouldn't just turn yourselves in?" She shot a beseeching glance at Ian. "What about Terry and your parents?"

Ian stiffened. "I'm keeping them as far away from me as possible. I would have done the same with you if I hadn't already unknowingly put you in danger."

"If I'd answered my phone, we wouldn't be in this situation, would we?"

Jackie hesitated and exchanged a glance with Ian. "Maybe. But the bad guys found you before we could get to you, so if you had been home when your apartment was trashed, you would most likely be dead. It's a good thing you were gone."

"Oh." Holly's jaw hardened and she lifted her chin. "Fine. Do you need anything else?"

"Food would be nice," Ian said. He glanced at Gus, whose ears pricked forward. "Yeah, dog food. I wouldn't forget about you, buddy." He rubbed Gus's ears.

"And more hair coloring or wigs, whatever you can come up with. I think I'd like to be a brunette." Jackie looked at the ID, then at Ian. "How do you feel about a new color?"

He grimaced, but nodded.

Jackie rummaged in the bag Ron had given her for the two IDs and showed them to Holly. "As close to these colors as you can."

Holly drew in a deep breath. "All right. I'll try to be back in thirty minutes or so."

"What about Lucy? Is she all right where she is for now?"

"For now," Holly said. "I always call her at night. I didn't call her last night and I'm sure my friend is worried."

"Call her from a pay phone," Jackie said. "Or borrow someone's cell phone. There's no reason to believe they know where Lucy is, so there's no reason to believe they'll be listening in on your friend's phone."

Holly nodded and turned to go.

Jackie stopped her. "I want to check outside before you go."

Ian stood and grabbed the laptop Ron had provided. "I'm going to do a little research on Wainwright."

Jackie stepped outside and pulled Holly with her.

"What is it?" Holly asked as soon as the door shut behind her.

Jackie hunched her shoulders against the cold and walked to a nearby van, sheltering herself and Holly from any prying eyes. "You weren't overseas."

Holly's jaw dropped, then she snapped it shut. She lowered her eyes to the concrete. "No. I wasn't."

"And you didn't land at any airport."

"No. I drove." She lifted her chin to look at Jackie.

"Why didn't you answer your phone?"

"I really did have it turned off most of the time."

"What about Lucy? What if she'd needed you?"

"I was only going to be gone two nights. Lucy was fine. I needed time to think, to process."

"Process what?"

Tears filled her friend's eyes. "I'm not ready to talk about it yet, but the friend who has Lucy understands." She sniffed. "Now let me go get what you need." She paused. "How did you know?" she whispered.

"Because the FBI is looking for you. They would have you on a watch list for flights. If you'd been overseas teaching, the feds would have known that. And when you were landing. They would have picked you up the minute you stepped off the plane."

"Oh." She frowned. "You thought they'd be at my apartment today."

Jackie gave a slow nod. "But you came back a day early. They probably checked with your work or your father and found out when you were supposed to come home."

"Only I came home a day early. I see."

Jackie squeezed her friend's arm. "When you're ready to talk, I'll listen."

"I know."

Jackie cleared her throat. "All right then, I'll let you get that stuff. If you feel uncomfortable at all at any time, if you feel like you're in danger, call 911."

Holly's eyes went wide, then she took a deep breath and left. Jackie closed her eyes and leaned her head against the cold side of the van for just a moment, then returned to the room.

Ian sat at the table staring at the laptop. He looked up. "Are we staying here for a while?"

"No. Not if we can get away. I don't want to stay in one place too long." Jackie rubbed her eyes. They were five minutes from Holly's apartment. Law enforcement had swarmed like ants on a hill at the report of gunfire this close to Central Park and Times Square. They'd barely managed to avoid a gridlock and roadblocks when Jackie had taken a chance and swept into the Park Central Hotel parking lot and handed over her keys to valet parking as they'd hurried into the lobby. Later, she'd gotten the car and pulled it around to park on the street and pocket the keys. They might need to leave fast.

She wondered if she'd made the right decision. She studied Gus, who sat on the end of the bed with his nose settled between his paws. "He's going to have to stay with someone else. The word is out now that he's with us."

"I know."

She'd turned on the television and flipped the channel to Fox News. They were still one of the top stories. "They've gotten new pictures of us."

"From the bus camera."

"Yes, I'm sure."

"So we change our appearances once again."

She nodded. "We may be regular chameleons before this is over."

"So what's our next move?" he asked.

She didn't answer right away. Instead she tapped her chin and closed her eyes. "Let's make a list."

He grabbed a pen and the notepad from the end table, then took the chair opposite her. "You talk, I'll write."

"First, we need to get that email to the FBI. Elizabeth Miller is the South Carolina FBI agent, right?"

"Right."

"So we send her the email. We'll fax it to her and be on our way. Holly can do it when she gets back. By the time they trace the number, we'll be long gone."

Ian rubbed his head. "Or just text it to them, then dump the phone."

Jackie shrugged. "Or that."

"I wish there was a way I could convince them I haven't done what they're accusing me of."

"We're working on that part."

"I know. Then what?"

"You said Wainwright is the one who actually sent the email."

Ian nodded. "It came from his account, yes."

"Then we'll assume he sent it."

"Just like they're assuming I sent the emails they found on my computer." His sour expression would have made her laugh if the situation weren't so serious.

"Who were the other recipients of the email?"

"I don't know. We were all blind copied so my name was the only one on there that I could see. I'm only going on the assumption it was supposed to go to Ian Peterson."

"Maybe. Probably. Unless it was just a huge slip of the finger on the key or whatever."

"Maybe."

"And if it was meant for you?"

He shook his head. "That's one thing I'm certain of. I wasn't meant to see this email. If Ian Peterson wasn't supposed to get it and I wasn't supposed to get it, I don't know who the intended recipient would have been."

"I want to know the other names on the email," she murmured.

"Unfortunately, the only way to do that is to see the original email."

She rubbed her chin, her eyes on the far wall. "From Wainwright's account."

"Yes."

She dropped her gaze to him and shrugged. "So then we need to hack into his account."

# 19

Victor tapped his fingers against the steering wheel as he waited for the young woman to exit the building. Hector sat beside him, still and silent. Almost too silent. The young man, a kid really, in his early twenties, was brilliant. If Victor wasn't quite comfortable with his position in the organization, he might feel threatened by Hector's presence. But Hector knew his place, so all was well. "You ready?"

"Of course." Hector reached into his shoulder holster and pulled out his weapon.

Doing a little research on the doctor behind the glass doors had proved helpful. Dr. Jason Arnold was in practice for himself. He had no partner and his two assistants shared the full-time position. The first assistant would leave at lunchtime and the second one would come in for the afternoon shift.

As soon as Dr. Arnold's morning assistant walked out to go to lunch like she did every day, he would be alone. And as long as she didn't lock the door behind her, she would live to see the sun set tonight. If she locked it . . .

It took ten more tense minutes before the woman finally

165

exited. She let the door shut behind her and walked to the beat-up Ford Taurus parked under the tree near the end of the sidewalk.

"She didn't lock the door," Victor said.

"Which makes things a little easier for us."

Victor waited another two minutes after she drove off before he nodded. "Let's go."

Hector and Victor exited the stolen car and entered the building. A small bell rang and Hector quickly twisted the lock on the door before moving like a silent shadow to the far door opposite him that led to the examination rooms in the back. Standing off to the side, he held his gun and waited.

As soon as the good doctor stepped through the door, Hector lowered his weapon against the man's left temple. Dr. Arnold froze and Victor stepped forward with a smile, ignoring the terror stamped on the man's suddenly gray face. "Hello, Dr. Arnold. So nice to meet you."

His throat worked and his Adam's apple dipped. "If you're after drugs, I'll give them to you."

"I'm not after drugs, I simply want the password to your computer files."

The man blinked. "My computer files? Why?"

"That doesn't concern you. Do you want to live?"

"Of course."

"Then stop asking questions and let's get busy."

Dr. Arnold walked slowly to one of the computers and slid into the chair. He clicked a few keys and brought the home screen up. The cursor blinked in the space that requested the password. He glanced up. Hector moved the gun closer.

Dr. Arnold swallowed and typed. The screen went black, then opened up to the software his assistant had been using just before she left. "What now?"

"Bring up the file for Ian Lockwood and get me the code."

The doctor jerked. "Ian?"

"Yes. Is there a problem?" The barrel of the gun rested against his temple.

"Yes, yes, there's a problem. Ian's a good man. He's not a terrorist."

"Correct," Victor said. "But we are." He reached around the doctor and picked up a picture. A blonde-haired girl with blue eyes had her arms wrapped around the man now seated at the computer desk. She smiled into the camera, looking happy and carefree. "'Love you, Dad. Corie.'" Victor smiled. "Pretty girl. Looks smart too."

"Leave her alone, please." The man's voice shook. "I'll do what you want."

Victor hardened his voice and threw the picture to the floor. He ground the glass with his heel. "Pull up the file or that will be Corie's face."

Knowledge entered Dr. Arnold's eyes. Tears appeared and his throat worked. He took a deep breath. "May I please call my daughter before you kill me?" he whispered.

"No. Now stop stalling and get me Lockwood's information. Or I will find your daughter next."

The doctor clicked the keys and brought up the file. Victor leaned in. "Excellent."

The doctor moved fast, grabbing Victor's head and slamming it against the counter. Victor yelled, his vision swirled as pain raced through the back of his neck and up into his head. Darkness threatened. His knees hit the floor, then his left cheek. He heard a pop and a cry. Fighting the nausea and desperate to stay conscious, he rolled. He could see Dr. Arnold on the floor next to him, blood pooling beneath his head.

Then Victor looked up, expecting a helping hand and, instead, finding the dark hole of the suppressor staring him in the eye. "What—"

"Just tying up a few loose ends."

Hector pulled the trigger. Victor felt one more sharp pain and knew no more.

---

*NEW YORK CITY*

Ian rubbed his eyes and stared at Jackie. "Where's Holly? I'm starving."

"She went to get lunch. She'll be back in a minute." She ran a hand through her hair and shoved the laptop from her. "We've been at this for three hours. Hacking into his computer remotely simply isn't going to work. At least not with us doing it. If I had the right equipment, maybe, but with this—" She gestured to the laptop. "It's hopeless." She stood and paced and glanced at her watch. "We need to come up with a different plan. And we need to move out of this hotel room soon. Where is Wainwright Labs here in New York?"

"It's in Armonk, about forty-five minutes from here."

"What's security like there?"

"Tight. And all kinds of firewalls on their computer systems. If you try to hack into it, alarms will go off."

She nodded. "I know. I was having to be too careful. I either set the alarms off or I just don't get in. Either way, it's an epic fail." She sighed and ran a hand down the side of her face as she thought. "What if we don't hack into it? What if we just walk into his office and get on his computer so the FBI can hack into it?"

Ian laughed. "That's insane. I don't see that happening." He sobered. "I mean, even if we managed to steal the computer, wouldn't they have to get some kind of order to justify searching it? The email's not going to be enough to prove I'm—we're—innocent."

Jackie nodded and Ian studied her. The faraway look in her eyes said she was hatching something. Ian glanced at the clock and sent up a silent prayer for Holly's safety.

Jackie stood. "As soon as we have the names of the others the email was sent to, we'll be able to start piecing this together."

"How do you propose we go about doing this?"

"We'll need help. I have computer skills, but not the kind needed for that."

Ian blew out a breath. "He has a laptop—or a tablet—that he carries everywhere. Rumor is he sleeps with it handcuffed to his wrist."

"Tell me more."

Ian shrugged. "It's just a rumor."

"You know what they say."

"What's that?"

"Where there's smoke, there's fire."

"Maybe, but if we steal the information, can it be used against him?"

"Why not? If we have evidence that he's a murderer, I don't think the authorities are just going to ignore that. The cops aren't getting the information in a questionable manner, we are. They're free to use it."

The hotel phone rang and they both jumped. Ian tensed while Jackie answered it. "Hello?"

She listened, then shot out of the chair to push the curtain back from the window. "Stay there, we'll be there in one minute." She hung up and turned to Ian. "Let's grab our stuff and Gus and go."

"They've found us?"

"The bad guys, not the cops. Holly said she was walking down the sidewalk and thought she recognized the car from yesterday afternoon's shooting turn into the parking garage of the hotel."

Ian started gathering belongings. Jackie did the same. Within seconds, they were out the door. "To the stairs, don't take the elevator."

The phone rang again. Ian paused and pushed back into the room to grab the phone. "Yeah?"

"Don't come down the stairs on the east side," Holly whispered. "They're standing just inside the door."

Ian tensed. "Where are you?"

"I followed them inside the lobby and to the stairwell. They're waiting for you to come down. There are two guys hanging around the elevator, also."

"Go outside and wait for us near the car."

"I saw guns, Ian. They're trying to hide them and act cool so people won't look at them twice, but they're there."

"We'll be all right. Don't let them see you," he said.

"No. I'm going to leave and go around the corner of the building next door, the one that faces the parking lot. I'll be able to see the car from there." He heard her footsteps.

"Do you see anything else?"

"I can see the car now. There are two men dressed in black near it. They don't have masks on, but they look suspicious." Holly's voice squeaked on the last word. She cleared her throat. "That means there are about six of them total."

"Can you get around to the other side of the hotel and meet us?"

"Yes, but what are we going to do? We need to get the car."

"We'll worry about that as soon as we're all together again. If you need to reach us before we get there, then call the cell."

"Okay. I—I'm coming."

Ian motioned for Jackie to follow him. With a raised brow, she didn't question him, just swept from the room again and kept pace with him as he went to the next set of steps on the opposite side of the building. Ian, Jackie, and Gus made their way down the stairs as silently as possible. Just in case the bad guys were coming up. He told her what Holly had said on the phone.

She thought about it for a brief second. "They've got the exits covered," she whispered. At the next level, she opened the door and led the way onto the floor.

"What's the plan?" Ian asked.

"Based on what Holly said, we're going to have to wing it. Top priority is to find a back way out. Head for the elevator."

"What if they're coming up?"

"It's a chance we're going to have to take. There are people all over this hotel. They're going to have to be a little cautious."

"They weren't very cautious when they were shooting at us in front of Holly's apartment," he muttered.

"Touché." She pressed the button to the elevator and motioned for him to stand to the side. Gus planted himself next to Ian's leg. Ian watched the elevators in the mirror opposite the steel doors, tension humming through him. "This hotel has an elevator that opens on the bottom floor and into the back of the hotel," she said.

He could see tightness in her muscles at the base of her neck. "Don't we need a key?"

She reached into her pocket and held it up.

Ian raised a brow. "You lifted it. From your scouting mission when we arrived?"

"Yes. My pickpocketing skills far surpass my lock-picking skills. Don't worry, I'll leave it where the housekeeper can find it."

The elevator dinged. Jackie's hand went to her weapon and Ian moved so he could pounce if he needed to.

The doors opened to reveal an empty car.

Jackie's breath slipped from her and she lowered her hand from her gun to grasp the bags. She set them inside the elevator and let her hand go back to the weapon.

They stepped into the elevator and Ian pressed the button she indicated. He prayed she was right about where the elevator would open up.

Jackie held her gun out of sight to anyone who might be waiting on the elevator. "I don't want to scare a housekeeper if she's waiting to come up." Seconds passed. The doors opened. "Lucked out again," Jackie said as the cell phone in Ian's pocket rang.

"It's not luck."

"Okay, you give God the credit then."

"I will, thanks," he said, then spoke into the phone. "Where are you, Holly? Same place?"

They stepped into the laundry area of the hotel and Jackie put her weapon away and placed the key on a shelf where it would be easy to spot.

They juggled the bags. Gus stopped and sat, staring up at Ian.

Jackie's tight lips and hurried steps shouted her impatience. She had her hands full with the backpack from Ron and Holly's rolling bag. Ian held Gus's leash and his own small bag. He hung up with Holly and tucked the phone into Jackie's coat pocket.

"Where is she?" she asked.

"Waiting on us."

"Let's find the back door," Jackie said.

They moved fast and easily found another door that led to a set of stairs that would take them up.

"Do we chance it?" Ian asked.

"We have to get out of here."

Ian cautiously opened the door. A woman dressed in a house-keeping uniform headed down toward them. She frowned.

Ian shrugged. "Sorry, we took a wrong turn. This will take us up and out, right?"

"Yes. You want me to show you?"

"I think we can handle it."

She continued on down, keeping her eyes on Gus.

Ian backed up. "He won't bite."

The woman nodded. But her hand went to her phone. Ian saw Jackie had noticed as well. He motioned to the steps and Jackie picked up her pace. They moved quickly up the stairs. At the top, Jackie pointed. "There's an exit, let's take it."

They moved toward a break in the hallway.

Ian turned the corner. "We're back up on level one."

"Yes, we're taking the long route out, but so far it's allowed us to avoid whoever's after us. By now, though, they'll have realized we're not in the room. The housekeeper may have called security. We'll have the bad guys and hotel security looking for us, searching inside and out. The sooner we get out, the better."

"All right, here we go." Ian beelined for the glass door, Jackie on his heels. He stopped and assessed the area from behind the glass. Not seeing anything, he pushed the door open. Two steps out, he felt something hard and cold press under his ear.

# 20

Jackie took in the scene before her in the time it took to blink. She dropped the items she carried and propelled herself out the door to ram her elbow up and into the side of the figure's jaw. Ian spun and the gun clattered to the ground. As he came around, his heel landed in their attacker's solar plexus.

The man went down with a quiet whoosh. Gus barked and lunged, baring his teeth inches from the man's face.

Ian stepped on the man's throat and pressed. "Off, Gus." Gus sat, but his body vibrated with the need to help his master. Ian turned back to the would-be murderer, who squirmed and gagged and tried to move Ian's foot without success. "Who are you? Why are you after me?"

Jackie touched Ian's arm. "Ease up. If he can't breathe, he can't talk."

"We don't have time for this," Ian muttered.

"No. We don't. Leave him."

He shot her a black look. "I can't." Ian leaned over and grabbed the gun. This time it was his turn to press it against the man's head. "What does that email mean?"

Dark eyes glittered from behind the mask. Jackie ripped it

174

from his head. He growled and she searched his pockets, careful not to place herself in a position that would allow him to grab her and turn this into a hostage situation. She found what she was looking for. "Zip ties."

Ian blew out a breath. "Hands behind your back, dude."

He lunged. Ian directed a hand chop to the side of the man's head to render him motionless. The attacker dropped like a rock. Jackie went to her knees beside him and made short work of zip-tying his wrists. "Nice."

"Thanks."

"He's unconscious now," she said.

"He should stay that way for a while." Ian paused, his eyes searching the area. "What are we going to do with him?"

"Leave him for the cops."

"Fine." They stepped into the shadows of the hotel. Jackie caught her breath. "All right. Let's find Holly and get out of here."

"How did you know?"

"What?" She frowned.

"That it was safe to attack him while he was holding a gun on my head?"

"He had the safety on."

Ian blinked. "Seriously?"

"Seriously."

"You could see that?"

"Yes. I looked for it. I recognized the M1911 model weapon and know they have a safety you have to thumb off before you can fire it. It was on. Now where's Holly?"

Ian looked around and spotted his cousin. "Right there. She said some of the people who shot at us were outside near the car. They're going to be looking for their buddy in a few minutes."

"How did they find us?" she muttered.

"Probably waited until we drove off and followed us."

"But we were careful. We were all watching. There's something else going on."

Holly hurried over to them. She carried three bags. Lovely, tantalizing scents wafted from two of them. Ian's stomach growled and Gus whined.

"Gonna have to wait, boy, sorry," Ian whispered.

Jackie nodded to an alley running between the hotel and the start of a strip of stores. "I want you two to wait in there while I go check out how difficult it's going to be to get the car. If they followed us here, then they know our vehicle." She led the way to the alley, glancing back over her shoulder as she talked. "If I can get the car, I'll text you and pull around, so be ready."

Ian stopped. "You're not doing this by yourself."

Jackie's gaze flicked to Holly. "You need to keep her safe."

"I'll keep myself safe," Holly said. "Let's just get to the car."

Jackie's lips tightened. "We have a better chance of this working if I go it alone. Three people and a dog aren't going to cut it."

Ian started to protest. "She's right," Holly broke in. "We'll wait here." She gathered the bags and backed into the shadows of the alley. "Come on, Ian. Let her do it."

Ian stepped next to Holly and Gus sat next to him.

"We don't have time to argue," Holly said.

Jackie breathed out in relief.

"But if you're not here within five minutes," Ian said, "I'm coming after you."

"Give me ten."

"Eight."

Jackie blew out a short humorless laugh. "Be ready."

SOUTH CAROLINA

Special Agent Elizabeth Miller slapped the laptop closed and rubbed her burning eyes. She was tired. So very tired. She didn't need to be sitting at home waiting. She needed a break on this case and fate didn't seem to be interested in offering one up. Heck, she wasn't asking for Lockwood to step up with his arms extended asking for her to slip the cuffs on him, she was willing to go get him—or send other agents after him—she just needed a location.

A knock on the door brought her head up. Her fingers wrapped around the grip of her weapon and she lifted it from the table to carry it with her. She stood to the side of the door. "Yeah?"

Her phone buzzed the same time Sam answered. "Open the door."

She holstered her weapon, grabbed her phone, and cracked the door. Sam slipped inside her foyer and shut the door behind him.

He carried a large pizza, a two-liter bottle, and another bag that probably held the salad they'd split. His phone was ringing too. He laid his cargo on the table and fished in his pocket. "Yeah?"

She spoke into her phone, trying to tune Sam out. "What is it?"

"We've got some information on the murder of Daniel Armstrong." Ray Mallard, one of the criminalists in the lab for SLED in Columbia, said the words slowly as though savoring them.

Elizabeth lifted a brow. "The Wainwright employee. The one Lockwood killed."

"That's the one, but it's looking like he didn't kill him after all."

Elizabeth blinked. "All right. I'm putting you on speaker so Sam can listen in."

Sam ended his call and Elizabeth pressed the button for the speakerphone. Sam began his meticulous preparation of what was to be their dining table.

"We're both here. Tell us," Elizabeth said.

"Daniel Armstrong was killed around ten o'clock. Interesting thing is, we had a tip that Lockwood was seen at a gas station around that time."

"You get the video footage and watch it?"

"Yes. It's definitely him and the Sellers woman. They've got a German shepherd with them too. He was wearing a service vest in the video. The time stamp on the video says there's no way Lockwood killed Armstrong."

"The dog was wearing a vest on the bus too," she said absently, her mind spinning to process this new information. "So if Lockwood was at the gas station at the time Armstrong was killed . . ."

"Right. He didn't do it."

"And the ME's sure about the time?"

"He's pretty sure. Armstrong was found in his home, a bullet to the head, execution style."

Elizabeth frowned. "We seem to be having quite a few of those lately, don't we?"

"What do you mean?"

She bit her lip. "It's nothing, I suppose." But for some reason the family who'd been found dead in their Georgia home, shot execution style, came to mind. It wasn't her case, but still . . .

"You there?"

"Yeah, Ray, sorry. Anything else?"

"Well, trace evidence found a hair that matches Lockwood on Armstrong's body."

"But if he didn't kill him . . ." She frowned.

"Well, they worked together. Other employees said they were in and out of each other's offices on a regular basis. He could have picked it up there."

"Right. True. Any prints?"

"Nope. Whoever killed him wore gloves. There was also some dirt on the tile in the kitchen that didn't match the dirt outside Armstrong's home. That's still being analyzed. I hope to have something for you on that soon."

"Okay."

"And last, I just talked to Detective Cliff Baylor who's the lead on the Armstrong murder."

"I know Cliff. We've worked together before."

"He said there were some threatening emails from Lockwood to Armstrong the day before the man died."

Elizabeth's frown deepened and she shot a glance at Sam. "That's pretty convenient, isn't it?"

Sam shrugged. "Coincidence?"

"Threatening emails to a man who dies the next day. Bomb items in his home, emails between him and Jackie plotting terrorism." She shook her head. "Something is smelling a bit rancid if you ask me."

Sam lifted a brow. "Don't tell me you think Lockwood's innocent. Do I need to remind you that he ran?"

"We've already been over what his reasons could be. If he realized how tightly someone had set him up, he might have decided he had no other recourse, nothing to lose by trying to find a way to prove his innocence."

Sam shook his head and took a bite of the pizza. "I'm not buying that. He's guilty."

She slapped the table. "There's nothing in his past to indicate criminal action—or a tendency for it."

"There's always a first time."

"Guys?" Ray came through the speaker. "I'm still here, remember?"

Elizabeth focused back on Ray. "Sorry. Keep your nose to this one, will you? Don't let anything slip by you." She stared at Sam and lifted her chin. "An innocent man's life may be at stake." Sam shrugged. Elizabeth rolled her eyes. "And Ray? One more thing if you don't mind."

"Yes?"

"Would you contact the ME or the criminalist who handled the ballistics for the mass homicide of the Anwar Goff family to see if striations on the slugs match up?"

"You think they're connected?"

"Maybe. The MO sounds the same."

"But one is in South Carolina, the other in Georgia."

"Killers can't cross state lines?"

"Of course, but . . . I'm just trying to figure out why you would connect the two."

"The Goff family has been on my mind. Lockwood's being set up as a bioterrorist."

"*Maybe* set up."

"Goff worked for the CDC, Lockwood and Armstrong work for a lab with close connections to the CDC. I want to know if the weapon that killed these five people is the same one or a different one, that's all."

"I'll check it out," Ray promised.

"Oh, and one more thing."

"What?"

"Could you put me through to the ViCAP unit chief?"

"Sure thing."

"You're the best, Ray."

"Remember that, will you?"

She smiled as she waited for the chief to pick up.

"Chief Craig Thomas, what can I do for you?"

"Chief Thomas, this is FBI Special Agent Elizabeth Miller. I'm working a case and have come across information that you might find interesting." She explained the situation.

"You have my attention. What do you want me to do?"

"Could you ask ViCap to run their database for any other unsolved or solved homicides using the same caliber weapon and similar MO as these killings?"

"Of course. Can I reach you at this number when I have the answer?"

"Yes sir."

"I'll get back to you."

*12:30 P.M.*
*NEW YORK CITY*

Jackie slipped around the side of the building, her blood humming. Adrenaline made her senses extra sharp and her ears picked up every little sound.

The men Holly had seen around the vehicle had moved. She hesitated, not seeing anyone. No one guarded the car. A shadow just ahead shifted and a tall man in a dark sweater and black hat and pants hovered at the base of the stairs. Jackie was willing to bet the others were around. Some still on the stairs, others up on the floor where they'd been staying.

She needed a distraction. A quick glance at her watch showed she had about five minutes left before Ian came after her. She saw the cruiser across the street, sitting on the curb. An idea sparked. She dialed 911. When the operator answered, Jackie was ready.

"I'm at the Park Central Hotel on 7th Avenue. There's a man dressed all in black and I'm scared to go up to my room. If I go in the lobby, he'll see me." She gasped. "There's another one at the top of the stairs and he has a gun. They both do. Please. Hurry. I don't know what they're doing, but it doesn't look good."

"Stay calm, ma'am." Jackie could hear the keys clicking on the keyboard in the background. "I've dispatched a unit. He's one street over so he should be there within seconds."

Jackie already saw the flashing lights headed her way. She looked at her watch once again. Three minutes. The cruiser spun into the covered area near the front door. The man hovering at the entrance to the lobby slunk away into the shadows around the side of the hotel. Jackie clicked the unlock button to the vehicle. The car chirped once and the lights flashed. She froze. The cruiser slowed and two officers exited the car.

Two people came out of the hotel lobby.

The officers met them. "Excuse me, we got a report of . . ."

There was no sign of the man she wanted to avoid and no one between her and the car. Jackie darted across the street to the SUV and climbed in the driver's side. She shut the door with a soft click and waited. Another glance at her watch. One minute before Ian came looking for her.

If he hadn't already.

The officer entered the lobby, speaking into the radio on his shoulder. Jackie cranked the vehicle and pulled out of the parking lot. Two more cruisers passed her heading for the hotel and she held her breath, but they never glanced her way. Slowly, she pulled around to the side alley where she saw Holly and Ian hurrying toward her.

They reached for the doors as she pulled to a stop. Ian motioned Holly into the front seat, then climbed into the back with Gus. "We were coming to find you."

"Good thing you didn't." She told them what happened as she drove. She heard Ian rustling in the bags and then heard the distinctive sound of Gus eating.

Holly had the food bags. Delicious smells emanated from them. Jackie kept her eye on the rearview mirror even as she took the hamburger Holly handed her. "How did they find us? I'm not getting it. No one followed us to that hotel." She glanced at Holly. "You didn't talk to anyone when you went out, did you?"

"Of course not."

"Sorry." Jackie tapped her fingers against the wheel. "We need to find another place to stay."

"Let's get out of the city while we can," Ian said. "I don't like the feeling of being trapped. All this traffic makes me nervous."

Jackie stayed silent as she thought. "Okay, we'll head for Wainwright Labs."

"Fine. Take Henry Hudson Parkway," he said.

Jackie maneuvered her way through the flow of traffic, an anonymous driver just like everyone else around her.

"I know that area," Ian said. "There's a hotel not far from there."

"We'll check in and get some rest." Jackie glanced in the rearview mirror. "We really need to get Gus somewhere."

"I don't have anyplace to leave him." Ian frowned. Jackie knew he hated the thought of giving up the dog even temporarily.

"What if Ron would take him? Keep him up at the cabin?" Ian hesitated and Jackie shrugged. "Think about it. You've got a little bit of time."

"But not much." He sighed.

"No, not much."

# 21

Thirty minutes later, Jackie was satisfied with the random hotel they'd found. "We can't be seen with Gus," she said. "It's best if the clerk doesn't even know we're here."

"I know." Ian fell silent and followed her around to the back of the hotel to wait. Holly went in the front door. Jackie shivered as the wind blew. She adjusted the collar of her jacket as though that would help. She and Ian didn't talk, they just waited.

Finally Holly came around and let them in.

"Any problems?" Jackie asked.

"No, not at all." Her pale, wan face tugged at Jackie's heart. "I got us a two-room suite," Holly said. She bit her lip and looked at Ian. "It was expensive. She looked at me funny when I said I didn't have a credit card and paid cash, deposit and all. She's definitely nosy and wanted to know why I needed so much space for just me. I said I liked to have room to think." She grimaced. "I don't think she believed me."

Ian shrugged. "It's not her business, but she'll remember you if anyone asks."

"It doesn't matter," Jackie said. "We're not going to be here that long. The suite is great." She gripped her bags. "Holly, why don't you take Gus upstairs to the room? I'm desperate for some coffee and maybe a snack." She looked at Ian. "Think we can manage to snag something without the clerk noticing us?"

"Probably. Let's try." He touched his cousin's hand. "We'll bring you something. What do you want?"

"Anything is fine. Some fruit and a granola bar." She shrugged. "Whatever they have." Holly went to the elevator, Gus trotting along beside her.

Jackie and Ian headed toward the lobby.

Jackie peered around the corner. "Hang on, she's on the computer, but will see us if she looks up." Jackie waited a minute, then tried again. Then again. Finally. "She's on the phone," she murmured. "Let's see what we can do." They went straight to the snack area that was conveniently located on the other side of a large fireplace. The clerk wouldn't be able to see them unless she came out from behind the desk. They helped themselves to coffee.

Jackie's phone rang. "Hello?"

"Turn on the television," Ron said. "National news is following the story and you need to see this. Stay in touch."

Jackie grabbed the remote from the end table next to the sofa. She pulled up the guide and found the channel for one of the news networks.

She nudged Ian and he looked up.

The closed captions scrolled while the reporter spoke into her microphone. "And now an update on the story we're all following. In a shocking turn of events, officials have released a statement saying that they have evidence to suggest that Ian Lockwood is not responsible for the death of Daniel Armstrong after all. They did go on to say that he and his companion, Jackie Sellers, *are* still wanted in the questioning of a possible terrorist act against the United States and are investigating several emails found on his work computer. They have not said what they found at his residence, but we have video of the FBI carrying several bags from the house." A short segment played showing FBI agents carrying black bags from Ian's house. "If you have any information about them, please call the number listed at the bottom of your screen."

Ian stared, shock blanching his face white, then red. "I didn't have anything incriminating in my house. Whatever they found, someone planted."

Jackie could feel the tension flowing from him.

"Interesting."

"Yeah." He rubbed his chin. "But announcing that I'm no longer a suspect in Daniel's murder, do you think it's a trick? A ploy to get us to come in?"

She shook her head. "They wouldn't have said we were still wanted for the terrorist acts. I'll call Ron and get the details, but it looks like that's one thing you can rest easy about. They know you didn't kill Daniel."

"Thank God," he breathed. They continued to watch the coverage of their case and learned nothing new. Ian looked at her. "How did you know?"

Jackie paused, tilted her head and frowned. "Know what?"

"That he didn't want me—us—dead."

"For one, the safety was on. If he'd wanted you dead, he would have shot you before you walked out that door. He would have gotten us both before we knew what hit us."

He blanched, then nodded. "Which is why you searched him."

She nodded. "I figured if he wanted us alive, he would have to have a way to restrain us handy."

Ian shook his head. "You're amazing."

She laughed. "No, not so much. Just trained." She paused. "Someone told him to bring us in alive. I wonder if it's because they want to question you about the email. Like who you've told, that kind of thing."

"They know who I've told, which is why they're after you and Holly."

"Yes, but maybe they're trying to make sure there's no one else." She paused. "I've been thinking."

"When?"

She shot him a glance. "Huh?"

"When have you had time to think?"

"Oh." She gave a low chuckle. "Right. Well, off and on." She turned serious. "We've put this off long enough. It's time to call Special Agent Elizabeth Miller and talk to her."

Ian went still. "She'll come with backup and plenty of firepower. We'll end up talking all right. From behind vertical bars and through a lawyer."

Jackie sighed, afraid he was right. "We're going to have to take a chance."

"I don't like it."

"I don't either, but we've got to go on the offensive. We've been running, trying to stay alive and one step ahead of everyone. It's time to figure out how to take control of this."

"All right. Let's get upstairs and see what kind of plan we can come up with."

Once inside the suite, Ian went straight to the television to turn the news on. Jackie noticed Holly had claimed the room with the two beds while Ian and Gus got the king. Holly rolled her carry-on into the room and left it just inside the door. She sank onto the bed closest to the bathroom. "Were we really shot at yesterday? Was it just yesterday that someone broke into my apartment and trashed it?"

"Yes to the part about being shot at. Not sure when someone broke in and trashed your apartment. Could have been yesterday or the day before." Jackie set her bag on the bed and pulled out the hair color. "Feels like a lifetime ago, doesn't it?"

Holly blinked. "Yes."

Jackie paused. "Is Lucy really all right? Can anyone find her?"

Holly rubbed her eyes. "I don't see how. She's staying with a friend of hers from school. Carissa has a little boy named Micah." She gave a small smile. "Micah and Lucy hit it right off the first day they met."

"Good." Jackie cleared her throat. "Good."

She flopped back and stared at the ceiling. "But I mean if someone tracked my cell phone calls and started tracing the numbers, they would come across Carissa's."

Jackie froze. "All right, then we're going to have to warn Carissa not to let on that Lucy's with her."

"How?" Holly sat up with a wince and pressed the heel of her palm to the side of her head.

"Are you all right?"

A long pause. "No, Jackie, I'm not all right."

Jackie moved to sit beside Holly, the bad feeling growing in her belly. "What is it? A tumor?"

Holly shot her a startled look. Then bit her lip and looked away. She took a deep breath before she met Jackie's eyes once again. "Yes."

"Cancerous?"

"Yes."

"How long have they given you?" she whispered.

"Three months."

Stunned, Jackie stared at her friend. Then grief welled and the tears spilled down her cheeks. She grabbed Holly in a hug. "We'll fight it. You can beat this. Lucy needs you. *I* need you."

"I'll fight it," Holly agreed slowly. "But I've been doing a lot of thinking since being diagnosed, as I'm sure you can imagine."

"Of course."

"And if—"

"No ifs."

"*If,*" Holly insisted. "If I don't make it, I need you to take Lucy. I've already put it in my will and my lawyer knows my wishes."

Jackie stared. "Holly, do you know . . . are you sure . . . I can't . . ."

"You can." She stood. "Now, I'm going to take some medicine and then a shower if that's all right."

Jackie's jaw worked. She didn't know what to say, so she settled for, "Sure." She held up the other box of color. "I'll . . . um . . . just give this to Ian."

Holly stepped toward the bathroom, then stopped and turned. "Don't tell Ian yet."

"I won't. That's not for me to tell."

Holly blinked back the tears that clouded her eyes and Jackie wanted to wrap her arms around her friend once more. Instead she watched Holly struggle with her words.

"What is it you're trying to say?" Jackie asked.

"Ian," she said. "He was completely in love with you, you know."

Jackie sighed. "I suspected."

"But you left him anyway."

"I had to."

"Why?"

Did she really want to get into this now? Holly seemed to need her to. "Because the social worker made me." Holly gaped and Jackie took pity on her. "I was an abused child, Holly. Verbally, emotionally, sometimes physically. The summer my parents finally split, I hitchhiked to stay with my grandfather in Virginia. He took one look at my broken nose and badgered me until I finally told him everything that was going on in my home. He called CPS, Child Protective Services. They gave him custody." She swiped a hand across her eyes. "I never saw either of my parents again."

"Oh my goodness. I'm so sorry. I never knew."

"No one did."

"But you came back. For a really short time."

"For about a week. Gramps told me I needed to say my good-byes." She swallowed hard. "I was seventeen years old, Holly. I was too ashamed to tell the truth about why I had to leave, so I just gathered my things and said I'd chosen to go live with my grandfather."

"Ian was depressed for months."

"I'm sorry. But . . . he looks like he got over it."

Holly gave a short nod. "He did. Eventually. He turned to working out. He says it was because of the bullying—and I'm sure that was part of it—but mostly I think it was to try and forget you. He stayed at the dojo from the time school got out until it closed. Every day and even on the weekends."

Jackie sucked in a deep breath. "I'm sorry. I wish now I had told him, but back then . . ."

"You were probably an emotional mess."

"To say the least."

"Where are your parents now?"

Jackie's fingers tightened around the box she still held. "They're dead. I'm just going to give this to Ian."

Holly studied her for a few seconds longer. "Okay. I won't be long."

"Take your time." Jackie heard the door snick closed behind Holly. But the woman's last question still echoed in her mind. *Where are your parents now?*

She knew where they were, she just wished she could have

made some kind of peace with them before they'd died. Her mother from a drug overdose, her father in a car accident. He'd been driving drunk. She knew she needed to come to terms with the fact that they never loved her, never put her first in anything. Didn't care enough to fight for her when her grandfather was given custody. But it was hard to accept those things. Hard to wrap her mind around what Ian believed. That God wanted a relationship with her. That he loved her. That she *mattered*. How could God love her when her own parents didn't?

A light rap pulled her from her thoughts. Ian stood in the open doorway. "You okay?"

"Sure." She tossed him the box. "Time for us to change identities once again."

## 22

James Walden threw the clipboard onto his desk and picked up the paper. LOCAL COUPLE MISSING. Mr. and Mrs. Bates smiled back at him from a photo he felt was several years old. She simply looked too happy and didn't have any new or healing bruises on her face.

The cops had just left and James knew that while he'd played it cool and offered the performance of a lifetime, he could only hope they hadn't noticed the sweat on his forehead. His armpits were soaked and he'd have to change before his next meeting. He glanced at his watch. He had an hour.

He walked to the small room where he kept several changes of clothing and toiletries. He turned on the water in the small sink and stripped off the wet shirt. The plan was going all wrong. And it had started with that stupid email. And while the email had been planned, sending it to Ian had not been. Ian's appearance into the mix was creating a set of problems he feared would destroy everything they'd all worked so hard for. He rubbed a warm, soapy washcloth over his face and upper body. Once finished, he rinsed, dressed, and returned to his office. He stared at the newspaper picture once again. He shook his head and wondered if it was time to bail. He had several million in an offshore account. If he wasn't greedy, he could disappear forever. But the millions he'd leave behind . . .

"Wainwright wanted you to know he's tying up loose ends."

James looked up. Bo Gaines, one of Wainwright's goons, stood there, his hulking six-foot-four frame making it look like the architects used the wrong measurements when building the doorway. "Tying up loose ends?" James asked. "What do you mean?"

"He feels like things have gotten out of control."

"Well, he's got that right. Red Peters is in custody."

"Red hasn't talked so far. He's too scared to, but we won't have to worry about him long. He and his family will be dead within the hour. Wainwright said your inside man is taking care of it."

James gave a slow nod. "All right." Fear slithered through him. Red wasn't just a hired killer like some of the others. Red knew things and could identify James and other key players. If he decided to talk and request protective custody before he could be taken out, the whole plan would implode.

He looked at the picture in the paper once again, then back to the man about to leave. "Hey, Gaines. Are you still looking for the woman? Mrs. Bates?"

"Yeah, we're keeping an eye out for her." He scowled.

James rubbed his eyes. According to his security feed, as soon as her husband had left the room with James, she'd grabbed the keys from his desk and walked out the door. Curious and perturbed, James had watched the feed that covered the parking lot. Mrs. Bates had gotten into her car and simply driven away.

Where was she?

James understood why Wainwright felt like there were too many loose ends.

There were.

And yet he couldn't help wondering when Wainwright would decide James was also a loose end who needed tying up.

---

Jackie stood while she watched the news. She didn't want to sit, refused to pace, and couldn't go for a jog.

So she stood.

Ian joined her. He settled his hands on her shoulders and leaned his forehead against the back of her head. She went completely still even while her pulse picked up speed. "Get some sleep, Ian."

"You're the one who needs to do that."

True enough. "Did you see that?"

"What?" He lifted his head, but his fingers began a gentle massage. A soft sigh slipped out and she closed her eyes, trying to focus on what she was going to say.

Oh yeah. "The media is speculating on reasons for the government's suggestion that everyone get vaccinated for smallpox. They're making the shots available at all flu shot outlets." She moved to the couch and he settled beside her.

"But why? Smallpox was eradicated years ago."

"Seems like there's been a very small and isolated outbreak here in the United States, but they're not saying where."

"If it's isolated, why offer the vaccine?"

"Good question," she muttered. "That's the same question the media is asking and no one in the government is answering. Tobias Freeman is the director of the CDC and he just offered a statement. He said that it was just a precaution. With the fact that smallpox had reared its head once again, he wanted to make sure that the American citizens could be proactive and get the vaccine."

Ian frowned and shook his head. "Something's not right about that."

"I agree."

Something niggled at her. Something she'd seen on the news. She tried to pull it from the depths of her brain, but it wouldn't come to the surface. But it would. Eventually. She rubbed her arms. "I'm going to grab a shower and some sleep. I recommend you do the same. But first . . ."

"But first what?"

"We're going to make contact with the FBI, give them that email, and figure out where to go from there."

Ian didn't offer the arguments she saw running through his mind. He simply nodded.

Jackie walked to the end table, picked up the handset of the phone, and dialed Ron's number.

"Can't they trace that?" he asked.

"No, they don't know where we are and I'm calling his throw-away phone."

"Oh."

"Jackie, you guys all right?" Ron asked, his concern evident.

"We're safe for now." She walked to the window and stayed to the side. She peered around the edge of the curtain and gazed out into the parking lot, taking note of the cars and the people. No one in dark clothes or masks as of yet. "I need the number for Elizabeth Miller."

"Hold on a sec, I'll have to switch phones and make a call."

Jackie held, tapping a foot against the carpeted floor. Her thoughts spun.

Gus rose from the floor and stepped to Ian's side and nudged his hand. "I'll have to feed him and let him out. I'll keep first watch."

Jackie thought they might be all right, but she'd thought that at the previous hotel too. "Fine."

Ian clipped the leash on Gus and they left the room. Jackie watched the news play while she waited on Ron. She could hear him speaking in the background, but couldn't make out the words. Five minutes passed and she started to wonder if Ron would be able to get the number after all. Fifteen minutes into her wait, Ian and Gus returned. The dog flopped onto the floor in front of the couch and stretched out.

A blip about a local couple in their mid-forties caught her attention. They'd been reported missing by their college-aged children. The couple had disappeared from a local mortuary and their car had been found abandoned in a grocery store parking lot with blood on the passenger seat.

"It's a shame," she said.

"What?"

"Life. The way it works out sometimes. Most of the time."

He lifted a brow. "Go on."

She nodded toward the television. "That couple is missing. They walked into a mortuary to finalize the plans to bury his father. And then . . . what? They disappeared. Why?"

"I don't know. Why?"

She shrugged. "I don't know either, but it's like you just never know when life is going to throw you a curve ball."

"I think our situation clearly demonstrates that point."

"Agreed." She couldn't help but think about Holly's staggering news too. And Lucy. Dear, sweet Lucy who would have to face such a thing at her young age. "So . . ."

"So?"

"So how do you keep your faith?"

"I make sure it doesn't get lost."

She shot him a black look. "That doesn't help."

"Sure it does. I stay focused on the One who really has control in this situation. He's allowing this to happen for a reason. I don't know what it is, but I trust that he's got my back."

"Your back's going to be in prison if we get caught."

"Exactly. Which is why I stay prayed up—and have my catcher's mitt on so I can field all the curve balls." His smile faded to a frown. "Look, I don't mean to make light of the situation. I'm scared, but that doesn't mean God has abandoned me. Life doesn't always work out the way you want it to, but . . ."

She frowned back at him. "Doesn't that just prove my point?"

"What point?"

"Jackie? Are you there?" Ron asked.

She jerked. She'd almost forgotten she was still connected to him. "I'm here."

"Here's the number."

Jackie memorized it. "Thanks."

"Let me know what happens and if you need any more help."

"Will do."

She hung up, tapped the number into the phone, then stared at the device.

"What point?" Ian asked.

She blinked and looked up. "What?"

"You said that just proves your point. What point exactly?"

"Oh. Right." She shrugged. "That God just gives up on some people."

"Gives up on them? Not at all."

She frowned. "How can you say that?"

"God never promised us perfect. Trouble is going to come." His brows dipped. "And unfortunately some people are going to seem to have more than their fair share. But he promised us he'd be with us in that trouble." He cleared his throat. "'Even though I walk through the valley of the shadow of death, I will fear no evil, for you are with me; your rod and your staff, they comfort me.'"

"I remember my grandfather quoting that just about every day," she whispered. "From the Twenty-third Psalm."

"Yes."

She nodded, then sighed. "It doesn't feel like he's with me."

"You can't rely on your feelings. Feelings can be deceptive and lead you down the wrong path. You have to rely on truth."

"And God is truth?"

"Not just truth. Absolute truth. I don't always understand him, but I do believe him. And I believe he's truth. So when he says he's with me in the midst of this mess, I believe him."

"But he still lets bad things happen," she whispered. Her mind flashed to her dead husband, to Holly's cancer, to her rotten childhood, to having to say goodbye to Ian, to his sister's death. To her baby. To being on the run from people who wanted to either put them in prison or kill them.

"Yes, he still allows bad things to happen. He gave us free will. And some people will choose evil. But . . ."

"But what?"

"He still lets good things happen too."

She snorted. "Like what?"

He took her hands and squeezed them. "Like bringing people into our lives just when we need them most."

Jackie tilted her head. "You're talking about me. You really think God put me in your life?"

"I have no doubt about it."

NEW YORK CITY FBI FIELD OFFICE

"Someone else is after them too." Elizabeth took a sip of the strong hot coffee and gave a blissful sigh.

"Yes." Sam set his half-empty cup on the table between them. "We've chased them from South Carolina to Virginia to New York. And someone keeps beating us to them."

"How are they tracking them? The only reason we know they were here last night is because someone reported seeing them and the dog get in the vehicle."

"They haven't changed their appearance yet."

"Which just means they haven't had time."

"His cousin is with them now."

"Yeah, I saw her on the surveillance video." He took another sip of the coffee and leaned forward. "Why would she go with them?"

"They probably needed someone who wasn't immediately recognizable. Her face isn't on the news yet. According to the report, Ian and his cousin were close as children and still keep in touch in spite of the physical distance."

"So she probably wanted to help them. What did Holly's father have to say?"

"Just that he told his daughter to stay away from Ian, but she was bullheaded and would most likely ignore him."

"Sounds like some interesting family dynamics."

They had more leads than they could possibly chase down, but the report of the dog with the couple had sent them after this one. And it had paid off. Security video had captured them leaving out the back of the hotel shortly after several black-dressed individuals were seen entering. They hadn't attracted any immediate attention with their entrance to the hotel. However another camera had caught the attack on Ian and Jackie.

And Jackie and Ian defending themselves quite well. They had skills. Good skills. Which explained why they were still not in custody.

Authorities now had the man Ian had knocked out in an interrogation room. Elizabeth couldn't wait to hear what he had to say. She itched to question him. Her phone rang and she picked it up. It was her Special Agent in Charge in South Carolina. "Hello, Cole."

"Elizabeth, I've got some news."

"What's that?"

"Red Peters, the man who was captured after attacking Lockwood and Sellers, was killed while in custody about an hour ago."

"What?" She shot to her feet and began pacing. "How?" Sam lifted a brow and she put the phone on speaker. "Sam's listening too."

"He was being taken to the magistrate's office along with several other prisoners when a fight broke out among two of the other inmates. There was some confusion and when the smoke cleared, Red's throat was cut and he was dead."

Elizabeth drew in a deep breath. "Someone got to another inmate. They didn't want Red talking. Cole, he was in custody. If someone could get to him there—"

"Yeah, we watched the video footage, but whoever it was knew the angles of the cameras, knew which area was slightly off camera, and that's when he struck. The fighting inmates covered him too. It was a tangle of bodies and everyone had blood on them by the time they were separated. It's impossible to see who actually did the murder. He was dressed in prison orange and blended in. The shank was on the floor and we'll check it for prints, but don't hold your breath. We're still picking apart the video and hopefully will be able to have something soon, but even if we know who it was, he might not be able to tell us who hired him."

"These people have power, but they're not perfect. They're scrambling. They're fighting to keep their plan from derailing completely, so they're having to wing it."

"Possibly."

"No possibly about it." The more she thought about it, the more likely it seemed. "They're going to mess up."

"Well, if what you say is true, they already messed up when they went after Lockwood and Sellers."

"Exactly. But who?"

"We're working on figuring that out now. We're also going to plaster Red Peters' face all over the news networks and see if we can get some solid leads to chase down. He has a rap sheet a mile long. He also recently made it onto the terrorist watch list."

Elizabeth's eyes burned and she pressed her fingers against them. Her phone beeped indicating another call. She glanced at the screen. "It's Yosef." Yosef Anschel with the ATF.

"Take it," Cole said. "I'll be in touch later."

Sam nodded. "Yosef's examining the explosives found at Lockwood's apartment."

"Bye, Cole. Keep me updated." She switched to the other call. "Hello?"

"How's my favorite Special Agent?" Yosef asked.

Elizabeth smiled. She really liked this serious man who never got ruffled. Steady, intelligent, quiet. She'd never heard him raise his voice. "She's wondering what you've managed to unearth."

"Your buddy didn't buy this stuff they took out of his home."

Elizabeth leaned forward. "Okay. Why not? How do you know?"

"Because it was stolen."

"By Lockwood? Stolen from where?"

"Doesn't look like it was Lockwood, but I'll get to that in a minute. It was taken from an area the highway department was working on. They were clearing out part of I-40 where there had been a rockslide. The guy I talked to said an inspection crew came by to do a routine check. Had all of the right uniforms and ID. The supervisor showed them all of the properly stored TNT, blasting caps, et cetera, signed the paperwork, and they took off. Later that same day, another inspection crew showed up. The supervisor was naturally confused, but agreed to another inspection. It was at that point they found the missing TNT."

"So we have a fake inspection crew who managed to steal the TNT. But Lockwood wasn't with them."

"Right."

"And you know this how?"

"We showed pictures. Ones of him in disguise and ones of him before he started changing his appearance. Lockwood wasn't identified as part of the crew."

"Then who was?"

"That, my dear, is the million-dollar question. We are working on it."

"So maybe Lockwood hired someone?" Sam said.

"Hmm," Yosef said. "It's possible, I suppose, but Lu doesn't think so."

Lu Gans, the profiler. "What does Lu think?"

"That someone's setting him up."

"What's her reasoning?"

"Number one—why would he keep the explosives in his home? Let's stretch it and say he was stupid and did so. The TNT wasn't stolen until after he was on the run and, from all accounts, in New York."

Elizabeth shook her head and paced from one end of the room to the other. "What else?"

"Number two—nothing in his past has even suggested he would sell out his country or consider mass murder. In fact, everything suggests the complete opposite. His sister served in Afghanistan. Ian was one of her biggest supporters. And before you ask, no, there's nothing in his behavior to suggest that he's bitter about his sister's death and wants to get even for it."

"And number three?"

"Number three—you have the video showing Ian at the convenience store around the time Daniel was killed. As skilled as he's been at avoiding capture, even he can't be in two places at once."

Her phone beeped in. "Hang on." She switched lines. "Hello?"

"Is this Elizabeth Miller?"

"It is."

"This is Jackie Sellers and we need to talk."

# 23

Jackie heard the woman's indrawn breath. "How did you get this number?"

"I have friends in high places too. I know you're not the Special Agent in Charge, but I know you're an agent from South Carolina and are part of the task force. I also know you're in New York. My friend said you're trustworthy and an outstanding agent, not prone to jump to conclusions and you think things out."

Silence. "Wow. I'm impressed. You do have friends in high places. Where do you want to meet?"

"I don't want to meet you anywhere. I'm going to send you a text. It's a picture of an email Ian Lockwood received from Cedric Wainwright. It's what started this whole thing. He saw something he wasn't supposed to see and now someone wants him dead. I'm helping him, so that makes me a target too."

"I see."

"No, I don't think you do, but you will. You'll need a cryptologist to work on it most likely. It's all in code."

"Why did you run to New York?"

"Because something's going to happen here and we need to stop it."

"How do you know?"

Jackie sighed. "Actually, I don't. It's a guess. But trust me, as soon as we know, you'll know." She paused. "I hope you figure it out before we do."

"Mrs. Sellers—"

"Jackie."

"Fine. Jackie. You and Ian need to come in and let's talk this thing out. There are agents working the case in New York. Just call the field office. I'll give you the number. Or if you don't want to do that, just tell me where you are and I'll come get you."

"Not yet. I don't think we have time for that."

"What's the urgency?"

Now Jackie was stuck. She nearly groaned her frustration. She didn't know exactly what the urgency was, she just knew she had to get off the phone. The minute she'd called, they'd no doubt pinged her location. She shivered in the cold and pulled the coat Ron had provided tighter against her throat. God bless Ron. He'd thought of everything. She'd walked at least four miles in the light snow to get away from the hotel. They might get her current location, but they'd have no idea which hotel they were in. Unless, of course, they started calling around and asking about three people and a dog.

Jackie pulled the phone from her ear, found the text she'd readied, and pressed send. "Did you get it?"

"Hang on."

She started walking. Couldn't stay in one place too long. She walked into the nearest bar and pressed the phone harder against her ear. "Well?"

"I got it." Elizabeth sounded distracted.

"Good."

"Don't hang up yet."

Jackie laughed. "Right."

"No. Wait. Please. Ian's not guilty, is he?"

"No."

"Then why run?"

"I think that's obvious. Because he can't prove it. Yet. Cedric Wainwright is one powerful man and he's trying to make Ian—and me now—the fall guy for seeing whatever is in that email. If he goes to prison and tries to wait on the feds to figure it all out, he'll be dead before you can prove his innocence. Our innocence." She sighed. "You know what I mean."

"I know you're getting ready to hang up. How can I get in touch with you?"

"You can't," Jackie said. "But . . . I have a feeling you're the only one who believes Ian and I could possibly be innocent. Stand by. I think we're going to need you."

"There are other agents—"

"No, you."

Elizabeth paused. "Fine. I'm here and I want to get to the bottom of this as badly as you do."

"I seriously doubt that. I'll call you soon." She hung up, dropped the phone onto the nearest table, and headed for the back of the bar. She slipped out the side door and into the falling snow.

---

Ian paced the floor of the hotel room, worry for Jackie eating at him. He should have gone with her, but she'd argued they were more recognizable as a couple. Gus whined from his spot on the floor. Ian sighed. "I know, buddy. She'll be fine. Right?"

Gus settled his nose between his paws and let his gaze follow Ian from one end of the small area to the other.

Until Jackie finally darkened the door.

Ian pounced. "Well?"

"She got the text. They'll have someone working on the code soon enough."

He sank onto the couch. "Thank God."

Jackie snorted. "Why do you have to bring him into this?"

He rubbed his eyes. "Because if it weren't for him I'd be falling apart."

She swallowed. "Oh." Then picked at nonexistent lint on her sweatshirt while she processed that. "I did notice that even as a teenager and all of the rotten things were happening to you in school, you never turned your back on God."

Ian shrugged. "No."

"Why not?"

"Because he was the only one I trusted enough to help me get through it."

She pulled in a breath and gave a short nod. "All right. But why?"

Ian ran a hand over his face. "I don't know really. I guess when I was little, all those Vacation Bible School weeks sunk in. My parents were absentee for the most part, more interested in traveling and doing their own thing than parenting. They weren't horrible, just uninterested in me or Terry and Gina. I suppose I decided that if my parents weren't going to be there for me, I'd let someone who wanted to. God proved himself over and over to me as a kid. It never occurred to me he wouldn't be there for me as an adult."

She stared at him. "I never had any of that. We had similar childhood experiences. You hung on to God and I pushed him away. Why do you suppose that is?"

He gave her a small smile. "Different personalities, I suppose."

"I suppose."

"But you're wondering if you were wrong to do that, aren't you?"

She blinked. "Hmm. Maybe. You ready to do a little midnight snooping?"

"Changing the subject?"

"Yes."

"Okay. So. Midnight snooping. I assume you're talking about Wainwright Labs?"

"Yep."

He frowned.

She leaned forward. "We've got to find something, Ian. Otherwise we're chasing our tails."

"Too bad we're not the only ones chasing them," he muttered.

She snorted a short laugh at his sour humor, then cleared her throat. "Where's Holly?"

"She was asleep last time I checked."

"I'm worried about her."

"She looks sick, doesn't she?"

"Yeah." And she was going to get sicker. Had Holly told him about the cancer? "Did you see the cache of drugs she has on her?"

"I did."

Jackie moved to the small table in the corner and took a seat. "Are you going to ask her about them?"

"Maybe. If she wanted to tell me about it, she would have."

"Okay, fair enough." So Holly hadn't said anything. Keeping Holly's confidence chafed at her, but she'd promised. She picked up the pen. "You've been to this facility before?"

"Yes." He shook his head. "But it's locked up tight. There's no way to get in there at night."

She pursed her lips. "All right, what about during the day?"

He blinked. "Well, yeah, we could get in, but getting out

would be another story. They'd recognize us as soon as we walked in."

"Not if we're in disguise."

"But—"

"You know where Wainwright's office is?"

"I do." He leaned back.

"Then let's plan. Who are the types that he meets with?"

"Executives, heads of charities, investors—"

She snapped her fingers. "That's it. Investors. We'll be investors."

"How are we going to do that when he knows what I look like?"

"He's not actually going to see us. You're going to create a distraction and we'll get him out of the office. Then while he's out, we're in and we get what we need to prove you—we—didn't have anything to do with any terrorist plot."

Ian stared at her, certain the stress had finally gotten to her.

She sighed as she returned his stare. "Come on, Ian, what have you got to lose?"

He thought about it. "Nothing. Absolutely nothing."

# 24

The night had been a long one of planning and gathering supplies needed to pull off the plan. Holly had done an excellent job of finding what they needed while Ian and Jackie kept their heads down.

Once everything had been finalized, they'd grabbed a couple of hours' sleep and now they were nearly ready.

Ian closed the expensive men's satchel that he'd just finished packing. "Three bombs and a detonator."

"Bombs?" Holly stood at the door, twisting her fingers together.

Ian gave his cousin a grim smile. "Not real ones. They're a combination of the stuff you gathered last night."

Holly looked at the table that held the leftovers. "So you were conducting science experiments while I slept?"

"Exactly. They won't hurt anyone, but they'll create a lot of smoke."

Holly nodded and blew out a breath. "I think I figured out part of this code."

Jackie's pulse jumped. "Really?"

210

"Yes." Holly walked to the table and set the paper in the middle, then slid into the chair.

Jackie sat next to her. "Show us."

Holly pointed to the first line, <u>NYonSTBY</u>. "I think this means what it says. Something is going to happen in New York and people are on standby—meaning maybe they're waiting for further instructions or something."

"Okay. What else?"

"This." She tapped the paper. "The key to the code is simply a computer keyboard. If you use each letter to the left of the one in the code, this is what you get." She pushed the paper across the table to Jackie.

Over each letter, Holly had written the letters to go with the coded letters. "Smallpox delivered," Jackie breathed. "Smallpox?"

"This must have something to do with the smallpox vaccine the government's encouraging the public to get," Ian muttered.

"'Smallpox delivered.' Delivered where?" Jackie frowned.

"Somewhere here in New York," Ian said. "It has to be."

"But why would you have to code a message about delivering a smallpox vaccine?" Holly asked.

"It didn't say vaccine. It said smallpox. What if it's not the vaccine?" Ian murmured.

"But what else—"

Jackie snapped her fingers. "The family that was murdered. The man worked at the CDC in Atlanta." That whole thing had been bugging her since she saw it on television and then saw the government's encouragement to get the vaccine.

"Yes." Ian drew in a deep breath.

"Someone got some of the virus and delivered it to be used here in New York," Jackie whispered. "There are only two places in the world that hold some of the virus. The CDC in Atlanta and the equivalent of the CDC in Russia."

"And most of the population under thirty-five years of age hasn't had the vaccination since it was deemed unnecessary once the disease was considered wiped out," Ian said.

"But someone stole the virus from the CDC and they plan to use it," Jackie said.

"As a bio-weapon," Holly said. "Which is why the government is covering their tails and issuing the suggestion that people get vaccinated now. What do you want to bet they're keeping it hush-hush while they try to find that missing virus?"

Ian blinked. "You've become suspicious in your old age, cuz."

"I agree with her," Jackie said. "But where? How? Who or what's their target?"

Ian shook his head and looked at his cousin. "What about the rest of it?" She rubbed her temples and winced. Ian touched her arm. "Your head still hurting?"

"Yes. I've been having migraines. I have some medication I can take once Ron gets here." She sighed and blinked. "As for the rest of the code, I may have it soon. I tried the same pattern for the other letters, but it's not working. It looks like each line is a different pattern, but I still think it's all connected to the keyboard. I'll keep working on it."

Ian nodded. "All right, Ron will be here soon. Use his phone to call if you figure it out." He paused. "Actually, call once you and Gus are safe with Ron in Virginia, okay?"

"What about Lucy? I didn't call last night. I know she's got to be wondering why. And so is my friend she's staying with."

"Ron's arranging to bring Lucy to you," Jackie said. "She should arrive at the cabin about the time you do."

Holly frowned. "Wait a minute. So far no one has tracked Lucy to my friend. If the FBI or someone go asking, I'm sure someone might mention her name and they'll find her that way, but so far no one has done that. Wouldn't it be safer for her to just stay put?"

Jackie bit her lip. She paced the perimeter of the room, then stopped. "I'm sure the FBI know you're with us by now."

"I'm okay with that," Holly said.

"And even if they figure out you have a daughter, which I'm sure they saw pictures when they trashed your apartment, there's no reason for them to believe she's not with you now. With us."

"Okay." Holly gave a slow nod. "That makes sense."

"I say leave her there. But, your friend will be worried and wonder why you haven't called. Does she know about your . . . ah . . . business trip?"

"Yes."

"Then I would say you can use one of the throwaway phones to call her. No one knows about her, they wouldn't have any reason to be keeping tabs on her number." Jackie gave a decisive nod. "Let Lucy stay there. I think it's safer than dragging her into the middle of this."

Ian took a deep breath. "I guess that's it then."

Jackie handed one of the remaining cell phones to Ian and pocketed the second one after a glance at the screen. "It's time. Wainwright should be eagerly anticipating our meeting."

"I feel like I should be doing something," Holly said.

"You are, you're deciphering that code. Ron will be here soon and you'll be safe while you work." Ian hugged his cousin for a long moment.

"I think I want to stay."

"Your dad already hates me. I don't want to give him a reason to try to kill me too."

Holly pulled back and for the first time since Jackie had seen her in the doorway of her apartment, she had some color in her cheeks and a faint smile on her lips. "He wouldn't."

"Maybe not, but I don't want to be the reason you two never reconcile."

The smile faded and Holly's eyes narrowed. "You wouldn't be the reason. He did that all by himself." Then her features softened. "But we'll have to make our peace sometime soon before I . . ."

"Before you what?"

"It's not important. We'll talk later."

Jackie felt awkward listening to the conversation, but it wasn't like she could avoid it.

Holly sighed. "What time is Ron going to be here?"

Jackie glanced at the clock on the wall. "Any minute. He's been hanging out at my grandfather's place in Virginia coordinating all kinds of help should we need it."

Ian stared at her. "Why haven't the cops been able to connect Ron as the one who's helping us?"

"Because Ron doesn't have any connection to Operation Refuge. He's strictly off the books and doesn't leave a trail anywhere."

"Why?"

She shrugged. "He has his reasons. I'm not at liberty to share them."

A knock sounded at the door and Ian checked the peephole. He opened the door and Ron stepped in.

He opened the door and Ron stepped in. His eyes landed on Holly and he gave her a smile. "Time to go, little lady."

Holly hugged Jackie, then Ian one last time. "Please be careful."

"We will."

"See you soon."

"Real soon."

As soon as Ron and Holly were gone, Jackie dropped an extra clip of bullets into her blazer pocket. And hoped she didn't need them.

# 25

At 26 Federal Plaza, on the twenty-third floor, Elizabeth hovered over the shoulder of FBI cryptologist Tyesha Lee. "Well?"

The pretty black woman turned from the printout and looked up at Elizabeth. "Well, your stalking me isn't going to inspire me to get this figured out any faster. I've been working on it all night and I'm a bit cranky. You might want to keep your distance." Elizabeth dropped back a centimeter and Tyesha sighed. "I ran it through the system and got nothing, so it's definitely a homegrown code."

"Can you crack it?"

"Of course." Tyesha shot her an insulted look. "It's just going to take a bit of time."

Elizabeth surrendered. "Sorry. Call me when you know something."

"You know I will."

Elizabeth headed for the door, then stopped. "Hey, Ty?"

"Yeah?"

When Elizabeth didn't speak, Tyesha lifted her gaze to meet hers. "I think this one is time sensitive," Elizabeth said. "Don't ask me why, but I think the sooner we know what this says, the better."

"Sure, Liz. It's my priority, I promise."

"Thanks."

Elizabeth checked her phone as she headed for the elevator. Her gut said Jackie had told her the truth last night. She and Ian were innocent victims in a super-powered game headed by super-powered people.

People who had a lot to lose because Ian had seen that email. Only now she had it. And she would have it decoded within hours. Hopefully. Cedric Wainwright. She had people looking into him with a magnifying glass. If the guy had any dirt to be found, they'd find it.

Her phone rang. "Hi, Mom."

"Elizabeth, honey, how are you?"

"Working a case as usual, but fine. You?"

"I'm lovely, dear, thank you, but I'll get to the point. I haven't heard from you about Thanksgiving. It's tomorrow, you know."

"I know." Actually she'd forgotten.

"Wonderful. Then can we expect to see you? And maybe a friend? We plan to go to the parade first thing in the morning, then head back to the house to eat."

Elizabeth grimaced. A friend. As in a male friend. As in a boyfriend. And the parade? No thanks. "I'm sorry, Mom. This case is taking all of my time and attention. If I can be there, you know I will." A heavy sigh filtered through the line, firing the guilt Elizabeth felt every time she missed a holiday or family celebration. But she had a job to do. A job she loved. But she loved her family too. "I'll do my best to make it to lunch, all right?"

"All right, dear."

She heard the resignation in her mother's voice and closed her eyes. "Love you, Mom."

"Love you too, dear."

Elizabeth hung up only to find her phone ringing again. She stepped off the elevator and headed for her car. "Yes, Sam, what do you have?"

"We found the phone Sellers used to call you. She left it at a bar on Garrison."

"Of course she did. She wouldn't carry it back to where she was staying. They must have an abundance of throwaway phones."

"Where are they getting their money?"

"We checked their bank accounts before we froze them. No significant withdrawals were made prior to Lockwood going on the run, so either he had a lot of cash on hand at home . . ."

". . . or someone's helping them. Someone in Operation Refuge is staying in touch with them."

"But who?" Frustration bit at her. "We've got eyes on all of them. They're talking back and forth about what's going on, but I would expect that. However, no one has left town or met them."

"What if it's someone not affiliated with Operation Refuge?" he asked.

"It almost has to be."

"There's no telling."

"Right. The best we can do is keep looking and hope someone spots them and calls it in." Her phone beeped in with yet another call. "Let me catch that. It's the SAC in South Carolina. I need to talk to him." She hung up with Sam and pressed the screen to answer the incoming call. "Elizabeth Miller."

"Elizabeth, this is Cole." Cole didn't stand on formality. As long as you did your job and respected the chain of command, he was pretty laid-back. In an intense kind of way.

"Hi, Cole, what have you got?"

"Have you been in touch with either Jackie Sellers or Ian Lockwood?"

"Yes. You know I have." She'd dictated the conversation with Jackie and emailed it to him, to Special Agent in Charge Rebecca Wilson in Atlanta, and to the ADIC in New York, Scott Mitchell.

"No. I mean since the last conversation."

"No, I would have let you know. But I expect to hear something soon."

"Try to set up a meeting. We need to get him and his accomplice off the streets as soon as possible. We've got to get some answers."

"What's happened?"

"A Dr. Jason Arnold was found in his office here in South Carolina with a bullet in the back of his head."

Elizabeth sucked in a breath. Another death? "Who's Dr. Arnold?"

"He's a veterinarian."

"A vet? As in someone who's a doctor for animals?"

"You get the gold star."

And then she knew. "Ian's dog."

"The dog, Gus, was once a service animal to Gina Lockwood, Ian's sister. When she died, he took in the animal."

The light went on. "And Gus has a GPS tracker embedded in him, doesn't he?" Elizabeth asked.

"Nothing gets past you, does it?"

"Save the sarcasm. So now whoever is after Ian and Jackie has Gus's code," she said. "And Gus is going to lead them straight to them." She paced. "We need to beat them there."

"We have the code and are running it now." Cole paused. "We're not sure how much of a head start the others have."

"He's innocent, you know," Elizabeth murmured.

"No. I don't and neither do you." He paused to take a sip of his drink. "But I must say I'm starting to lean in that direction."

"When . . . if . . . Jackie or Ian call me, I'll let them know about Dr. Arnold."

"And get them to meet you. Set it up and get them in custody. If he's innocent, we can protect him."

"Right." Elizabeth pressed her fingers against her eyes. "He's innocent, I know he is."

"I don't know. Could be he's as guilty as they come, and his partners just want him out of the picture for some reason."

"Or he's innocent and is running from everyone until he finds a way to prove it."

"Or that."

"Well, the vet's not dead. Seriously wounded with a bullet in his skull, but he's still breathing."

"So when he wakes up, he can probably ID his shooter."

"If he's not permanently brain damaged." She heard talking in the background. Cole came back on the line. "We just got an ID on another man found murdered in the vet's office. Victor Stroebel."

"Who's he?"

"He has connections with Wainwright Labs. His sister married Cedric Wainwright."

Elizabeth frowned. "Jackie is convinced Wainwright is behind the attempts on their lives, but why would the man take out his brother-in-law?"

"Maybe he doesn't want to split the profits from whatever they're doing?"

"We need to find out if the bullets match Stroebel and Arnold." She thought for a moment. "And see if they match the Goff family and Daniel Armstrong."

"All right. Working on it. And speaking of the Goff family and Daniel Armstrong."

"Yes?"

"They match. It was the same weapon."

Elizabeth let out a puff of air. Her hunch had paid off. "All right. Keep me updated. We've got to find that dog before the wrong people do."

"I just got a text." His voice sounded farther away, as though he were looking at his phone. "Says they're in Virginia. I've contacted the Richmond office and they have agents on the way to the GPS coordinates."

"Virginia?" Her frown deepened. "That can't be right."

"Why not?"

"Because Jackie said something was going down in New York. She and Ian are here in New York."

"Not according to the dog's GPS."

"You follow that. I'm going to stay here and wait for Jackie to call me." She looked at her phone. "Come on, Jackie, call me," she whispered.

They were ready.

"Thank goodness for the city that never sleeps," Jackie muttered. She adjusted the collar of her pin-striped blouse and tugged at the waistband of her black slacks. Not her usual attire. But she'd be comfortable and confident wearing it. Or die trying. Hopefully not literally.

Ian sported a dark blue Versace suit, and frankly Jackie thought he rocked it. She shoved aside the desire to take his hand and suggest they just run away to a deserted island and live happily ever after.

She scoffed, shocked at the turn of her thoughts. Happily

ever after would be great, but if she didn't want to spend it behind bars, she'd better get focused.

"You all right?" Ian asked.

"Peachy. You?"

"The same." He swallowed hard and tugged at his tie. "You made the appointment?"

"Eleven o'clock sharp."

"What if he recognizes you?"

She lifted a newly arched brow and looked at him over the top of the black-framed glasses. "Would you recognize me?"

Ian sighed. "I don't know. Probably not. If I was suspicious of you, then yes, I would see the resemblance."

"Then let's hope he doesn't suspect anything."

Ian watched her, his eyes intense, new lines etched on his face. "Are we really going to try and do this?"

"Absolutely. And we're not going to try, we're going to do it." She studied him. "You don't look anything like Ian Lockwood."

"I hope that's a good thing."

"Today it is."

They walked out the door and Jackie couldn't help winging a small prayer heavenward. She figured it couldn't hurt. And if it helped . . . well. That would be a very good thing indeed.

---

*10:30 A.M.*

Ian wanted to fidget. Instead he held himself still, gripped the satchel, and took a deep breath. The back of the cab smelled like pine cleaner and reminded him of the lab. A wave of homesickness rolled over him. He wanted his life back. "Are you going to text Elizabeth Miller and let her know what Holly deciphered?"

he murmured. He kept an eye on the rearview mirror, making sure the cabbie couldn't hear him.

"Yes. As soon as we're finished with this."

"What if we get caught?"

"Then we have some leverage to get someone to listen to us." She reached over and gripped his fingers. "You can do this, Ian."

The look in her eyes, the determination to help clear him, and her willingness to put her life on the line for him did him in. His head dipped and he swooped in to land his lips on hers. Jackie froze and for a moment he did too. Then he felt her lips soften, respond, and he kissed her the way he wanted to back in high school. Every word he never said, every emotion he ever felt, came out in the kiss.

When he lifted his head, the stunned look on her face nearly made him smile. If only—

The cabbie cleared his throat. Ian jerked but didn't turn away from Jackie. "I've wanted to do that for a long time now."

"Well . . . ah . . . well."

He smiled. "Yeah. Me too."

"You folks getting out or you need me to drive you to the nearest church and preacher man?"

Jackie's face lit up like Rudolph's nose on Christmas Eve. Ian wanted to laugh. And couldn't. His throat closed. "I don't want to die without telling you how I feel about you, how I've always felt about you," he whispered in her ear.

The color drained from her cheeks as fast as it had appeared. She placed a finger over his lips. "Don't. Don't say anything else. Let's focus on what we need to do here." She frowned. "And don't talk about dying."

He gave a slow nod. "Right."

Jackie straightened her hair, handed him a tissue from the

purse she'd clutched on her lap, then reapplied the lipstick he'd just kissed off.

Ian felt the heat climb into his face as he swiped his lips. He looked at her. "Better?"

She gave a brisk nod. "Yep."

Ian paid the patient cabbie and gave him a generous tip. "Can you hang around for about thirty minutes?"

The man counted the money and nodded. "If there's more where this came from."

"There's more."

"I'll circle the block and find a place to park. Meet you back here in thirty."

"Or before."

"Got it."

Ian and Jackie slipped from the cab.

"I hope this works," Ian breathed.

"It has to." Jackie grabbed her purse and the black briefcase she'd brought and strode to the glass doors of Wainwright Labs. Ian shook his head and took a deep breath even as he admired the confidence she emitted. He followed her, prayers on his lips that they would get what they needed and get out without trouble.

Somehow he didn't hold out much hope of that.

# 26

Jackie and Ian rode to the fourth floor and stepped off the elevator. A woman in her early thirties, seated behind a mammoth desk, complete with three flat-screened monitors and a bookshelf crammed with binders, stared at them over the rim of her glasses. Her red lips pursed as they approached.

Her nameplate read Brenda Newall.

Jackie forced a small, mysterious smile to her lips. Aloof, she hoped. "Hello."

"May I help you?"

"I'm Sharleen Howard." She flashed the fake ID Ron had provided. "This is my associate, Joseph Terrell. We represent the Johannsen Estate and are here to see Cedric Wainwright."

"Do you have an appointment?"

"Yes, of course. He said he would be able to meet with us at eleven."

The receptionist looked at her computer screen and her face brightened. "Ah yes, there you are. You're the investors Mr. Wainwright was so excited about this morning."

Ian lifted his nose a fraction and kept the haughty expression on his face. "I suppose five million would go a long way in the R&D department," he said in a perfect English accent.

Jackie did a double take and hoped the receptionist didn't notice.

"Absolutely. If you could just wait a moment, I'll let him know you're here." She pressed the button on her earpiece.

"Before you announce us, do you mind if I use your facilities?" Ian asked.

She paused and pressed the earpiece again. "Of course, of course. Follow me. I could use a bit of a break myself. It will take a few minutes. The restrooms are at the very end of the hall."

"I'll just wait here, take your time," Jackie said. She walked to the sofa.

Ian shot her a look that said he was worried, but he'd do his part. Jackie gave a slight nod. The adrenaline flowed and her hands held a faint tremble. But she was ready. Ready to stop this nightmare and put whoever was responsible behind bars.

Jackie settled herself on the couch and waited.

---

"Thank you so much, Mrs. Newall," Ian said.

She smiled. "It's Ms."

"Have you worked for Wainwright Labs for a while?"

"Twelve years," she said.

Ian stopped in front of the restroom door. "Is Mr. Wainwright a good boss?"

Her eyes flickered. "He can be a difficult man to work for, but I know it's just because he's so busy running the company and needs to make sure everything is done exactly like it's supposed to be done."

Ian cleared his throat and gave a light cough. "Why stay?"

She gave a light snort. "Jobs aren't exactly growing on trees, you know."

Ian coughed again. "But twelve years? Surely that's enough

time to—" He stopped and coughed, a deep hacking cough that had Ms. Newall backing up, concern etched on her face.

"All you all right?" she asked.

"Yes, yes. Do you think I could trouble you for a bottle of water?"

"Of course. I'll have to run downstairs and get it."

Ian nodded, coughed again. "I'll just meet you back at your office. Thank you."

"I'll be right back."

Ian watched her go, cleared his throat, and took a deep breath. Now that he had her out of the way, he could get busy.

---

Even though she'd been expecting it, when the alarm sounded, Jackie jerked, then she stood and walked behind the desk to crouch. And wait. She peered around the edge, her heart thudding. *Please let this work.*

Within seconds, the door to her left opened and Cedric Wainwright came out, his expression clearly unhappy. Another man followed him. Cedric stopped and looked toward the desk. Jackie eased back. "Brenda? Brenda!"

"She probably left the minute the alarm sounded," Cedric's companion said. Cedric cursed. His buddy took his arm. "Come on, let's get out of here."

"It's probably some stupid false alarm. Let's just wait it out."

Jackie tensed. If they stayed, it was over.

Sirens sounded and Cedric strode to the window, the one nearest Jackie. She held her breath. If he looked down and to his left, he'd see her. Adrenaline pumped, her breath caught in her throat, and she stayed as still as possible.

Another curse slipped from the man's lips. He spun on his heel. "Let's go. This better not take long."

As his footsteps carried him further and further away, Jackie wilted. She waited until she knew they were in the stairwell, then dashed for the office door. Her fingers curled around the handle and pushed.

Locked.

---

Ian held the stairwell door open and directed people to it. They muttered their thanks as they hurried past. No one made eye contact. The smoke drifting up convinced them their lives might actually be in danger.

At last, he was alone. He raced back down the hall, checking the rooms. Soon the firefighters would be in the building. He found Jackie kneeling on the floor, her face at doorknob level. "What are you doing? We don't have a lot of time."

"He locked the door behind him," she growled. "And I can't pick the lock."

Ian froze for a millisecond. "It's got a key card slot too."

"Yep, but I don't have the card."

Ian bolted to Brenda's desk. He opened the large drawer in the middle.

Nothing.

Slammed it shut.

The sirens grew louder.

He tried the next drawer, then the next. He stopped and ran a hand down his face.

"What are you doing?" she asked, head tilted, fingers working.

Ian looked at the phone, the stapler, the bin with the Post-it notes.

And a small item that looked like a credit card. He grabbed it and loped back to the door. "Let me."

Jackie moved out of his way and Ian swiped the card.

The lock gave a soft snick and Jackie pulled the handle down. "Nice job," she whispered.

"Anytime." Ian pushed the door open and ushered Jackie into the office.

She went immediately to the tablet on the desk.

Ian went to the items on the desk, papers. He read notes Cedric had written to himself on the legal pad next to the phone. "He was expecting us," he murmured. "Has big dollar signs next to our names."

"Of course," Jackie said. "Money always talks. Now hurry."

"I don't even know what I'm looking for."

"You'll know it when you see it." She tapped on the tablet screen and it jumped to life. She slapped the desk and Ian jerked. "Password protected, of course."

"Of course." He tossed the stack of papers onto the desk and moved to the next drawer.

Jackie folded the screen protector over the tablet and jerked the cord from the wall.

"What are you doing now?" Ian asked.

"Taking this with us."

"Hello? That's stealing."

"It's evidence collection. Just a little before the warrant is issued."

She shoved the tablet into her purse and started helping him go through the drawers. "It's too much," she whispered. "We don't have the time."

Ian dumped the trash can and dropped to his knees to pick through the papers. He shoved aside a paper coffee cup, found a sticky note, a business card. "Something," he muttered. "There's got to be something."

The door slammed open.

Ian spun, Jackie whirled.

To face Cedric Wainwright holding a small gun like he knew how to use it.

# 27

Jackie's heart raced even while her mind flashed twenty different scenarios in less than a second. "Mr. Wainwright? Why do you have a gun? We came looking for a way out." She played innocent, knowing he wouldn't fall for it, but hoping it would buy her a little time.

"Which explains why you're going through my trash and have my tablet in your bag." He held out a hand. "I'll take it back, please."

The alarm still blared. She couldn't tell if the sirens had stopped or not, but figured the fire trucks were right outside. She decided to try the direct approach. "You're setting us up to take the fall to keep us from stopping you from whatever it is you're doing. At least have the decency to tell us what it is," she yelled and covered her ears. How long would it take for the firemen to clear the first three floors?

Wainwright's eyes narrowed and his finger tightened on the trigger. Jackie ducked as the bullet smashed into the wall behind her. Ian gave a yell and tackled the man, sending his weapon

229

spinning across the hardwood floor to the edge of the expensive oriental rug.

Jackie grabbed the gun and rammed the barrel against the side of his head. "Don't. Move." She spoke loud enough to be heard.

Cedric froze. Ian grabbed her bag. Jackie removed the weapon from the man's head, but kept it trained on him center mass. Three firefighters came into sight of the office and she tucked the gun behind her.

"Go!" Jackie yelled at Ian.

They turned as one and burst from the office. The firefighters stopped and waved them toward the exit stairs. Jackie and Ian darted past them, hit the stairs, and shot out the door at the bottom.

The crowd milled. Jackie slipped Cedric's weapon into her purse next to the tablet. They pushed through the chaos. Jackie gripped Ian's arm and he steered her to where they'd left the cabbie. He was gone, of course.

"Keep walking," Ian said.

"You have any idea where we are?"

"Yes. A vague one. When we were here for a seminar not too long ago, we walked to a nearby restaurant. I think this is the right way."

Several shops lined the street. Traffic had been redirected so no cars passed them. They walked and Jackie's nerves continued to twitch. Sirens sounded in front of them.

"The cops aren't going to be the only ones stepping up the search," Ian said. "Cedric is going to double his efforts to find us now that we have his tablet."

"I know. We need to get off this street." Jackie saw a cruiser turn their way and she gripped Ian's arm to propel him onto a side street. The tall buildings offered some shelter and comfort, but she knew they were being caught on camera. The FBI would track them in no time. The side street opened up onto another busy avenue. They were far enough away from the lab that life moved as usual.

Which meant cabs.

Jackie raised her arm and waved. The taxi pulled to a stop and she and Ian slipped into the back.

"Where to?" the cabbie asked.

"Where's the nearest quiet restaurant where you can get good food and have a little privacy?" Jackie asked.

The cabbie smiled in the rearview mirror. "I've got just the place." He pressed the gas and Jackie pulled Cedric's tablet from her purse. "Call Ron for me, will you?"

Ian didn't ask questions, just dialed the number. He handed her the phone. Ron answered on the second ring. "Are you all right?"

"For now."

"What do you need?"

She glanced at the cabbie, bent her head close to Ian's, and kept her voice low. She hoped the cab driver just took them for lovebirds who were snuggling. "I need for you to arrange a meeting with Special Agent Elizabeth Miller and I need you to do it without giving her enough notice to have backup waiting."

"Consider it done."

"We're going to give her the tablet?" Ian murmured in her ear.

"We are." His lips brushed her ear and she shivered, pulling back and clearing her throat. "Thanks, Ron." She hung up and shook her head. With another glance at the cabbie who didn't seem to be paying them one bit of attention, she leaned even closer to Ian. He wrapped an arm around her shoulders and pulled her closer. She breathed in his unique scent, musky cologne, and hotel soap. "This is bigger than us. This has something to do with a smallpox virus being delivered, the rest of that code, you—us—being set up as terrorists. This is so huge."

"That guy who was killed, we saw him on the news."

"Who?"

"You were pointing out the news scroll going across the bottom of the screen and I thought you wanted me to watch what was on the television. I don't remember the guy's name, but he and his family were killed. Remember?"

Jackie frowned. "Yes, actually, I do remember that."

"So, he was killed, the government issues statements that the public needs to get a smallpox vaccine. And Holly decodes 'Smallpox delivered.'"

Jackie swallowed and rubbed her forehead. "Someone's getting ready to release the smallpox virus somewhere."

"That's what I've come up with."

"Then we're on the same page."

"But where?" His frown deepened.

"New York on standby," she whispered. "Right here in New York obviously. Just like we suspected, but *where* in New York?"

"And when?" They fell silent for a moment. "So how do we stay out of jail and stop them?" he asked.

"We're out of our league. We need to invite the big boys to the party."

"The FBI."

"And whoever else wants to get in on the action," she murmured.

---

James Walden paced while the fires burned at their hottest. Two thousand degrees Fahrenheit would take care of the wood coffin and the body. He glanced at the clock. About another hour and the cooling process would begin.

His phone rang. He picked up the handset for the cordless phone and began his ascent that would take him up to the main level. "Walden's Mortuary."

"They're moving again."

"Where to?"

"Looks like they're headed back to Virginia. At least that's what the dog's GPS says."

"Follow them. The dog will lead the way."

"We're on it. Oh, and one more thing."

"What?"

"There was some commotion at Wainwright Labs."

James stiffened. "Commotion?"

"There was a small fire. Or some kind of smoke bombs that were released. Wainwright said Lockwood and Sellers were in his office."

James swore. "How did that even happen?"

"I'm not sure of the details, but they grabbed his tablet and he wants it back."

"What do I need to do?"

"Be ready with the fire when we bring them to you."

James swallowed. "Fine."

"Also Red Peters. I had to take care of him yesterday."

"Take care of him?"

"He's dead. He got into an argument with two inmates at the prison. Poor guy came out on the losing end and had his throat slit. He won't be talking anymore."

For a moment, James couldn't breathe. Red had taken care of a lot of the details of the plan. If he'd talked before he'd been silenced—

He struggled to keep his cool. "Look, if anything else goes wrong, I'm—"

"You're what? Bailing?" The voice on the other end let out a laugh. "Right. Try it and see how long you live."

*Click.*

James lowered the handset onto his desk and leaned his head against the back of the leather chair. He could leave now. Leave the country and never look back.

But the money. What if they actually pulled this off and he'd run to safety? He would be out millions. And if they got caught, he would know in time to escape anyway. He rubbed his chin and considered his options.

The millions.

And knew he'd stay.

*6:00 P.M.*

Jackie pulled in a deep breath and picked up the phone to punch in a number. After grabbing food they'd eaten on the run, she and Ian had managed to hide out in a small hotel off one of the side streets for the past six hours. Long enough for David and Adam to fly to New York. Ron was busy at the cabin in Virginia with Holly and she needed outside help.

David answered. "I'm here."

"Good. You have Elizabeth's number?"

"I do. Ron gave it to me."

"Okay, you set up the meeting with her and call me back."

"I'm on it."

"Have you heard from Ron?"

"He and Holly are tucked away. She's still working on the code."

"The FBI is too. I wonder if they're any closer to figuring it out."

"Haven't heard."

"Yeah. Okay."

"Stand by," David said. "Hope to have something for you soon."

She hung up and leaned back against the sofa of the common room in the hotel suite they'd managed to snag. She'd tried to rest, but sleep had eluded her and now she felt punchy with exhaustion.

The door to the hotel room opened and Ian stepped into the living area. "I've got food," he said.

Jackie swung her legs over the side of the bed and walked to sit at the table. Ian held up a huge bag of fast food. Jackie's stomach rumbled its anticipation and he smiled. A real smile. Not forced, not strained.

"Glad I could do something right today."

She shot him an answering smile. Thank goodness, money wasn't an issue and they could afford the large suites with two or three rooms. It made it so much easier to have each other's back—and not worry about the awkwardness that sharing a hotel room would bring on.

Ian distributed the food and took the chair opposite her. "Do you think this is going to work?"

"It has to."

He took a bite of his hamburger and studied her. She sipped on her milkshake. "What?"

"What?" he echoed.

"You're staring at me."

"I was just wondering about your husband."

She froze for a second before reaching for a French fry. Chewing slowly, she finally swallowed and managed to nod. "What do you want to know?"

"He must have been special. He would have had to have been in order to capture your heart."

"He was special." She sighed and closed her eyes for a brief moment.

"You're still in love with him."

She thought about that, then opened her eyes. "No. I'm not."

Ian stilled. "Really?"

"Really." She pursed her lips. "It's been over six years. I think about him, I miss the way things were, and I'll always hold a special place in my heart for him, maybe even a special love, but no, I'm not *in* love with him anymore."

"Then why does it look like you're in agony when you talk about him?"

"Agony?" She gave a sharp, humorless laugh. "No, that would be guilt, not agony."

"Oh." He took a bite of his hamburger. "Guilt because he died and you didn't?"

"Yes. Among other things."

"Can you tell me about it?"

Jackie's mind spun. "He was a great guy. I already told you the story of how we married and how he was killed at a convenience store."

"Yes."

"What I didn't tell you was that . . . I sent him there. I sent him to the convenience store in the middle of the night for an ice cream sandwich." She cleared her throat at the sudden tightness. "I was pregnant," she whispered. "And I wanted ice cream. And John wanted to give me anything I desired. To satisfy my every craving. And I was happy to let him do it." She drew in a shaky breath. "And he died because I made him go out in the middle of the night when he should have been home in bed next to me."

# 28

Ian stared at Jackie. He understood a little more about why she blamed herself for her husband's death. And shock zipped through him at the fact that she'd been pregnant. "You were pregnant?"

"Yes."

"What happened to the baby?"

Jackie let out a tearful laugh. "It doesn't matter," she whispered.

"Of course it does. Did you . . . ?"

She jumped to her feet. "It doesn't matter. It's in the past. Let's leave it there." She went to her room and slammed the door.

Ian stared at the barrier as he worked through this new information. The past was painful for her, he understood that. There were parts of his past that he still avoided thinking about too.

Jackie had unresolved issues that she needed to deal with. Issues he'd help her work through if she'd let him. But he had a feeling she'd closed a part of herself off from people for so long, she might not remember how to share. To let someone in and be a part of her healing process. Just like he'd like to let her be a part of his.

He debated whether or not to press the issue. Should he go after her or leave her alone? Before he could make a decision, Jackie came out of the room, phone pressed to her ear. "Okay, I'll fill him in." She hung up.

"What's the plan?" he asked.

"David has contacted Elizabeth Miller. He's set up a meeting with her, telling her that he may know our location, but wants to meet with her before saying anything."

"And she bought that?"

"David didn't give her a choice. She'll take a cab to the location he tells her, then she'll get in the car with him and he'll bring her to meet us. He wants to make sure she doesn't bring anyone with her to surprise us. After the meeting, she can grab a taxi and head to wherever she needs to go to report in."

"What if she's wired?"

"She probably will be. But as soon as she gets into the car with David and Adam, they have a way of blocking any radio signals, including cell phones and body wires." She paused. "But we'll tell her to get rid of her phone just in case. There's new technology out there that allows smartphones to stream live. All they need is a computer to track us. The app runs on the background of the phone even when the phone looks like it's turned off."

He nodded.

"Once he's sure it's safe, he'll tell us where to meet them."

"How long do we have?"

"Not long."

Less than a minute later, Jackie's phone rang and Ian lifted a brow. "That was fast."

She shook her head. "It's not David, it's Holly." She slid her finger across the screen.

"Put her on speaker."

Jackie did. "Hello?"

"I'm at the cabin with Ron."

Relief tugged at Jackie. "Good."

"I talked to Lucy. She sounded great." Jackie could hear the tears in her friend's voice.

"She'll be just fine."

"She's excited. She gets to ride on a float in the Macy's Thanksgiving Day Parade. Maria, another friend who also has a little boy in Lucy's class, works for a float building company. Somehow Maria arranged for the whole class to ride."

"The whole class?"

"Well, there are only twelve in the class, but they're so excited."

"That's awesome," Jackie said, but frowned.

"Lucy actually had to go stay with Maria. Carissa's son, Micah, has strep throat. She couldn't reach me so made the decision to send Lucy over to stay with Maria."

"Are you all right with that?"

"Yes, Maria's wonderful, she's just really busy right now, so her mother's going to have to take care of both kids. She says she's fine with it. Lucy adores Lewis so she's happy too. I guess it's all right. I don't like not being there for her."

Jackie heard the underlying meaning behind her friend's words. "You'll be there for her."

Holly changed the subject. "I worked on this code the whole way here and I think I've figured more of it out."

"Great. What?"

"Okay, the first two lines I'm still pretty sure about: New York on Standby and smallpox delivered. The third, fourth, and fifth lines I just can't figure out what they could be. I think if it's underlined, it means what you think it means."

"So Cnt:T8R. That's underlined. What does that mean? Contact Tater?"

"Or someone named Tate R. And I think the symbols to the right are a phone number."

Jackie bit her lip. "What number?"

"I've worked it several different ways, but when I do it one way, I get a number with a 212 area code."

"Which is New York."

"Exactly. I'm not a hundred percent sure, so I want to keep playing with it."

Finally, they were getting somewhere. "Good job, Holly. I'll pass this on to Special Agent Miller."

"Be careful."

"We will."

---

"The FBI are watching me. Lockwood and Sellers must have delivered the tablet to them," Wainwright told the person on the other end of the line.

"You were stupid leaving it lying around like that. Is my name on there anywhere?"

Wainwright drew in a deep breath and decided to ignore the insult. Besides, it had been stupid. "Of course not. Have you located them?"

"In the mountains of Virginia."

"How soon can you take care of them?"

"We're on our way now."

Wainwright clicked a few keys on his keyboard. It was time for him to vacate the United States. Looked like his pilot was going to earn a bonus this flight. He'd schedule the flight, then have the pilot take him somewhere else off grid. Once the plan was carried out, the money would be wired to his offshore account that was in another name. He didn't have to be in the United States to get the money.

"If you fail, we're done," the voice hissed. "I chose you because you were the one person I thought I could count on."

"You chose me because I could be bought."

"Well, yes, but—"

"Don't worry. Failure isn't an option. My whole future is riding on this deal."

"I'm glad we agree."

---

Ian and Jackie sat in the back of the cab for ten minutes while they watched the restaurant and those who entered and left.

"You think it's all right?" Ian asked.

"David texted me and said to come on in. She's here."

Jackie took one more look around. "If there are feds here waiting to pounce, I don't see them."

"Isn't that the point?"

She gave a low laugh. "True, but I can usually pick them out when I know they're around."

"Hopefully, David was able to keep them from getting directions."

Ian paid the driver and they slipped from the back of the cab. Jackie had the tablet in her bag. She wrapped the straps around her hand and followed Ian into the restaurant. Adam stood guard just inside the door and gave them a slight nod as they walked past.

Immediately, her eyes landed on David and a woman with jet black hair. Her Asian heritage was evident with her almond eyes and olive complexion. She stood, her expression guarded. Wary. Jackie held out her hand. "Jackie Sellers."

"Special Agent Elizabeth Miller. Call me Elizabeth." She dropped Jackie's hand and let her gaze land on Ian.

"I'm Ian Lockwood," he said.

He and Elizabeth shook hands. She glanced at David. "I'm feeling a bit outnumbered."

They all sat. "No need to worry," David said. "No one here wants any trouble."

"On the contrary," Jackie said, pulling the tablet from her bag and pushing it across the table to the agent. "There's proof of all kinds of trouble on here. You just need to find it."

"What kind of proof?" Elizabeth didn't touch the device, instead she reached into her own bag and pulled out a pair of gloves and a large paper bag. She slipped on the gloves and powered the tablet up. "Password?"

Jackie shook her head. "I have no idea."

Elizabeth turned the device off, slipped the tablet into the bag, and sealed it. She then proceeded to write the contents, the date, and time on the outside of the fold. "Then how do you know there's evidence of anything on here?"

"Because of whose office I took it from."

"And if there's nothing on here, he'll press charges of theft."

Jackie held her gaze. "That's the least of my worries right now. The proof is there, you just have to find it. Of course, I can't prove the tablet actually belongs to him and he will say it doesn't if you ask him, but it does, and I'm sure there's something on there that will prove it."

The woman nodded. "It's probably as simple as it being registered in his name or his company's. I'll get this to someone who can find out what's on here. In the meantime, I'm going to have to ask you to turn yourselves in. It really is in your best interests. Obviously you've made someone mad and they're out to get you. We can protect you while you're in custody."

Jackie sighed. "We can't do that. That was the whole reason for meeting you here without any of your backup. Has your cryptologist figured out that coded email yet?"

"Not yet."

"We've got more."

Elizabeth held up a hand and looked around. "Hold on, where's the dog?"

Ian and Jackie exchanged a glance. Jackie lifted a brow and shrugged.

"He's with a friend," Ian said. "We thought it would be less conspicuous if we didn't have him with us. Why?"

Elizabeth pinched the bridge of her nose. "So he *is* in Virginia."

Jackie stilled and looked at David. "How would she know that?"

David shook his head and they stared at Elizabeth. "Dr. Jason Arnold was shot in the head yesterday," she said.

"What?" Ian yelled and surged to his feet. Jackie grabbed his arm and pulled him down beside her. "Why didn't you say something?"

"I'm saying something now. He's hanging on to his life by a thread at a hospital in South Carolina."

Ian blew out a breath. "Oh no. No. This can't be. He has a daughter—" He swallowed. "Why? Why would they do that?"

"The GPS code."

"To track us," Jackie muttered. "Of course." Her eyes widened. "Ron. Holly," she whispered.

"Your friends?"

"Yes. They're not involved in this, but we had to send Gus somewhere. Ron took him and Holly to keep them away from the danger." She groaned. "Instead, we've sent them straight to it."

"The FBI also has the code and are on the way up there. Your friends will be fine."

"If the FBI gets there first," David said. He stood and pulled out his phone. "I'm going to call Ron."

Ian's face had lost most of its color. Jackie decided she might start praying after all.

"Is there anything else you can tell me?" Elizabeth asked.

Jackie blinked, trying to wrap her mind around the fact that Holly and Ron *weren't* safe. Gus would lead the killers straight to them. Then again, the FBI were on the way too. "Will they get there in time?" she asked.

"What?"

"The FBI. Will they get there in time?"

"If I had my phone, I could tell you."

Jackie shot a look at David, who paced in the small hall that led to the restrooms. "He'll find out."

Elizabeth's facial expression didn't change. "In the meantime, you said you had more. What else?"

Ian still looked shell-shocked. Jackie didn't blame him. They'd thought they were being so careful. "Um . . . yeah. Yeah." She filled her in on what Holly had discovered.

Elizabeth reached into her coat pocket then stopped. "One of you have a phone I can borrow?"

"Later," Ian said. "Let's finish this. Tell her the rest, Jackie?"

"Unfortunately that's about it." She looked at Elizabeth. "Can you tell us anything that you've found? What does the 'smallpox delivered' mean?"

"I'm afraid I'm not at liberty to discuss that."

"Well, why don't I tell you what I think?" Jackie leaned forward. "I think that the man who was murdered, the one who worked with the CDC, Anwar Goff, stole the last remaining smallpox virus from the freezer of the CDC and he—and his family—were killed once he turned it over to the people who forced him to steal it. How's that for starters?"

Elizabeth met her gaze. "Go on."

"I also think that when Wainwright sent the email and discovered Ian had read it, he had to come up with something fast. Something to send Ian running or have the authorities on his doorstep before he knew what hit him."

"And?"

"And when Ian ran, they had to regroup. They took the information they had—the fact that Ian was working with malaria—and simply twisted his research to look like he was going to sell it to the highest United States enemy bidder."

"Thereby taking the attention away from the whole smallpox theft thing," Ian said.

Jackie nodded. "So, the CDC and law enforcement are keeping the smallpox theft as quiet as possible. However, they can't just do nothing, so they're encouraging the population to get their vaccine. Against a virus that was eradicated back in the seventies."

Elizabeth's expression gave nothing away. "You think a lot, don't you?"

"It's caused me a lot of sleepless nights, that's for sure. Ian was working for Wainwright Labs. He gets an email meant for another person. Once they realize he and his co-worker, Daniel Armstrong, have seen it, they have to do damage control. Daniel is dead. The only person standing between these people and their terrorist plot is Ian. And maybe me."

Elizabeth looked at the man sitting at Jackie's side. "So who's trying to kill you?"

"Cedric Wainwright. Or someone who works for him. I don't know how far this organization reaches, but it obviously has a pretty long arm. From Atlanta to South Carolina to New York."

Jackie glanced at David. He still paced, the phone pressed to his ear.

*7:00 P.M.*
*VIRGINIA*

Ron's shoulders itched, and when that happened, bad things were getting ready to go down. He stood in front of the big picture window processing Holly's side of the conversation. Holly had called Jackie as soon as they'd stepped in the door. Gus had gone to the sink and Ron took that as his cue to fill the bowl Ian and Jackie had left on the floor of the kitchen.

Gus now lounged in front of the fireplace, ears pricked, but not exhibiting any concern. Ron wondered how good a watchdog the animal was.

Holly had her eyes closed and rested her head against the back of the recliner. Something was wrong with her and it worried Ron that he didn't know what it was. She'd slept the entire trip and had seemed disoriented when he'd awakened her. She was still, but he didn't think she was asleep. "Are Jackie and Ian still okay?" he asked.

She didn't open her eyes. "Yes, they're meeting with the FBI agent soon and plan to turn over all the information they have."

Ron nodded. David had texted him a brief, coded update. "What's wrong with you?"

She blinked and focused her gaze on him. "Brain cancer."

He sucked in a deep breath. "I wasn't expecting that one."

She gave a humorless chuckle. "Me neither."

"How long?"

"Three months without treatment. Maybe six with."

Ron gave a short nod. "I'm sorry."

"I am too."

"Where are you spiritually?"

She huffed a soft laugh. "I'm good spiritually. The Lord has allowed all of this for a reason. I don't necessarily like it, but I'm trusting him. I know where I'm going when I die and I know I'm going to be just fine when I get there."

"But?"

"Lucy," she said. Her eyes teared and she swallowed. "My dear, precious Lucy."

"Your daughter."

"Yes."

"It was you, wasn't it?"

Holly frowned at him. "What do you mean?"

"You were with Jackie during those horrible months after John was killed. You were the only one she could stand to have around her."

A sigh slipped from her pale lips. "Yes. I was with her."

"Thank you," he whispered, then cleared his throat.

"I'm sorry she wouldn't let anyone else with her. I'm sorry she shut you out."

"I am too." He paused, then rose to pat her hand. "But I'm glad she had you." His phone rang. He glanced at the screen. David.

Gus stood, hackles raised. Ron paused, finger hovering as he watched the animal. A low growl rumbled in Gus's throat and he took a step toward the front door.

Holly stood and met his gaze. "Something's wrong."

Ron pulled his weapon with one hand, slid his phone into his pocket, and grabbed Holly's wrist. He propelled her toward the front door and held his breath. If they'd been found, they probably had the house surrounded.

He paused at the front door and peered out the window.

"What's happening?" Holly whispered. "How did they find us?"

Her body trembled and Ron felt anger surge through him. Gus barked. Three sharp warning barks.

"I'm not sure how, but they have." And all of his backup was in New York. In hindsight, he should have had more help, but he'd truly thought if he kept it just him and Holly and the dog, everything would be simpler and off the radar. "Guess not," he muttered.

A loud bang echoed through the house. Then the front door

rattled. Holly gasped and shrank against him. Ron put her behind him and aimed the weapon at the door. Another house-jarring boom sounded and the front door flew in.

Gus growled and launched himself at the intruder and latched on to his outstretched hand. His weapon fell to the floor and Ron acted. He lunged toward him and placed his weapon against the man's dark head. "Gus! Off!" Gus didn't act like he was ready to relinquish the man's arm. "Off!" Gus backed up with a whine.

"Freeze or die," Ron told the cursing individual now cradling his bloody arm to his stomach.

"FBI! Freeze!" The shout came from just inside the door. "Drop the weapon! On the ground now!"

Ron tossed the weapon and lay on his stomach. "Do it, Holly. They'll sort us out when they figure out who all the bad guys are." Holly went to her knees. Then to the floor. Ron's arms were jerked behind his back. The man who'd kicked in the door rolled and punched the agent. The agent dropped. More agents moved in, shouting, weapons drawn.

"Don't shoot him!" Ron shouted. He needed the man alive. Ron rolled to his knees and shot forward, head down. He caught the man in the stomach. They went down together. The FBI agent landed on top of both of them.

Once the intruder was subdued, Ron lay still, panting. "I'm getting too old for this," he muttered.

"What was that?"

He looked up. A young agent, probably in his mid-thirties, held a weapon on him.

Ron shook his head. "Nothing." He looked past him to find Holly still on the floor. "Holly." She didn't move. "Holly? It's okay. You can sit up." Still no response. "Hey! She needs an ambulance, now!"

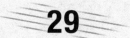

# 29

*WEDNESDAY*
*7:15 P.M.*
*NEW YORK CITY*

David shook his head and frowned. "Ron's not answering and neither is Holly. Are we done here?"

"I'm done," Jackie said. "We'll be waiting to hear what you find on the tablet," she said to Elizabeth.

David nodded. "You two get out of here. I'll call when I know something."

Elizabeth stood. "Wait. I can't just let you walk out of here." Her hand went to her weapon, but she didn't pull it.

"Don't do that," David said, his voice low. "You've got evidence. Take it and examine it."

"And figure out what that code is," Jackie said. She stood and Ian pushed his chair back to follow her.

"I'm sorry. I still can't let you take me in," he said.

"You're resisting arrest?"

"No, I'm not giving you the opportunity to arrest me." He nodded and turned to head for the door.

Jackie raced after him, glancing back over her shoulder to see David and Elizabeth in a heated debate.

But Elizabeth wasn't stopping them.

"Wait!" David's call spun her around. He rushed toward her with Elizabeth on his heels. "Hold on."

Elizabeth reacted to Jackie's sudden defensive stance by holding up her hand. "I'm not taking you in. I'm getting a cab back to the office. David can give you the news." She gave all three of them a fierce look. "Don't make me regret this. Stay in town and keep in contact with me." She stepped around them and out the door.

"We just got word," David said. "The FBI has Holly and Ron in custody, but they're just being held as victims right now. Ron saved one of the agents' lives when he head-butted a guy."

"So they're all right?" Jackie asked, relief flowing.

David nodded, but frowned.

"But?" Ian pushed.

"Your cousin's in the hospital. She's unconscious."

Ian sucked in a breath. "What happened? Did one of them get to her?"

"No, she wasn't shot or hit. She went to the floor when ordered by the FBI and then passed out. They're checking her out now."

Jackie bit her lip. Should she say anything? Holly hadn't wanted her to, she'd wanted to be the one to tell Ian about her illness. But . . .

As she wrestled with an answer, Adam stepped over to the three of them and introduced himself to Ian.

Jackie glanced at Ian, then pulled David aside. "She has brain cancer," she whispered.

"Oh." Sorrow flashed in his eyes and he glanced at Ian. "He doesn't know?"

"No, Holly wanted to be the one to tell him."

"Okay. I'll make sure the doctors know." He shot a look at

Ian and Adam. "Now get out of here before Elizabeth changes her mind and has you picked up."

Jackie grabbed Ian's hand and let him lead the way out of the restaurant. It took a few minutes for him to flag a cab.

Jackie buckled her seat belt and leaned her head back against the seat. "She's going to try and track us."

"I know."

"Go two blocks, turn left, and then go three blocks. Then let us out," she told the cabbie. "I'll let you know when to stop."

"I need to go see Holly."

"No. You need to stay put. As soon as you walk into that hospital, you'll be in cuffs."

Frustration glinted in his eyes—along with a mixture of worry for his cousin. She thought she saw some guilt there too. Guilt for getting her involved in this craziness, she was sure. "She'll be okay." Which wasn't exactly true for the long term unless a miracle happened, but for now, it was.

He shook his head and shoved his hands into his pockets. And paused. He pulled out a business card.

"What's that?" she asked.

"I found it in Wainwright's trash can."

Curious, she leaned closer. "What made you keep it?"

"I don't know. It just caught my eye so I shoved it in my pocket." He handed it to her.

"Walden's Mortuary," she read. "Think Wainwright's planning for a funeral?"

"Yeah. Ours." Then he shrugged. "It probably doesn't mean anything."

"Might as well find out what the connection is." She tapped the cabbie on the shoulder. "Never mind about letting us out. Take us to Walden's Mortuary."

He nodded and took the next left.

Ian frowned at her. "I thought you were worried about being followed."

"I was. But we might be able to use that to our advantage."

"How so?"

Jackie started to answer, then spotted the van careening toward them. "Watch out!"

The cabbie tried to swerve but wasn't fast enough.

The blue van came fast and hard through the intersection and slammed into the side of the cab.

---

Maria was worried. Holly had called but she hadn't had good news. Grief threatened to consume her and she blinked the tears from her eyes. No. She wouldn't act like her friend was already gone. Holly would fight and she would win. She had to.

Maria studied the float, absently noting the details, doing her best to make sure everything that could be done was. She felt a surge of satisfaction overshadow the worry for a brief moment. The float would be the talk of the parade. And Lewis and his classmates had been approved to ride. Excitement threaded through her. She hoped Leo would be as thrilled as she about the unique opportunity Lewis was going to have. A once-in-a-lifetime thing.

She rubbed her tired eyes and her thoughts went back to Holly only to be interrupted by her cell phone ringing. "Hello?"

"Hey, babe."

"Hi, Leo."

"Just wanted to check in with you. How's everything going?"

She smiled. He was making the effort to show her he cared and wanted to know about her work. "It's going fine, thanks for asking."

"How's Lewis doing?"

"He misses you, of course, but he's all right. I think Lucy is a pretty good distraction for him right now."

"Yeah. Where's her mom again?"

"She had some doctor appointments. Carissa, another mom, was keeping her for Holly, but her son has a bad case of strep so she asked me to keep her. As for Holly, it's not good, Leo. She has brain cancer."

"Aw, man. That's awful." The words were right, but he sounded distracted.

Maria sighed. "I know."

"Okay, well, give Lewis a hug for me and I'll be in touch."

"Wait, you didn't say how everything was going for you. Are you being careful?"

His voice softened. "You know I am. I love you, Maria. You know I'd do anything for you and Lewis. Anything."

"I know."

"I just want you to be happy. I'm so sick of this debt that's still hanging over our heads. That's the only reason I'm working two jobs."

Maria's throat tightened. "I know, hon. It's hard, I'm not going to lie, but I know. And," she injected some cheer into her voice, "we're making progress, right?"

"Right. Right." He sighed. "Okay, I've gotta go. I'll try to call Lewis later tonight."

"Bye."

She hung up and stared at the phone for a brief moment, then shook her head. She was sick of the debt too, but she was almost willing to just live with it if it meant Leo could be home with her and Lewis. With another sigh, she turned back to the float. "Thank you, Lord, for this job," she whispered.

7:35 P.M.

Elizabeth slapped a fist against her thigh as the taxi fought the traffic to the FBI field office in downtown New York City. She wanted to hit something. Instead, she answered her buzzing phone. "What's up, Ty?"

"I'm working on this code."

"Yes?" Elizabeth could picture Tyesha's office, visualize the woman bent over the email paper with numbers and letters surrounding her—on the floor, under her desk, scattered across her keyboard. "Anything?"

Elizabeth heard the squeak of Ty's chair. "Okay. Maybe. Your girl who figured out the other line is good. We should bring her on board."

The cab pulled up to the entrance and she paused to pay the driver, grab her satchel, and hurry inside. "So did that help you figure anything out?"

"Maybe. How far away are you?" Ty asked.

"Heading upstairs to see you now."

When she entered Tyesha's office, the woman motioned for Elizabeth to have a seat. "Here's the code."

She gave Elizabeth her own copy. "Don't worry about the last line. Holly's already come up a suggestion for that one and I like it."

NYonSTBY. NEW YORK ON STANDBY
d,s;;[pcfr;obrtrf. SMALLPOX DELIVERED
H4W9 ____?
aasjl;; - 1127900
/fg'g[.jl]]u
Cnt:T8R sas1sjg2hjha3

254

Elizabeth looked up. "What's that? 1127900?"

"Might be nothing. It's just one of the combinations I came up with, but when I use letters, nothing makes sense. If I use numbers, this is what I get. It's simply two steps up to the left on the keyboard. For example, the letter A. If you go up, you hit Q, then 1. And so on."

"And is this significant?"

"It might be. Look at the calendar."

Elizabeth frowned. And studied the November calendar. "Eleven twenty-seven. November twenty-seventh. That's Thanksgiving Day."

"If there's a terrorist attack, what would you hit in New York on Thanksgiving Day?"

"The parade," Elizabeth whispered. "Oh my—they're going to hit the parade. 9-0-0. That's the time the parade starts."

"That's what I think. I'm going to keep working on the rest of the code. I'm hoping it'll give me more information."

"Like a location. What part of the parade? The beginning? The end? How are they going to release the smallpox? Work fast. I'm going to let everyone know."

Rafe Clements appeared in Tyesha's office door. "You need to come with me. I found them." Elizabeth followed him back into his office. He sat at his desk and clicked a few keys. The café building appeared. The video cams showed Lockwood and Sellers getting into the back of a cab, driving down the street, and turning left. And then nothing. "Where did they go?"

"Working on it. Give me a minute," he said as he clicked more keys and pulled up different cameras around the area. Rafe could do anything with a computer.

"Anything?" ADIC Scott Mitchell asked from the doorway.

Elizabeth turned. "Yes." She quickly filled him in on their deductions about the possible terrorist attack.

"Do we have any proof?"

Elizabeth hesitated. "Not solid, but it's a well-educated guess on the intel we have. And with the bomb materials that were found in Ian's home, there could be some kind of explosives too."

"I'll alert the NYPD, the ATF, and Homeland Security."

"They need to cancel the parade."

He shook his head. "The parade is tomorrow. Even if we sent it out over the news stations and made announcements on the radio, there would still be people who showed up. And besides, can you imagine the widespread panic that would ensue throughout the city? Not to mention the staggering financial loss?"

"Who cares about money?" Elizabeth argued. "Think of the people, the families."

"I'm not saying we're not going to act, I'm saying we better find that smallpox virus before it's released."

"Got 'em," Rafe said.

Elizabeth whirled and Scott stepped into the room. Elizabeth moved closer to the computer. "There, at the intersection of—" A blue van ran a stop sign and T-boned the cab. Elizabeth gasped. "Holy cow. Did that just happen?" She gaped at the tangled mess of blue van and yellow taxi.

Scott was already on his phone ordering agents to the scene.

"Scott," Rafe said. "You gotta see this."

Elizabeth turned her attention back to the computer. Just in time to see two men jump from the back of the van and race to the car that held Ian and Jackie. The van backed away from the scene, smoke leaking from the hood, but still operational. One of the men dragged Ian from the totaled taxi, another grabbed Jackie.

"Get me the face of that driver," Scott ordered.

"They're kidnapping them," Elizabeth whispered.

*7:52 P.M.*

Ian felt someone latch onto his left shoulder and pull him out of the back of the cab. "Jackie!" He tried to turn to see if she was hurt. Hard hands prevented him from moving.

"Get him in the van, I've got the girl."

Ian felt the fog of shock begin to lift. Van? A van had hit them.

Someone carried Jackie in a fireman's hold from the cab. Her eyes were closed and blood ran from a gash on her forehead. People tried to offer to help.

"Hey, put her down, you idiot! She could have a neck injury," one bystander called.

The man carrying Jackie pulled a gun, turned, and fired above the crowd's head. Screams echoed through his pounding head and the people vanished in the time it took to blink. Ian finally understood the men pulling them from the cab weren't there to help them. In fact, they had probably caused the wreck.

The person who had him by the arm propelled him toward the van. Ian let him since Jackie was already in the back. His head spun and nausea pounded at him. Had he hit his head? Reality punched him.

If he landed in the back of that van, they were both dead. He gathered his strength as the gaping entrance to the back of the van yawned closer.

Hoping for the advantage of the element of surprise, Ian swung around with his elbow and caught the man behind him in the face. His attacker went down with a yell. Ian went after the next man, desperate to get to Jackie. He spun into a kick that was as second nature to him as breathing. The side of his foot caught the man in the chin.

Sirens screamed.

The two men Ian had attacked threw themselves into the back of the van. The vehicle peeled away from the curb and Ian stumbled after it. An officer leapt from his cruiser and pointed his weapon at Ian. "Police! Freeze! Hands in the air!"

Ian's strength deserted him. His legs gave out and he dropped to his knees, slowly lifting his hands as he watched the van turn the corner.

# 30

Her head pounded a merciless beat. Little people with jackhammers had taken over her skull and were ignoring her eviction notice. Jackie reached for the glass of water by her bed and frowned when her hand struck something solid. She blinked.

Darkness.

With one hand she reached up and rubbed her eyes. Something flaked off onto her fingers and she felt the gash in her forehead. She winced as sharp pain shot through her head.

She moved her other hand and felt something soft. Silky. Nausea swept over her and she swallowed hard.

Why did her head hurt? Why couldn't she see?

"Walden will be here soon. He'll take care of her. Come on."

Who was there? She blinked, trying to see something.

Anything. Even a sliver of light would have helped. But there was nothing but darkness. Total, encompassing, breath-stealing darkness.

But she could hear the voices. "Hello?" She pushed herself up and her head cracked against a hard surface. She gasped. Bright colors spun before her eyes and she lay back down.

259

On a pillow.

*Oh God, oh God, where am I? Are you there?* "Hello?" Her voice cracked on the word and she cleared her throat. "Hello?"

No one answered.

*Think. Think!*

The car wreck. The blinding flash of pain, then oblivion. And now more darkness.

She beat on the wood overhead until her palms were bruised. Winded, she sucked in air and the horrifying thought that she could suffocate crossed her mind. She flipped on her side. Her head and neck protested the movement and she winced as she ran her hands down more wood.

Blinding terror filled her. She couldn't get out. She banged on the side of the wood with her foot.

Again, again, again.

Her head pounded almost as hard as her heart.

She was in a box.

She felt the silk beneath her fingers again.

Felt the pillow cushioning her pounding head.

No, not a box.

Her breath whooshed from her lungs.

Her coffin.

# 31

Elizabeth paced the floor. Ian sat across from her, looking bruised and battered from the wreck. However, the fire in his eyes said he wasn't down for the count. Not by a long shot. An EMT had checked him over and suggested he go to the hospital. He'd refused.

"Where were they taking her?" she asked him again.

"I don't know!" He slammed a fist onto the table. "If I knew, I'd tell you. You've got to go after her, track her somehow. If you don't, they'll kill her, then come back for me."

"We've got people looking for her."

"It's not enough," he whispered. His agony touched a spot in her that she'd thought she'd closed off a long time ago. But this case had been different than anything she'd dealt with. Not the case necessarily, but the people involved. Innocent people wrongly accused.

"Our computer forensics agent got into the tablet without any trouble. You were right."

"What?"

"You were right about Wainwright. It's all there. Emails about setting you up to be the fall guy, talking about how much money they would lose if the plan doesn't succeed. We were even able to connect the IP number to the emails. They came from several locations, but one of them was Wainwright's office."

"What about the other people on the email. Did you find out who they were?"

"All except one. We're in the process of acquiring search and arrest warrants."

"Which one?"

"The one we don't know about?"

Ian gave an impatient nod.

"His email address is simply Armed&Dangerous2009@gmail.com. There's no name attached to it."

"Okay. So what now?"

"Every attempt our computer forensics people have made to trace it has come up empty. He knows how to cover his tracks."

"And the code? There could be something in the code to tell us where she is. You've got to break it."

"One of our most talented people is working on it. So far, your cousin has managed to figure out more than we have."

Ian dropped his head into his hands.

---

A knock on the door caught their attention. Ian lifted his throbbing head and squinted. Another agent he hadn't been introduced to stepped inside. Annoyance flashed across Elizabeth's face. "What do you need, Sam?"

"Sorry to interrupt, but we've just had an interesting development in this case. Could I speak to you a moment?"

Elizabeth frowned and stood. She nodded to Ian. "Excuse me."

Ian stood. "Jackie's in trouble. We need to find her now!"

Didn't they get it? He was wasting time trying to cooperate. He'd go after Jackie himself except he didn't know where to start looking. And where were David and Adam? Were they looking for her? Of course they were. And if they had any news, they would have called him.

"We have agents looking for her and trying to track the van. We hope to have some answers soon."

"Hope to?" He sighed. "Could I borrow a phone please or have mine back?" They'd taken his personal items when they'd brought him into the building.

"Looks like you've been cleared of all charges. There's even a picture of the receipt from the purchase of the bomb materials that were planted in your home. There are pictures of everything. The man was an idiot to record all that stuff, but I'm not complaining. Made our job easier." Elizabeth pulled her phone from her pocket. "Here. It's a secure line."

Ian dialed and David answered on the first ring. The door shut behind Elizabeth. "Did you find her?" Ian went to the door and pulled it open a crack. He could see Elizabeth and the man she'd called Sam standing in the hallway talking to two other agents. Probably the New York agents they were working with.

"We have a lot of the same capabilities as law enforcement when it comes to the ability to view traffic cams and that kind of thing," David said. "I'm on the computer at the hotel searching. Adam's tracking street cams. Do you have *any* idea where she could have been taken?"

"Why would I know that? Solve that code and maybe that will give us a hint." He regretted the harsh words as soon as they escaped his lips. He closed his eyes. "Sorry, I'm just worried."

"We all are."

"I know. The FBI and local police are looking for her, but

I'm afraid they're not going to find her. At least not alive. The longer she's gone—"

"Yeah. I know."

"Where's Ron?"

"With Holly. And mobilizing his friends to help should we be able to let them know how."

"How is Holly? Has she woken up?"

"Not yet. I'm sorry."

"What's wrong with her?"

David fell silent. "I know Holly wanted to tell you herself, but she has brain cancer, Ian."

The floor tilted. Ian stumbled back to the chair he'd vacated and slumped into it. "What?"

"I'm sorry. They've called her parents down."

"You were able to find them?"

"Yes." He gave a small snort. "They were super easy to find in comparison to keeping you and Jackie hidden."

The door opened. "I've got to go," he told David.

"I'll call back when I can. Don't worry, we won't stop looking for her until we find her."

"Yeah." He just prayed it wasn't too late.

Elizabeth stepped inside. "We had someone come forward and tell us something about the case."

"Who? What did he say?"

"Not he, she. Mrs. Bates, who's been missing since she and her husband visited a funeral home. She said she's been fanatically watching the news every chance she got."

"What does she have to do with this case?"

"Her husband was abusive. She's been waiting for just the right moment to run from him. At the funeral home, he went down to where they keep the bodies and she didn't go. As soon as her husband walked out of the room, she did too. She got in her car and ditched it, sliced her arm with a pocket knife to leave some blood . . . and walked away."

"Okay." Ian was confused and wished she'd get to the point.

"She said she saw Red Peters on the news and recognized him."

"Red Peters?"

"The man you knocked out at the hotel and left as a gift for us to bring in."

"Ah. And she recognized him?"

She stuck her hands in the front pockets of her coat. "He was killed in a prison brawl yesterday. We flashed his face on television hoping someone would come forward. The missing woman did."

"And?" Ian wanted to shake the information from her.

"She said she saw him at Walden's Mortuary."

"Walden's Mort—" Ian broke off and pulled the card from his pocket. "That's where we were headed when we got T-boned."

Elizabeth snatched the card from his hand and pulled out her phone.

---

*9:30 P.M.*

"Where's Walden? Do you know how to fire this thing up?"

"Me? No way. I don't even like being in this place. Creeps me out."

Jackie blinked. The voices were back. How much longer did she have before her air ran out? How long had she been in there? And what did he mean, "Fire this thing up"?

Who was Walden? Wait a minute. Walden's Mortuary? "Fire this thing up?" she whispered.

Her sluggish mind put it together.

She was in a coffin.

They were going to cremate her.

Alive.

She wanted to scream, to cry, to demand they let her out. And knew it was futile. They had put her in the coffin with the intention of killing her. By suffocation or cremation. They probably weren't concerned which happened first. So . . . unless someone opened the lid to the coffin, she would die.

Very soon.

Jackie drew in a deep breath, savoring the feel of the oxygen filling her lungs. And then let the air out. She had to breathe shallow breaths to conserve her air. She had to give Ian or the FBI or someone time to figure out where she was.

So she had to control her panic and use as little of the oxygen as possible and pray whoever was supposed to turn on the retort didn't arrive in time. She'd rather suffocate.

A tear slipped down her temple. "Actually, I don't want to die, God," she whispered. Then clamped her lips shut. Conserve the oxygen. She closed her eyes and imagined herself at home in her bed. Don't think. Pray.

*God, please tell me you haven't abandoned me. Tell me you love me. Tell me you know I'm here. Tell me someone's going to come get me.* The tears continued to fall. She had to distract her mind. Dwelling on what was going to happen was simply going to send her further into uncontrollable panic mode. Which would send her into hyperventilating. Which would use up the oxygen that much faster. She drew in a shallow breath and let it out.

How much oxygen did she have?

Think about it. Don't think about the cremation part. Do the math. She'd been a good student in school, excelling in math and science while letting the English grade slide. Social studies had fascinated her because she loved learning about new places. Jackie corralled her thoughts. Math.

She vaguely remembered a math problem that had to do with how much oxygen was in a sealed container. She needed to know the volume, right? So volume was length times width times height, right? So how long was the coffin? No, not a coffin. Box. It was just a box. She needed to know the volume of a box. So if she was five feet six inches, that was sixty-six inches. The box was bigger than that. Not roomy, but . . .

Slowly, in painstaking slow motion, she moved until her feet touched the end. Maybe another foot and a couple of inches. Eighty-four inches total from head to foot. She reached up with her right hand to touch the lid and pressed with her left hand on the bottom. Maybe twenty-six inches to twenty-eight inches? A little more than two feet? That was it? The lid was close to her face.

Too close. Her breaths came faster. She couldn't breathe!

Stop! Be still. Breathe. In. Out. She remembered the same feeling she'd had when she'd been buried under the manure. Breathe. Shallow breaths.

*I will never leave you nor forsake you.*

Jackie stilled. Where had that thought come from? Her grandfather. She kept her eyes closed and pictured him sitting at the kitchen table, his Bible opened, his mouth moving in prayer.

*Ian! Please find me!*

Her fingers closed into a fist as she remembered the feel of his hand around hers. She wanted to feel that again. She wanted to hug him. To kiss him. To tell him she never forgot him and had thought of him often over the past years.

Focus, Jackie. Finish the math problem. Eighty-four by twenty-eight by—she stretched her hands to feel from side to side—twenty-two? Twenty-three? Twenty-four?

So multiply the three numbers. She did the first two. Eighty-four by twenty-eight. Two thousand three hundred fifty-two. Then that times twenty-four. She pictured writing the numbers on the dry erase board in her senior math class. Fifty-six thousand four hundred and forty-eight. So the total volume would be fifty-six point . . . something cubic centimeters. Which would be around eight hundred and ninety liters.

*Oh God, help me!*

What was her body's volume? She had to figure that out so she could subtract it from the total so she would know how much space she took up. How many liters was she? And how many liters of air did that leave if she—

Her brain froze. She couldn't do it. At best she probably had a couple of hours. At worst—

*God, I want to believe you're there. Show me you're with me. I need you. Please get me out of here!*

# 32

Ian insisted on going. There was no way they were leaving him behind. "I can ride with you or I can follow you there."

"Or I can arrest you for obstruction of justice," Sam shot back.

"And I can sue you for false arrest," Ian countered.

"Boys, we need to go. Save the schoolyard arguments for later." Elizabeth nodded to Ian. "Get in the backseat. I think we're better off keeping you with us since we don't know if there's still a hit out on your head."

"Thanks." He walked out of the FBI office and hit the elevator at a run. Elizabeth and Sam followed.

"Other agents are already en route."

"Don't go barging in and get her killed," Ian said. "But don't waste precious time trying to figure out what to do."

She shot him a perturbed look. "I think we can handle it. We'll assess the situation and figure out what we need to do. We don't even know Jackie's there. It's a long shot."

"I'll take it. It's the only one we have." Ian stepped into the elevator and pressed the button. After an eternity, the elevator finally stopped on the first floor and opened with exaggerated slowness in Ian's opinion. He bolted as soon as the metal doors parted. Then had to stop and wait for Elizabeth and Sam.

Elizabeth's gaze was understanding. Sam's not so much.

He slid into the backseat of the sedan and glanced at his watch. Two hours had passed since Jackie had been taken. *Please let her be all right, God. Be there with her. Let her know she's not alone. Tell her we're coming. Don't let her die.*

The memory of their shared kiss swept over him and he realized he'd never gotten over Jackie. He'd moved on with his life and he'd had a good one. But he'd grieved her loss almost as though she'd died. She'd rebuffed all of his efforts to communicate with her and he'd finally given up. Now he wished he hadn't.

"Turn here."

Sam did. Ian looked back to see several other agents in similar cars behind them. *Hang on, Jackie, we're coming.*

---

9:50 P.M.

"I'm here."

"'Bout time."

Jackie heard the exchange through a sleepy fog. Her brain registered that she was getting sleepy due to the oxygen running out. Every time she breathed in, she now inhaled carbon dioxide along with what little oxygen was left.

At least it would be a pretty painless death. *God, if I'm going to meet you soon, I need to be honest. I'm a little scared to come face-to-face with you. Okay. A lot scared. I haven't done much to earn my way in to heaven.*

*For by grace are you saved through faith, not as a result of works.*

Jackie blinked. Another verse from her childhood. From her grandfather. How she missed him. "Please . . ."

". . . the parade tomorrow. The smallpox is going in as we speak."

Parade? Smallpox going in? Going in where?

They were going to hit the parade. She gasped. All those innocent people. Children. Lucy!

"Walden, get this thing going and let's get out of here."

"It will take it awhile to heat up," Walden said.

"How long is awhile?"

"About an hour."

"An hour!" Curses riddled the air. "Just turn it on and get her in there. We need to get moving."

No! Jackie tried to lift her arms, but they felt weighted down, too heavy—just like her lungs. She closed her eyes and tried to drag in another breath.

She heard the machine groan to life. The bottom of the coffin rumbled beneath her. She pictured the box moving toward the flames and wondered how much it would hurt before it stopped. Before it was all over. Probably not that long.

Acceptance set in. Sobs escaped her. She didn't care about using up the oxygen now. Suffocation seemed preferable to being burned alive.

*Ian! Lord . . . I'm sorry . . .*

---

*10:00 P.M.*

"Leo!" Maria put the paintbrush down and raced over to her husband to hug him. Shock and sweet pleasure ran through her. "What are you doing here?"

"I decided to stop by and see you. It's late. You need to come home." He shifted the bag he had on his back. A pack that looked stuffed to the brim.

She ran her hands over his face and kissed him. "I can't believe it. You're here. I thought you were working through the holidays."

He gave her a surprised smile and kissed her back. "I told them I needed the time off to spend with my family."

"Oh! I'm so glad." She hugged him again.

"We're going to be okay, you know that, right?"

"Of course we are." How could they not be when it was obvious he was trying so hard? She patted the pack. "What's in there?"

"Just some work stuff I didn't have time to leave at the office if I wanted to get over here and see you." He kissed her again. "As soon as this parade is over, we're going to take some time for ourselves. You, me, and Lewis, all right?"

"That sounds lovely. What are we going to do?"

He kissed her. "It's a surprise."

"A surprise?" A thrill shot through her. "You don't do surprises."

"I'm doing this one." He patted her cheek. "Now, when can you leave?"

She glanced at the clock. "I have a few more things to do to make sure everything is running smoothly and then I'll be able to leave." Only to be back about five in the morning. Her mother would bring Lewis and Lucy at eight to get them settled on the float. Leo would be so surprised. He'd get such a kick out of seeing his son in one of the most prestigious parades. It would give him bragging rights at work, which was very important to him. "Go home and kiss Lewis good night for me."

"You should be home." His jaw tightened and his gaze darkened. He looked around the busy place. She tried to see the place through his eyes. They all looked like worker bees, people moving, painting, testing, doing whatever it took to make sure each float was perfect and ready to be lined up.

Satisfaction filled her, though. As an artist, she'd found that jobs could be hard to come by. But Leo had known someone who'd known someone, and before she knew it, she'd been working on the floats. The Lord had provided.

"What time will you leave tomorrow?"

"After the parade, I suppose. Why? You're coming, aren't you? You said you'd be here."

"Yeah, baby, yeah. I'm coming. Are you going to be at the parade or back here cleaning up?"

Maria bit her lip. She didn't want to lie, but she didn't want to spoil the surprise either. "I'm going to have to clean up some, but maybe I'll be able to make the parade too."

"Text me before you go and I'll meet you. We'll go together." He glanced at his watch. "Now, I've got to go."

"Where are you going?"

"You know the work never ends, baby."

His eyes flashed with annoyance at her questioning, but elation filled her. "I know. Okay. Tomorrow sounds just perfect, though." She couldn't have worked that out any better if she'd tried. They'd be able to watch Lewis on the float and cheer him on, then meet him at the end.

Together.

---

*10:30 P.M.*

Ian held his breath and Sam pulled up to the front of the mortuary. He parked in a handicapped spot near the door. Double white doors with glass-paned windows stared back at them.

Six brick columns graced the front, forming a bow-shape exterior. Cement benches sat in between the columns. The two sedans behind them split off and went in opposite directions to head around to the back. The place looked deserted with the exception of a white pickup truck, a low-slung Mercedes, and a Buick out front.

"I'll run the plates," Elizabeth said. She tapped the information into her phone and Ian watched her press Send. "We'll have that back in no time."

Elizabeth and Sam exited the vehicle and Ian opened his door.

"Stay here, please," Elizabeth said.

Ian sucked in a deep breath and slid back into the seat. He left the door open, his muscles tense, ready to spring. Prayers slipped from his lips as he watched Elizabeth and Sam try the front doors.

Locked.

They knocked and stood on either side of the doors while they waited.

No response.

Ian's fingers curled into fists. It was taking too long. Jackie's life hung in the balance and they acted like they had all the time in the world. In reality, he knew they had to be careful, to make sure there wasn't a threat nearby, but he wanted to burst through the door, grab the first person he saw, and demand answers.

Which was why he worked in a lab, not in law enforcement.

Through the open door, Ian could hear the second knock. Then Elizabeth shook her head. "No one's answering."

"No," Ian got out of the car. "We're not leaving until we look inside."

"I'm not planning on leaving yet." She spoke into her radio. "Anything?"

Ian waited, his heart thudding against his ribs. Two sharp pops sounded and he jerked. "What was that?"

Sam spun toward him. "Get back in the car! We've got shoot-ers around the back!"

The front doors opened and bullets spit into the air. Elizabeth dove sideways, firing back. Sam hollered and went to his knees. Ian slammed the door shut and ducked down across the backseat while grabbing the phone Elizabeth had left in the console up front. He dialed 911 and lifted his head to peer out the window.

"911, what's your emergency?"

"I need an ambulance at Walden's Mortuary," he said, his breaths coming in short pants. "There are several shooters and officers down." His blood pounded in his ears. He didn't know if anyone was down or not, but figured it might get help on the way a little faster. He opened the passenger door and turned back to the scene.

Sam was definitely down.

Ian raced over and reached for Sam's dropped weapon. Bullets kicked up the asphalt beside him. Wrapping his fingers around the man's gun, he shoved his forearms under Sam's armpits. He grunted as he pulled the SLED agent to safety behind the car. There he checked for wounds. Sam pushed him away.

"Just got the vest," he croaked. "Knocked the breath out of me." He struggled to his knees. "Elizabeth!"

"She dove out of the way, I don't think she was hit."

Sam tried to stand. His legs gave out and he coughed, then gasped. He sighed and sat down, hand pressed against his side. "Think I broke a rib."

"Don't move, you could puncture a lung."

Sam glared at him, pushing to his feet once more. "I'm not leaving Elizabeth unprotected." He went back to his knees with a pained cry.

"More help is on the way and I'm not going to leave her unprotected." Ian glanced around the side of the vehicle. The shooting had stopped. Where *was* she? He couldn't spot her.

But one thing he was sure of. As soon as he knew she was okay, he was getting in that building to find Jackie. He heard the sirens approaching. Ian just hoped the front doors were still unlocked. He pressed Sam's gun into the agent's hand. He couldn't leave the man without a way to defend himself. "If someone starts shooting at me, shoot back, will you?"

"What—"

Once he was sure Sam had a good grip on the weapon, Ian bolted from behind the cover of the vehicle.

"Hey!" Sam hollered at him. "Are you crazy? Get back here!"

Ian's feet pounded up the steps.

No bullets came his way.

"Ian! What are you doing?" Elizabeth's hiss came from his left. He turned to find her crouched behind one of the brick pillars. "Get away from the door."

"I'm going after Jackie." Expecting to feel bullets riddle his body at any moment, he yanked open the heavy white door and ducked inside, staying low, hoping if anyone decided to shoot, they would be aiming high.

A black-clad figure stepped from the adjoining room to the left and lifted his weapon.

Ian hit the floor and rolled right as several bullets passed over his head. He pushed himself to his feet and threw himself into the opposite room. An office. With a door that led into the next room. Ian moved fast.

Where would she be? How many more people with guns waited inside? How long would it take for the feds to swarm the place?

He didn't stop to try to figure out the answers as he moved into the next room. Another office with another door straight ahead. Ian stopped and gave a cautious look around the edge of the frame. The office led into a short hallway with a door that opened into a larger room just across from him.

A bullet zipped past his nose and he ducked back, heart thundering in his ears. Footsteps hurried toward him. "You get him?"

"No! He's still here."

"The feds are outside. How did he get in? We need to get out of here now!"

"What about the girl?"

"She just rolled into the fire. She's done for. Let's go!"

Ian heard the man curse and footsteps retreat. In the fire? Chills and nausea swept him. The cremation room. Downstairs. He needed to find the stairs.

"FBI! Freeze! Hands in the air!"

Gunshots.

Ian flinched, hoping the feds had subdued the shooters. He moved again. This time through a lounge area and past the bathroom.

He found the stairs.

Footsteps pounded behind him, shouts reached his ears, three more loud pops. He couldn't stop now. *She's in the fire.*

At the bottom, he stopped and took a deep breath. Then rounded the corner into the large cremation room. The retort hummed just ahead and the fires burned bright.

The wooden coffin sat in the middle of the flames.

"No!" Ian bolted forward as the FBI broke down the external door.

"FBI! Freeze!"

Ian ignored them and figured he could keep moving long enough to reach his goal even if they shot him. He reached the front of the retort and slapped the emergency shutoff valve just as one of the agents tackled him to the floor.

"Get her out of there! Please!"

## 33

Hot. So hot.

And sleepy. Did she have a fever? She wanted some water and her throat hurt. Actually, she wanted ice. On her face. No, she wanted to dive into it, be surrounded by it. Was she sick?

No. Wait a minute. She was going to burn alive. That's right. She was going to be toast. Literally.

She wanted to giggle at her joke and then wondered what was wrong with her. Oh right. Lack of oxygen. Or too much carbon dioxide.

Or something like that. Why couldn't she think?

Heaven. She was going to see God. Would he let her in heaven? *I want to come to heaven, God. I want to see you. I want to ask you all kinds of questions. And I want to see Grandpop too, okay?* She tried to drag in another breath and just couldn't find the air. *I don't want to die alone. Please, God. Not alone.*

*I will never leave you nor forsake you.*

*You're here with me now, aren't you?* The strange calm that had settled over her not too long ago still held. *I can feel you*

278

*with me. Thank you for that. I still don't want to die, but I'm not so afraid now. Just hot. Really, really hot.*

Darkness crowded in on her thoughts. She tried to focus, to stay awake, to ignore the pressure on her lungs, the increasing heat, the feeling of fire all around her, but she drifted.

Away.

Into the darkness.

Something jerked.

"Jackie! Jackie!"

Ian?

She must be already in heaven if she was hearing his voice. At least she wasn't so hot.

"How long was she in there?" Another heavenly voice. "Ian, she could be—"

"Jackie! Someone get this lid off!"

A rattling sounded, then a sucking pop made her frown. Cool air drifted over her. Definitely heaven.

"I need paramedics here."

Was that Ian? How was that possible?

A hand brushed her hair back. She sucked in. Air! Greedily she grasped at it, fought for consciousness, and blinked.

Her eyelids were too heavy.

She felt herself lifted, cradled against a hard chest, then placed on something soft. A mask slipped over her mouth and nose and blessed oxygen filled her lungs.

"Jackie, honey, look at me. Can you open your eyes?"

She managed. Barely.

And looked straight into Ian's tear-filled gaze. "Ian. Hi," she whispered. She pushed the mask off. "Are you dead too?"

A paramedic moved the mask back into place. Aggravated, Jackie ripped it off. She didn't need a mask in heaven, didn't they know that?

A tear slipped down his cheek and he ducked his head. "No. And you're not either."

"I'm not?"

"No."

"Are you sure?"

He gave a soft laugh, but the tears on his cheeks said he didn't find the situation humorous at all. "Oh yeah. I'm sure."

"Prove it."

"My pleasure." He touched his lips to hers and she was so glad God hadn't given up on her after all.

---

THANKSGIVING DAY
1:15 A.M.

"You were almost cremated alive, Jackie, you need to stay put and rest," Ron said.

Jackie rubbed her eyes and glared at those who made a semi-circle around her hospital bed. Ron, David, Adam, Elizabeth, and Ian. Dear sweet Ian. She needed them all to leave so she could get dressed. But in a minute. First she needed some answers. "Where's Holly?" she asked.

"Down the hall," Ian said. "She's stable, so they transported her here. I just checked on her a few minutes before you were rolled into this room."

"Has she woken up yet?"

"No." Ian cleared his throat. "Not yet."

"We need her to wake up, Ian," Jackie said. "We have to get her friend's name. They're going to attack the parade." She looked at Elizabeth. "You have to find Holly's friend and warn her. Lucy's class is going to be on one of the floats. What are you doing to stop it? Have they canceled it yet?" Jackie felt uncharacteristic hysteria rising up in her and she swallowed, trying to force it back.

Elizabeth pinched the bridge of her nose and shook her head. "I recommended canceling it when we first found out, but it's simply too late. There are already people in the city at the hotels and just . . . everywhere. If we cancel the parade, these people will just find another way to release the virus. And," she drew in a deep breath, "we have to consider the source. Even though you've been proven innocent, for the past few days you've been a terrorist doing everything you could do to elude capture. My Special Agent in Charge still isn't 100 percent positive you're not involved somehow and is reluctant to trust anything you have to say."

"What?" Ian shouted.

"But the people—" Jackie said at the same time.

Ian pressed the palms of his hands against his eyes. "You've got to be kidding me."

"And I heard them talking," Jackie said. "I heard them while I was shut up in that box—" Her voice shook and she pulled in a deep breath. She didn't know if she'd ever be able to shut her eyes and sleep again. Not without horrific memories crowding her brain.

"I know. I know."

"No, you don't. I heard them specifically say they were going to target the parade. You *have* to convince the FBI to cancel it, postpone it, whatever."

"They won't," Elizabeth said softly.

David rubbed his chin and exchanged a glance with Adam. "Please tell me they're upping security."

"Of course. While they can't cancel it, they *are* taking it seriously and pulling out all the stops to make sure security is extremely tight. They're doing metal detectors, all bags will be scanned." She shrugged. "It will be like going through airport security."

"This is crazy," Adam said and shook his head.

"What are we going to do?" Jackie whispered.

"You're going to stay put and rest," Ian said. "We'll figure something out."

"Jackie," Elizabeth said. "One of them escaped. He had a motorcycle hidden off the property. We chased him, but he got away. Did you see any of them? Could you describe them to a sketch artist?"

"No." She rubbed her eyes. They felt gritty and burned. "I remember the crash and then nothing until I woke up in the box." She just couldn't say "coffin" yet. "But—" She gasped and sat up.

"What?"

"I heard them clearly."

"Yes?" Elizabeth asked.

"So I could identify their voices. One spoke with a slight accent."

"What kind of accent?"

She shook her head. "I don't know, I'd have to hear it again. I wasn't exactly filing that kind of information away at the time."

"Of course."

"But—"

Elizabeth's phone rang and she stepped out of the room to answer it. Jackie wished she could listen in on the conversation. "Okay, y'all need to leave. I'm going to get dressed and get out of this hospital. We've got terrorists to stop."

---

*1:45 A.M.*

"I've got more on this code. It's all related to the keyboard," Tyesha said.

"When was the last time you slept, Ty?"

Ty huffed a soft laugh. "I don't remember. It's not important. You ready?"

"Sure. Go ahead." Elizabeth pressed the phone to her ear and walked to the nurse's desk to find a pen and paper.

"Okay, we've got New York on Standby and smallpox delivered. I had all kinds of combinations for the third line, but one stands out to me."

"What?"

"MTDP," Tyesha said.

"What does that—" It clicked. "Macy's Thanksgiving Day Parade." She wrote it down.

"That's what I think, but we already figured that out from the date."

"Right. Okay, then the next line was the date and time of the parade." She went ahead and wrote that too.

"Right."

"The next line says 'masks in floor.' It didn't take me long to find the pattern. It's three letters to the left of the symbol written in the code."

"Masks in floor. In the floor of what?"

"Maybe the floor of the float? Whoever's going to release this virus isn't going to want to take a chance on exposing himself. Unless he's suicidal. The mention of masks makes me think that's not the case."

"Yes, that makes sense."

"But which one?"

"I have no idea. You've almost got it all."

"I think Holly's right and the contact person is Tate R. No last name of course, but I think the letters after that are a phone number. It's tricky and I don't know if it's the right one, but I came up with 212-264-5651. Moving up two from the initial letter in the code to the left and picking the number. I'm pretty sure the 1, 2, and 3 are in there as a distraction. They're not necessary. I think."

"Did you try the number?"

"No. I didn't want to. If there's a bomb involved—"

Elizabeth rubbed her gritty eyes. "Calling the number could set it off. Of course."

"We traced the number, though, but nothing. It's probably a throwaway phone."

She nodded. Figured. "Okay, thanks. Has there been any change on the status of the parade?"

"It's still a go."

She closed her eyes. "Then we're going to have to work fast."

"Let me know if you need anything else."

"Will do."

Elizabeth hung up and turned to find Jackie standing behind her, dressed and looking extremely rough around the edges. Ian stood beside her, hands held as though he figured he might need to catch her when she toppled over. "You need to rest."

Jackie didn't topple. She stepped forward, a ferocious frown on her face. "You really think I can do that when you and I both know terrorists are going to strike soon? My friend's daughter is in danger. I need to know Maria's last name."

"Her last name is Fox."

Jackie blinked, the frown faded. "Okay. How did you find that out?"

"We called the principal and got the name of the children's teacher. She answered and we got the last name from her."

"Oh. Well, good. So did you call Maria?"

"Yes. Well, someone did, but she's not answering. I'll know as soon as they get ahold of her."

"Okay. So now what?"

"We start screening every single person involved with the parade."

Jackie's eyes widened. "There's no time for that."

"We don't have any other choice. It's a place to start until we come up with a better plan."

---

*4:16 A.M.*

Maria rolled over to look at the clock. She gave a contented sigh and snuggled back into the warmth of her husband. She couldn't believe it when he'd said he could stay the night and even take her to work in the morning. When they'd walked in the door, he'd given her a gentle shove toward their bedroom. "Go pack a bag. A big one for you and Lewis."

At his voice, Lewis had looked up from his game of Sorry with his friend Lucy. His eyes had flown wide and he'd given an ecstatic cry, bolted across the den and into his father's arms. Lucy had clapped her happiness at seeing her friend's joy. Lucy. Such a sweet child. Maria could only pray her mother would pull through and live to watch her grow up.

She pushed the sad thoughts away and let her lips curve into a smile. Lucy would go back to Carissa's, and she and her family would go on a well-deserved vacation. She'd packed her bag and then, unable to help herself, went snooping. She'd found the brochure and plane tickets in her husband's coat pocket while he and Lewis had wrestled on the den floor. They were going to Mexico to an all-inclusive resort. Today. After the parade.

Together.

## 34

Jackie rubbed her eyes and tried to shove aside the fatigue that wanted to grip her in a headlock. She looked at the others around the table in the FBI conference room. David, Ian, Adam, and Sam, who'd left the hospital AMA—against medical advice—and looked like he was on the verge of passing out.

"We're running out of time," Jackie said.

Elizabeth looked up from her computer. "I know."

The door opened and Scott Mitchell stepped into the room. Elizabeth shot to her feet. "Anything?"

"We've done background checks on all of the float companies and their employees that are working directly on the floats. There's nothing that raises a huge red flag. There are some employees that have previous records, but no one with any outstanding warrants and no one with terrorist ties. There are only thirty-one floats. We've started checking them all, but it's going to take time."

"We don't have time," Jackie said and popped to her feet to pace the room. "There's got to be a way to cancel the parade or at least warn people not to go."

Sam snorted. "Do you know how much money is involved in that parade? How many people and volunteers? Spectators are already lining the streets as we speak. People camped out in Central Park last night. Canceling isn't an option."

"So how many people will die today because no one wants to call off a parade? A *parade*!" Jackie asked. "Would you want to die for that? Wouldn't you want some notice if you were going to take your kids to watch it? At least a chance to say, 'I'm not going'?"

Sam started to respond, then went white, grabbed his side, and settled back in his chair with a grimace. Jackie almost felt sorry for him. He shook his head. "No, I wouldn't want to die for it, but I also understand that calling it off at this late date would be useless. Whatever they're going to do, they can still do."

"Then they have to be stopped," Ian said. He held up his phone. "I still can't get Maria."

Jackie closed her eyes, the stress sending her blood pressure sky high. She pulled in several deep breaths, sending up a prayer of thanks for the ability to do so. When she opened her eyes, Ian was staring at her with concern. "I'm fine," she said before he could ask.

She turned to the ADIC. "How many float companies are involved in this parade?"

"Three," Mitchell said.

"Can you check their financials? See if any of them have made a significant deposit?"

"Of course. And we're working on that. But if there are explosives involved or even someone in the actual parade who plans to unleash the virus among the crowd, there are over ten thousand participants to clear. We can't do that in the next—" he glanced at his watch—"two hours."

Jackie sighed and buried her face in her hands. Waiting for

something, *anything*, to come through, was sending her impatience levels soaring. She needed to be *doing* something. She lifted her head. "I'm going down there."

"Where?"

"To where the parade begins. They'll be lining up the floats shortly. I'm going to listen."

"Listen?"

"To people talk. I'll recognize the voices from the mortuary if I hear them."

Elizabeth huffed. "That's a needle in a haystack."

Jackie strode to the door. "I know, but it's better than sitting here doing nothing."

Ian stepped beside her. "I'll go too."

She clasped his hand in hers and looked at Elizabeth. "We'll need your badge to get into the secure areas."

The woman studied her for a moment, then nodded and told Mitchell, "I'm going with them."

"Thank you." Jackie pulled open the door and headed for the elevator.

---

Ian stepped to the back of the elevator and dialed the nurse's station on Holly's neuro floor.

"Regional Neurology. How may I help you?"

"This is Ian Lockwood. I'm Holly Kent's cousin. I just wanted to check on her condition." The doors slid open and he followed Jackie and Elizabeth out to the car.

"She seems to be trying to wake up. Her vitals are good."

He slid in the backseat of Elizabeth's car and let Jackie have the front. He felt bruised and battered. Every muscle ached and he had a headache that made him halfway sick, but there was no way he was staying behind.

Ian closed his eyes and sent up a prayer of thanks. "Thank God. Will you be sure to call me as soon as she wakes up and can talk?"

"Of course."

"And if she asks about her daughter, Lucy, tell her everything is just fine." It wasn't a lie. Lucy *was* fine right now. And they were going to make sure she stayed that way.

"I'll be glad to."

"Thanks."

Ian hung up and leaned his head against the back of the seat. *Lord, please let her wake up.*

"Any change?"

Jackie's worried question brought his head up. "Yes, the nurse said she was trying to wake up, but wasn't all the way there yet."

She frowned and nodded. Her top teeth settled into her lower lip—a sure sign she was working on some problem. "Which float is Lucy on?"

"The toy store one," Elizabeth said. "Manguson Toys."

"If we pull her off of there, she's going to hate us forever," Ian said.

"If we can figure out what the threat is and where it's coming from, we won't have to pull anyone and no one will even know danger was anywhere near them," Jackie said.

Elizabeth nodded. "That's the plan. But if we don't, then I want to get her and get out of there."

---

7:10 A.M.

Leo rolled over with a groan. He was so tired. He'd been running on fumes the past week, trying to make sure he kept all of his plates spinning. He reached for Maria and frowned when he only felt cold sheets. He forced his eyes open and they landed on the alarm clock.

With a curse, he shoved off the blankets. He'd overslept. Maria had turned off the alarm. Adrenaline blazing, he grabbed his clothes and his uniform and dressed in record time. He was supposed to be there. He couldn't botch this. His marriage depended on it.

He raced into Lewis's room to find his mother-in-law making up the child's bed. "Naomi, where's Lewis?"

She looked up and gave him that special frown she always seemed to reserve for him. He knew she didn't approve of him, thought he wasn't good enough for her precious Maria. And she was probably right, but . . .

"Maria wanted him and Lucy to be with her this morning."

"What? Why?" He didn't have time for this.

Her eyes slid back to the bed and she fluffed a pillow. Her shoulder lifted in a small shrug. "I cannot say."

"Of course you can say. Why would she take Lewis and Lucy to work with her on one of the busiest days of her job? She won't be able to watch him properly. The children could wander off and get lost."

Naomi waved a dismissing hand. "They will be fine. It is a special day and I suppose Maria wanted to share it with them. She said you would be coming shortly."

"Look, I know you don't think I'm good enough for Maria, but I'm trying. I really am." Why did he blurt that out? He cursed his wayward tongue. The stress was getting to him.

She lifted a brow. "No, you're not good enough, but it doesn't matter because no one would be good enough."

"Well, you got that right." He glanced at his watch. "I'm supposed to be working security at the parade and I'm late."

He closed his eyes and took a deep breath. "Why didn't you go with her to help?"

"I'm an old woman. Parades are not for me."

"Old woman? You're only fifty-five years old."

"Exactly."

Leo rolled his eyes and raced back into the bedroom to gather his things. He spun to head to the front door and pulled up short when he came face-to-face with his mother-in-law. "What?"

"You think a trip to Mexico will make everything all right?"

Leo drew in a sharp breath. "What are you talking about? How do you know—"

"I know a lot of things. I may be an old woman, but I have friends. Like Greta at the travel agency."

Seriously?

"It's just a trip, Naomi. Don't get snippy because you weren't invited."

She narrowed her eyes. "My daughter and grandson are everything to me. Hurt them and I'll make you pay."

Make him pay? Who did she think she was? He was the one with the gun. He shook his head. "I don't have time for this."

She stepped in front of him. "I'm serious. I think I will be coming to the parade after all. I think I will be watching you."

He stared at her. "Watching me?"

"You plan to leave and not come back, don't you? You plan to take my daughter and grandson and disappear." She gave a laugh, devoid of humor, and her eyes hardened. "I don't think you want to do that. You really don't want to cross me."

A sliver of unease traveled up his spine. He'd mostly ignored his mother-in-law over the past few years, but today, he took another look at her. And wrote her off. "I don't know what you're talking about." He shoved past Naomi and, with one last look around, stepped out the front door. Today was the day he and Maria would start over and he couldn't wait to see the look on her face when he presented her with the plane tickets.

Satisfaction filled him as he grabbed his backpack and shut the door behind him, all thoughts of his mother-in-law's threats already forgotten.

---

*7:30 A.M.*

Jackie waited for Elizabeth to flash her badge and gain entrance to the back area of the parade where everyone was already lining up. The air crackled with the electric excitement the participants exuded.

And the noise was deafening. How did she ever think she would be able to hear anyone talking in order to identify a voice? Everyone talked and voices blended together into one loud roar.

Jackie had to admit security was tight, tighter than she would have expected. Elizabeth had to show her credentials and explain their presence to more than one police officer. Finally, they arrived at the Manguson Toys float and Jackie stopped. Parents milled around, but no children were in sight. "Where's Lucy?"

"I don't know. I'm going to find her, though." Ian gripped her fingers and stepped forward.

"May I help you?"

A pretty dark-haired, dark-eyed woman barred their approach. Ian held up his driver's license. "I'm Ian Lockwood, Lucy's uncle. I'm here to get Lucy Kent."

The woman's eyes widened. "I'm taking care of Lucy right now. I won't let her go with you until I talk to her mother."

"You're Maria," Jackie said.

"Yes."

"Holly's in a coma in the hospital," Ian said.

292

Maria gasped. "What? Oh no." Tears filled her eyes. "When she called me, she said it wasn't good." She wiped her tears and her gaze flicked over Jackie's face. A small frown gathered between her brows and Jackie wondered what she was thinking. Then she sighed.

Elizabeth showed her badge. "Where is Lucy?"

"She's with the class. They're back at the warehouse about a mile and a half from here. Their teacher and several chaperones will be bringing them shortly. We didn't want them waiting out in the cold for such a long time." She glanced at her watch. "They should be heading this way shortly." When she looked up, a brilliant smile crossed her lips. "Leo, you came! I thought you had to work right up until the—"

"You turned off the alarm."

"Oh. I'm sorry."

"But I am working."

Jackie turned to see a man in his early thirties. He blinked and thunderclouds rolled in his eyes. She thought his smile was forced, but he leaned over and kissed Maria. "What's going on?" Maria asked.

"There's been a threat." He flashed his badge toward them. "ATF. Explosives Enforcement Officer."

"What? What kind of threat?"

"One dealing with bombs, sweetheart. I'm here to check the float. No way I'm letting anyone on there without checking it out myself."

Maria swallowed and stepped back, motioning for the man to go ahead. Jackie tilted her head, wondering if her foggy brain was playing tricks on her. She squinted at the man. Had she met him before?

"Christine has Lewis and Lucy at the warehouse and they'll

be here shortly," Maria said. "Do I need to text her and tell her not to bring them?"

"No," he said.

Jackie stepped forward, her eyes on Leo.

He scowled and shot her and the others a dark look before taking a deep breath and walking to the float. He ran his hand over the edge of the trailer, then hopped on. Maria sighed and watched, her concern and anxiety clear on her pretty face.

Elizabeth's phone rang and she answered it. Jackie tried to listen in, but it was impossible. She didn't talk long, though. "Other agents are checking the floats for any masks in the floor."

"Can someone please tell me what this is all about?" Maria asked.

"Like he said, there's been a threat."

Leo looked down at them. "It's all clear. No explosives."

Elizabeth stepped forward. "Do you mind if I check the floor of your float?"

Maria looked shaken. "The floor? For what? And what kind of threat?"

"One against the parade."

She swallowed and looked around. "But why check the floats? Security has been tight. No one has gotten on without clearance." She glanced at Leo. "Someone's threatened to plant a bomb on one of the floats?"

"Something like that, but it's not going to happen on my watch." His phone rang. "Excuse me."

"Since it's been cleared, do you mind if I go up there?" Elizabeth asked Maria.

"Okay, just be careful to step around the perimeter. There are clearly marked areas for the children. You can step in those too."

Elizabeth walked up the steps and onto the platform. Jackie watched, but her gaze was riveted on Leo, who'd moved to the front of the float to take his call. She moved closer. Uneasiness flickered across his face and he turned his back on her to finish his conversation.

She went around to the side and climbed the steps. Maria frowned at her and Jackie ignored her. She stepped carefully along the side of the platform. Elizabeth saw her. "Nothing here. Nothing on the floor. No trap doors." She threw her hands up. "Just nothing."

"Maybe," Jackie muttered.

"What?"

"Sh."

Elizabeth's brows drew together, but she hushed. Jackie eased up behind Leo. She didn't care if it was rude, she needed to listen in on his conversation.

". . . a go. The feds are everywhere, it's taking time."

He turned and locked eyes with her.

She drew in a deep breath. "It *is* you."

# 35

Ian gave a shout when Leo shoved Jackie out of his way and jumped to the ground, his backpack bouncing with every step. Jackie threw herself right after the man while Ian pushed forward to see what the problem was.

"Stop him! It's him!"

Ian understood and gave chase, his stiff muscles protesting the continued abuse. He kept going, kept pushing. He didn't bother glancing back to check on Jackie, he knew she was right on his heels.

Leo dodged the parade participants, weaving in and out like a professional football player. Ian kept pace. He didn't even know what street he was on, he just didn't want to lose the man who'd put Jackie in a coffin and tried to burn her alive.

Only Leo didn't play nice. He shoved people into Ian's path, knocked over anything that could cause Ian to stumble.

And finally he did. Ian went down with a hard thud on the sidewalk. Pain raced through him. He rolled and bolted to his feet, nursing a bruised elbow and scraped hip. Jackie flew past him, followed by Elizabeth and several other agents.

And then the man was gone.

Ian pulled to a stop. "Where'd he go?" He did a one-eighty. No sign of the runner.

"No. No, no, no," Jackie pounded a fist against her thigh. "He can't just disappear."

A flash of black backpack caught Ian's eye. "There!" The three took off once again, running, weaving, shouting apologies to those they bumped or jostled. "Stop!" But of course the man didn't. He ran. Fast. Ian gasped, side aching, muscles protesting the further abuse. Leo turned the corner. Ian pounded after him. How long had they been running? Elizabeth had dropped back, shouting orders into her phone. Jackie stayed with him. Sirens sounded in the distance.

Where was the guy headed? It was like he had a destination in mind, something other than just a random run to escape.

And then he was gone again. Ian pulled up short and gasped. He was in good shape, but that had been at least a two-mile run at top speed. Throw in the sore muscles and pounding head from the car accident and Ian knew he wasn't exactly at the top of his game. Jackie pounded up beside him and Elizabeth joined them, panting, her phone now held to her ear.

"Where did he go?" she asked.

Ian pointed to the entrance to a warehouse just ahead of him. "In there, I think."

"What's in there?"

Elizabeth gave their location into her phone. "This is the warehouse where Maria said the teacher and the kids were."

"He's going after his son," Jackie said. "His son is in there."

A cab pulled up and Maria jumped out. "What's going on? Where's Leo? Why did he run?"

Within seconds, the police were on the scene and no one had answered Maria's questions.

Jackie stood beside the woman. "Would your husband hurt his son?"

"What? No, of course not. Why would you even ask that?" She rushed toward the door of the warehouse.

"Ma'am! Wait!" an officer called out.

Maria kept going and opened the door. Jackie stayed right behind her with Ian on her heels. Elizabeth waved her badge at the NYPD. Even if someone had tried to stop them, it would have been too late. Jackie stepped inside the warehouse with cautious steps, not sure what she would see. Her eyes landed on Leo first. He held his son on his left hip, his weapon in his right hand. The black backpack lay on the ground.

The door slammed shut behind them and Leo spun, his son in his arms, his weapon raised to point toward Jackie. "Back off!" The rest of the children cowered against the back wall, their teacher and other adult chaperones huddled around them, protecting them.

"Leo! What are you doing?"

"Mama!" Lewis cried. He wiggled in his father's arms, but Leo just held him tighter.

Jackie stepped forward. "You have the virus. What'd you do with it?"

"What I was paid to do," he sneered. His eyes landed on Maria and frustration glinted. "We almost made it, baby."

"What are you talking about? Made what? Put Lewis and the gun down and tell me what's going on."

Leo barked a laugh. "It's all over now. I accomplished the mission, but I failed in every other way."

"What mission, Leo? Start making some sense, will you?" Maria's voice held an edge, not hysterical, but rather a calmness that had Jackie looking at her twice.

The other children, chaperones, and teacher cowered against

the wall. Children cried and the adults whispered in their ears, offering what little comfort they could.

Jackie found Lucy's eyes and the child gasped and squirmed to get a better look at her. Her gaze bounced to Ian, and Jackie saw his name form on her lips. Jackie held up a finger, praying Lucy understood what she meant. The little girl frowned, but settled back against the wall, her eyes on her uncle.

"Officers are outside, Leo," Elizabeth said. "You're not going to get out of this alive unless you give up."

"Actually, Lewis and I are going to walk out the back door of this warehouse. Anyone tries to follow . . . well, let's just say, I'd rather take Lewis with me into the afterlife than let him grow up without me." He stared at Elizabeth. "And you'd better leave your weapon in your holster or I'll just use the gun and finish this right here, understand?"

Jackie sucked in a deep breath and knew the man was serious.

Maria gave a sharp cry and dropped to her knees. "Leo, no, you wouldn't. Let him come to me, please."

"Not a chance." He glanced at his watch and started to back toward the rear entrance.

Jackie turned to Elizabeth. "Where's the cavalry?"

"Surrounding the building. I managed to get a message out. He can't get anywhere without someone spotting him or following him." She glanced at her phone. "There'll be a sniper on one of the buildings, maybe two, but they won't endanger Lewis." She stepped forward, following Leo, who kept glancing over his shoulder, but not dropping his gun. Lewis cried, but didn't fight his father.

Elizabeth motioned to the others. "I'm going to send the others out of the building, Leo, all right?"

Silence.

"Leo?" Maria's voice wobbled. "Leo, think about this. How are you going to get away? The police are everywhere."

Leo didn't answer, just stood by the window. Lewis's head swiveled in the direction of his mother's voice. "Mama! Come get me."

Maria took a step forward and Leo met her gaze. "Don't do it."

The woman fell back and tears dripped down her cheeks.

He glanced once more out the window, then looked back at them. The children and the other adults were almost to the door, ready to slip out to safety. Leo lifted his weapon and pulled the trigger. Screams echoed through the warehouse as the bullet hit the door. The adults pushed the children to the floor and covered them. Jackie dove for Lucy the same time Ian did.

Jackie got there first. She hovered over the child and those next to her as best she could.

Elizabeth's phone rang.

She reached for it and Leo swung the gun on her. "Answer it and you die." Leo stepped away from the window. "It looks like we're surrounded."

"What are you going to do, Leo?"

"If I'm not leaving, then neither is anyone else."

# 36

Ron stood outside the police barricade and rubbed his chin. He waited, nerves tense, ready to burst through and drag Jackie out of the situation. But he couldn't. What he could do was continue to wait. He'd provided David with more information about the terrorist trapped inside with innocent children.

His phone rang. "Please tell me you have something."

"Leonardo Alexander Fox is married to Maria Fox, born Mariya Oksana Bashmakov," David said.

"Russian?"

"Yes. And get this. Her father was Vasily Bashmakov, who worked with an Islamic militant group."

"A terrorist."

"Yes. Fifteen years ago, Homeland Security got intel about a plot that he was instigating. He was closely monitored, and when he ordered a hit against the US ambassador to Moscow, US Special Forces intervened. He must have gotten wind of it just before it was to go down because he was in the process of running. When he realized he was trapped, he killed two of his children. The Special Forces team had no clue what he was going to do until they heard the shots. By the time they got inside, it was too late."

"What? Why would he kill his kids?"

"I'm getting to that part. He held a gun to his head with one hand and the phone to his ear with the other. When our guys entered the house, he had his wife on the phone."

Ron blew out a breath. "I think I can see where this is going."

"He waited for them to enter. Of course when they saw his weapon, they shouted at him in Russian and English to put it down. He told his wife the US monsters were there to kill him, that he loved her very much and would see her on the other side of eternity."

"Let me guess. He pulled the trigger."

"Yes."

"And she believed that US soldiers killed her family."

"Indeed."

Ron shook his head and muttered under his breath. He'd seen a lot in his time, evil stuff he sometimes still dreamed about, but people who could just kill their kids . . . "Anything else?"

"She has a nephew. We got a hit using the facial recognition software. He was the one who shot the vet and Stroebel. The picture was blurry and he was only facing the camera for a nanosecond, but we got it and finally got it cleaned up. It took awhile, but his name came back as Hector Mann."

"What's his real name?"

"Miloslav Bashmakov. He was taken into custody about thirty minutes ago."

Ron shifted his gaze back to the building. "Good. Good. Now just pray for Jackie and the rest of those being held."

"What's the status?"

"It's quiet, but crowded around here. ATF, FBI, the whole alphabet soup of law enforcement. Snipers are on the roof, waiting, trying to get a shot." Tension threaded his shoulders into knots. "What's it looking like for the start of the parade?"

"It's still a go for nine o'clock sharp."

---

Elizabeth's phone rang again.

"Don't answer that phone! Everybody up and in the corner," Leo shouted.

Jackie peeled her body from Lucy and helped the little girl to her feet. She threw herself into her uncle's arms and clung to his neck. "Uncle Ian, I want my mommy."

"I know, sweetheart," he whispered.

Jackie's heart lurched and she patted the little girl's back. Leo waved his weapon in the air.

"You have your gun?" Ian asked.

"No, it was missing when I woke up in the coffin."

"Should have asked Elizabeth for another one."

Jackie grunted. "Elizabeth won't draw hers until she can do so without risk of him pulling the trigger."

"Too many children's lives at stake."

"I can't believe Leo hasn't demanded she turn it over to him. He knows she has it," she murmured. "Why hasn't he asked for it?"

Ian drew in a deep breath and hugged Lucy to him, using her to shield their conversation. He slid down the wall, his eyes on Leo. Jackie did the same, her mind spinning. Ian settled Lucy in between them and she knew it was so she felt protected on both sides. He helped another little girl sit on the other side of him, and Jackie placed her arm around the child who'd sat next to her. Adult. Child. Adult. Child. Scared whimpers rose from around her and she clamped her jaws hard in order to control her tongue. Lashing out at the man wouldn't help the situation.

Something nagged at her. It was something Leo had said. "Did you catch what he said about completing the mission?"

"Shut up!" Leo pointed the weapon in her direction and she clamped her lips together. Sweat dripped into his eyes and he had a frantic energy about him that said he might be close to losing control.

"This wasn't supposed to happen, huh, Leo?" Elizabeth asked from her position on the floor. He swung his attention to the agent. "Let me help you."

He waved the gun at her. "You don't want to help me, you want to stop me."

"Well, yeah, but if I can help you out at the same time, I'm not opposed to the idea."

Her honest answer seemed to stop him for a moment, then he simply shook his head and glanced at his watch.

Elizabeth glanced at her phone. "They're calling."

"Hang up."

"Come on, Leo, you know how this works. If you don't communicate with them, they'll come in."

"You're right, I do know how this works and they won't risk the kids getting hurt. Leave it, I'm not interested in negotiating."

"He did something to the float," Jackie whispered.

"What?" Ian asked.

"What time is it?" She had her arm around Lucy and couldn't see her watch.

He glanced at his. "8:45."

"We don't have long. We have to end this."

"What are you going to do?"

She shot a look at Elizabeth and Leo, who were still going back and forth. What was the woman doing? What was Leo doing? The man was a highly trained ATF agent. There was no way he was going to fall for anything Jackie tried. She wouldn't be able to lure him in front of a window for a sniper shot and he probably knew all of the negotiating tricks. He'd probably even been involved in some hostage negotiations when explosives were involved and listened in. So what was the deal? She went around and around it in her mind. And saw him take another glance at his watch. "He's stalling," she whispered. "He did something to the float and he's stalling."

"You mean he lured us away from it on purpose?"

"Yeah." Elizabeth still had Leo's attention so she kept whispering. "He wants the parade to start on time. He knew where the kids were staying and he led us directly here. All of the attention is now focused on this area about two miles away from the start of the parade. Far enough away, they might not postpone it because of what's going on over here. The parade route is in the opposite direction of where we are so the floats won't be anywhere near here. You still have your cell phone?"

"Yes." He slid it out of his pocket and passed it across to her behind Lucy's back. The little girl snuggled closer to her uncle.

Her eyes on Leo, she wrapped her fingers around the device and pulled it to her. "And that doesn't make sense either. He should have taken our phones, but he didn't do that."

"Then your conclusion could be right. He just wants to stall."

"Will you two shut up before he decides to start shooting?" The woman to her right hissed. Her frightened blue eyes seemed overly large in her very white face. She shot Leo a scared look. "He said to be quiet. Can't you just do that?"

Jackie patted the woman's shoulder. Her ID badge read Mrs. Thompson. "I know you're frightened, but we're going to get out of this, just give us a chance, all right?"

"Are you a cop?"

"Something like that."

That seemed to mollify the woman and she sat back, her eyes closed, lips moving.

Jackie leaned closer to Ian. "The virus is on that float, Ian," she whispered. "I don't know where, but I'm willing to bet that Leo put it on there on the pretense of inspecting for explosives. He was on there a good long time."

"We've got to stop him."

She slid the phone down to the floor next to her thigh. In between her and Lucy. She hit the text message icon, then pretended to look down and rub her eyes. While she massaged her forehead with her right hand, she punched in Ron's number with her left. Then in the message box, she typed,

WE R DISTRACTION VIRUS IS ON TOY FLOAT

"Hey! What are you doing?" Leo's narrowed eyes met hers as he stormed toward her. "Give me that!"

She hit Send. Leo grabbed the phone from her fingers, threw in on the floor, and stomped on it.

Ron's phone vibrated. He raised it to take a look at the text message.

WE R DISTRACTION VIRUS IS ON TOY FLOAT

His heart thudded an extra beat and he looked at the time. 8:53. He spun on his heel and made his way through the crowd that had gathered behind the police blockade. He hit the number he'd put on speed dial early that morning.

"Special Agent in Charge Scott Mitchell."

"I'm at the parade. The virus is on the Manguson Toy float."

"What?"

"Don't let anyone on that float. Stop it now."

"How do you know? Who is this?"

"I'm a friend. Do you want to risk the lives in this city or just cause it a bit of inconvenience? We're running out of time. Get the float out of the lineup and let the rest of the parade go on as planned." He kept his voice calm, his temper in check.

"I have a hostage situation going on right now with twelve children involved."

"It's a distraction. The man who's holding everyone hostage is just waiting for the parade to start. Somehow, when the float starts moving, it's going to release the virus."

Silence. Ron let the clock tick. There was nothing else he could say. Either the man would believe him and act. Or he wouldn't.

"I'll see what I can do."

Ron hung up and dialed David's number. 8:59.

"Is Jackie all right?"

"Not yet. Nothing we can do for her at the moment." He gave David a fifteen-second summary of his conversation with the Special Agent in Charge. "I don't know if he's going to stop it or not."

"Then Adam and I'll have to find a way."

"It's 9:00, David. Hurry."

Ron hung up and looked back at the warehouse. "Come on, Jackie," he whispered. "Do something. Just don't get killed doing it."

---

"We could get killed, you know that right?" Ian whispered.

"We could, but we have skills. It's time to use them."

Ian started to respond, then snapped his lips shut when Leo

turned his attention from his watch to his hostages. "Just a little longer folks, then you can all leave." He gave them a grim smile and focused back on Elizabeth. Ian caught the agent's eye. She looked back at Leo, but Ian thought she might be watching him from the corner of her eye. "You grab Lewis, I'm going to knock his feet out from under him and get the gun," he said to Jackie.

She nodded. He stood slowly, ever so slowly, not wanting any movement to catch the man's eye. Jackie did the same.

Ian looked at the adults who were watching and held a finger to his lips. Some frowned, some shook their heads, eyes pleading for them to sit back down. Ian tensed. The children whispered amongst themselves, but Leo didn't seem to care if they talked. And their whispering covered any slight noises he and Jackie might make. However, if any one of the hostages called out—

Jackie stepped softly. Elizabeth drew in a deep breath and turned her body, keeping Leo's attention on her. Ian knew the parade had already started, he could only pray Ron managed to stop the toy float from being a part of it.

"What is it you're waiting on, Leo? The parade to start? Well, it has. Now what?"

"Just a little longer."

Ian needed Elizabeth's help. He held his hand in the universal shape of a gun and gestured to the right. Leo still held the weapon on his son and he needed it to be aimed at Elizabeth. *Please let her understand*. Then he changed his hand shape and pointed to her, then the floor. Would she get it? Was she even watching?

Elizabeth's facial expression never changed. Not even a twitch or a blink. "I think it's time for me to pull my weapon and call your bluff."

Leo went still. "What?"

Elizabeth's hand crept toward her shoulder holster. Leo swung the gun away from Lewis to aim it at the agent.

Ian exploded into action. He pulled his leg back and kicked straight out, catching Leo in the trunk. He cried out and staggered, but didn't go down. Elizabeth hit the floor.

Jackie snagged Lewis from Leo's left arm even as the man spun around, swinging the weapon with him, aiming at Ian's solar plexus. Center mass. She bent with the child in her arms and gave a backward kick, keeping her body between the gun and the child. The side of her foot caught Leo in the throat, then scraped up and hit him in the chin. Holding Lewis knocked her off balance and she fell, rolling, protecting the boy.

She could hear Leo gagging.

And saw that Ian didn't hesitate. He stepped forward and grabbed Leo's arm with his left hand, turning his body clockwise and pivoting on his left foot. He grabbed Leo's right hand and moved his left foot backward, throwing Leo off balance. The move allowed Ian to shove the gun aside, aiming the weapon up and away from his face. With one last move, he pulled, then twisted Leo's hand. Leo went down with a hard thud on his back, his fingers flexing, leaving Ian in possession of the gun.

Which he pointed at Leo's shocked face.

---

Jackie passed a shaking and whimpering Lewis to his weeping mother. She then spun back to the scene where Elizabeth had drawn her weapon and now held it on the subdued man who was still trying to catch his breath. Jackie grabbed Ian's phone from her pocket. 9:06.

"We're too late," she said.

Leo gasped a pained laugh and said something.

She leaned closer. "What?"

"Yes," she heard. "You are too late. It's done."

The door to the warehouse crashed open. Law enforcement rushed in, rifles held next to their faces, pointing low, ready to raise and fire in a split second.

Elizabeth didn't look up from the man she still held her gun on. "Ian, pass me the weapon."

He did and lifted his hands.

Jackie looked around for Lucy. The adults and children still lined the wall. Several wept and laughed at the same time. But Lucy simply huddled against one of her teachers, her eyes bouncing from Ian to Jackie. When she saw Jackie's attention on her, she pushed away from the teacher and stood. Jackie met her halfway across the floor and picked her up to cuddle her against her. She inhaled her little girl fragrance. "Thank you, God, for keeping Lucy safe."

"For keeping all of us safe," Lucy whispered.

"Amen."

Lucy leaned back and cupped Jackie's face. "I want to see my mom."

Jackie's heart constricted. "Okay, honey, I do too."

But she had to find out about the float.

# 37

Jackie followed Elizabeth and Ian to the car. Elizabeth had ushered them out as fast as she could, flashing her badge and talking police lingo.

As they pushed through, she thought she saw Ron in the crowd and broke away. "Wait for me. I'll be there in just a second," she told them.

"Jackie—"

She ignored Ian's protest and grabbed Ron by the jacket sleeve. He spun to gather her in a quick hug. "I've got to go," she said. "Can you get Holly life-flighted to Mount Sinai where her oncologist is? One of Lucy's teachers is taking her there now and will meet you."

"Consider it done."

She pressed a kiss to his cheek and bolted back to slide into the car. Elizabeth shot her a dark look, but kept her thoughts to herself.

Jackie had encouraged all of the students, parents, and teachers to vacate the city until they got word that it was safe. Elizabeth had echoed her suggestion.

*Please let it be safe.*

"Did they stop the float?" she asked Elizabeth.

The agent's phone rang and Jackie groaned at the interruption. Ian wrapped his arm around her and pulled her close. She lifted her head and kissed him. "You were awesome in there."

He shrugged. "Just did what I needed to do."

"Yes. And you were awesome." The red tinge that rose in his cheeks fascinated her.

"You were pretty spectacular yourself. That kick was amazing."

This time it was her turn to feel the heat in her face. "I just did what I had to do," she muttered.

He laughed, but it was strained. She knew he was thinking the same thing she was. Had they stopped the float or not? Had they found the virus or was there still a danger out there?

Elizabeth looked in the rearview mirror. "Thanks for letting me play chauffeur."

"Sorry," Jackie said.

"Yeah," Ian said. "Sorry."

Elizabeth grunted. "Right. I hear the sincerity in your words."

"The float?" Jackie demanded.

"It never moved. It's still parked where it was when all of this started. It was quite a to-do to get Santa around it, but the parade is on and everything seems to be fine."

"The virus?"

"No word on that yet."

"I wonder how Ron convinced them to keep the float from moving?" she murmured.

Elizabeth smiled into the rearview mirror. "Someone stole the keys right out of the ignition. David has them in case they're needed."

"Yes!" Jackie hissed and pumped a fist in the air.

Ian nodded his approval.

Elizabeth put her light on the dash and moved through the empty street. She headed for the area where they'd left the float around the corner of 77th and Central Park West. The crowds had been ordered away from the area. Elizabeth had to weave through the mess of NYPD vehicles. ATF and FBI bomb techs, the backs of their jackets identifying their branch of law enforcement, littered the area. Jackie even saw a Department of Homeland Security vehicle.

Finally, after flashing her badge an infinite number of times, Elizabeth pulled the vehicle to a stop and grabbed her handi-talkie, a handheld radio referred to as an HT. Jackie popped the door. She stepped into the street, her gaze flicking from one person to the next. David sent her a concerned two-finger salute. She waved back and gave a nod, hoping he understood she meant she was all right. Two hazmat-suited professionals were visible on top of the float. They'd dismantled the large green dragon.

"You shouldn't be here." Scott Mitchell approached with a frown.

"Did you find the virus?"

"We're working on it." He glowered at her. "This better not be some hoax you two have hatched."

Jackie frowned right back at him. "If it was just some elaborate hoax, Ian and I wouldn't have been running for our lives over the past few days."

He grunted and glanced up at the two on the float. "Parker! Anything?"

One of the alien-looking agents stepped to the side of the float. "We've got a positive. It's in the bubbles. Right now it's contained. As long as no one turns on the bubble machine, it looks like we'll be all right, but we need to get a perimeter set up around the whole float to prevent any particles from becoming airborne and then everybody in the vicinity needs on a hazmat su—"

A loud crack sounded, the man gave a sharp cry and went to his knees as a red stain started to spread across the front of his white protective suit.

---

"Shooter! Down!" Ian reached for Jackie at the same moment she grabbed his hand and yanked him to the sidewalk, up the stairs of the New York Historical Society Museum's steps, and under the cover of the building's overhang. The others weren't far behind.

Mitchell was yelling into his HT.

Bullets continued to hit the float. David dove for shelter and something fell from his pocket next to the front of the float. Keys? The other agent in the hazmat suit had dropped off the other side. Ian assumed he was hiding out waiting for the assault to stop. Elizabeth was on her HT too.

"Where did he shoot from?" Ian asked Jackie.

She shook her head. "I don't know. Somewhere from this side of the street."

The gunfire finally stopped. Only to pick back up again. Ian's ears rang.

"He's shooting at the tanks!" he yelled.

Jackie paled. "He's trying to release the virus. We've got to stop him!"

Ian glanced around to see David and several other agents had scattered to find cover. The other agent from the float had climbed back on and now worked to pull his friend away from the open area. For the moment the bullets had stopped.

Mitchell broke away from the cover of the building and raced across the street to his agents. "Is he still alive?" Ian couldn't hear the answer.

Sirens sounded, law enforcement descended once more. His gaze was on the float. "Did any of the bullets hit the bubble tank?"

Jackie drew in a deep breath as she stared too. An ambulance screamed in the distance. And once again, 77th and Central Park West was drop-kicked back into chaos.

But the gunfire wasn't finished. The dinosaur popped and danced under the hail of bullets. Ian glanced at the keys on the ground. "I'm going to move the float. If the bullets hit that tank of bubbles, the virus will be released."

"And if they hit you, you'll be dead!" But her eyes were also on the keys.

With a prayer on his lips, he darted for the keys, ignoring Jackie's harsh yell for him to stop. He snagged them, rolled under the edge of the float, and yanked the driver's door open just wide enough for him to slide into the driver's seat and onto broken glass. The windshield had been blown apart. He prayed he had the right keys. With shaking hands, he found the one he thought would work and shoved it into the ignition.

He turned it and was rewarded with a low growl. He could hear agents yelling at him as more gunfire hit the hood, pinging off the metal. He ducked down into the passenger seat and pressed the gas pedal. The float lurched forward. The bullets stopped. Ian lifted his head and peered through the tiny hole that was supposed to allow the driver just enough space to see, but not enough to ruin the magnificence of the decoration. Of course there were several holes to choose from at the moment, the bullets creating a kaleidoscope pattern. He floored the gas and prayed no one stepped in front of him.

No more bullets rained down. He glanced down to make

sure he wasn't bleeding. Had he really managed to avoid being shot? He'd expected at least one or two bullet holes. Of course when his adrenaline calmed down, he might find one or two.

He opened the door and slid out of the battered float.

The first bullet caught him in the shoulder. He cried out and went down. The second bullet hit the pavement in front of him. He managed to roll under the belly of the flatbed of the float. The fire in his shoulder took his breath away. Booted feet stopped in front of his. The shooter dropped to the ground and dark green eyes met his through the slits in the mask. The gun centered on his forehead.

---

Jackie grabbed the legs of the person who'd shot Ian and yanked. The shooter gave a startled cry and rolled. Lifted the weapon. With a fast kick, Jackie disarmed the man, then balled her fist and struck the mask-covered chin. The person went limp. Jackie kicked the weapon away and stared down, making sure he wasn't planning on moving again. Fiery pain shot through her knuckles, up into her wrist and arm. She didn't care. It was finally over. She leaned over and yanked off the mask.

And gasped.

A gray-haired woman lay unconscious. Jackie blinked as she and the shooter were surrounded by law enforcement once again.

# 38

On the sixth floor of the hospital, Jackie leaned against the wall and fought the desire to simply pass out. Her head pounded and every muscle in her body ached. But she'd been determined to hang on to consciousness until she knew if Ian would be all right.

He had required surgery to remove the bullet and repair the damage to his shoulder. He'd just been rolled in from post-op and had fallen asleep as soon as the nurses left.

But he would live. Relief—and staggering fatigue—combined with the adrenaline crash nearly made her knees buckle, but she couldn't give in yet. She had one more person to check on. She kissed Ian on the cheek and moved toward the door.

On the elevator, she pressed the button for Holly's floor and fought to keep her eyes from closing. The elevator's smooth ride didn't help. The doors opened and she stepped off, moving down the hall to Holly's room. The door was closed.

Jackie rapped her knuckles on the wood.

"Come in."

She pushed the door open and slipped inside. Holly sat on the bed, looking pale and sick and very tired. But at least she was awake. Jackie's adrenaline surged and she felt life return. Lucy sat next to her mother, her fingers wrapped around Holly's. "Hey," Jackie said. She went to her friend and hugged her, then Lucy. The little girl's red eyes said she'd been crying. She sniffed. "My mommy's sick, Jackie."

Jackie bumped noses with Lucy and nodded. "I know."

"She said she might even have to go to heaven."

Jackie swallowed. "Yeah, I know that too."

"But I don't want her to because then I can't go see her."

Jackie's eyes met Holly's. Tears streamed down her friend's face and Jackie cleared her throat to try to loosen the sudden tightness. "Well, not immediately, no, that's true. But you would see her again one day."

"That's what she said."

"Well, that's good, then. Right?" *Oh Lord, help me, I don't know what to say to this child.*

"No. It's not good. It's not good at all." She turned wet eyes back to her mother. "Why do you want to leave me?"

Holly cried out and grabbed Lucy in a fierce hug. "I don't want to leave you. I would stay if I had a choice. I would, I promise."

"Promise pinky swear?"

Holly nodded and hooked her pinky around Lucy's small one. "Promise pinky swear."

"Okay then. I believe you." She looked at Jackie. "Is Uncle Ian okay?"

Jackie swiped tears from her cheeks and sniffed. "Yeah, honey, he's going to be just fine."

"Well, that's a relief."

Holly gave a weak chuckle. "Yes, it's definitely a relief."

Her gaze met Jackie's. "Thank you."

"For what?"

"For everything you've done." She drew in a shaky breath. "And everything you're going to do."

Jackie could only nod. *Oh God, this hurts.*

"He'll be there for you," Holly whispered, then closed her eyes and sighed. "I think I need a little nap."

Lucy snuggled down beside Holly. "I'll take one too."

Jackie kissed both of them on the forehead, then stepped out of the room to find the bathroom. Once inside, she gave in to the pain. A sharp cry escaped her lips and she slid to the floor, arms wrapped around her knees. She sobbed until her jeans were soaked, then drew in a deep breath, washed her face, and vowed to be strong. She would be strong for Holly and Lucy. And she knew now where her strength was going to come from. "Okay, God, I'm trusting you to be there for me," she whispered. "I will get through this only by leaning on you, I get it. Now help me live it."

---

Ian woke to find Ron, David, Adam, and Jackie sitting in his room. His parents and brother had left two hours ago when the pain meds had taken him back under. He blinked and sat up. Jackie handed him the plastic cup of ice water and he drank deeply. With a sigh, he put the cup on the tray and eyed his visitors. "Please tell me I didn't drool."

Jackie smirked, but Ian saw shadows in her eyes. "How's Holly?"

"Hanging in there. She's going to do chemo and radiation and whatever else it takes to fight for as much time with Lucy as possible."

Ian swallowed and nodded. "Where's Lucy?"

"With Holly. I think she's afraid to leave her."

"Oh boy."

"Yeah."

Ron cleared his throat. "We were just discussing the latest. You want to hear it?"

"Sure."

"For the record, when you leave here, you better don disguises again. The media is camped out all over this hospital."

"Great." Ian rolled his eyes and took another sip of the water.

"The woman who shot you was Maria's mother, Polina Bashmakov," Ron said. "Wife to Vasily Bashmakov. She's in custody—with a broken jaw—" He shot a look of pride at Jackie, then continued. "But it didn't stop her from vigorously writing out her story. In detail. Apparently, she vowed revenge for her husband's and children's deaths fifteen years ago. She hates Americans. All Americans."

"She must have been planning this for years."

David nodded. "She had the connections because of her husband. All she had to do was make a few phone calls, present her idea. One of the top terrorist groups with ties to al-Qaida funded it. Millions of dollars were on the line yesterday. If the virus wasn't released, there was no money transferred."

"Which was why she was so determined to shoot up the float when she realized her son-in-law, Leo, had failed," Adam said. "She had to get that virus released into the air or she was one very poor dead woman."

"Thank God she failed," Jackie said.

"But to risk her daughter and grandson . . ." Adam shook his head.

"She had them vaccinated the minute the call went out. She had the plan so detailed, we found that she actually arranged for her daughter's marriage to the ATF agent Leo. Apparently the man was in love with Maria, and Polina pushed that relationship. She even proudly explained how she hired Leo without him knowing she was the mastermind behind the plan. She knew the lure of the money would be too much for him to resist."

Jackie shook her head. She just couldn't fathom it.

Adam leaned forward. "We showed her the video of what really happened with that mission. Her husband had already killed his two children by the time the team breached the inside, but they got him pulling the trigger on himself."

"What did she say?"

"Nothing. She just wiped tears from her face, but her expression never changed."

"So it's over?" Ian asked.

"Yes."

"The feds even picked up Wainwright before he could get on the plane to some private island he has in the Caribbean," Ron said. "More feds raided the homes of all the people involved in that email—which the FBI's computer forensics expert managed to pull off of Wainwright's tablet. The remaining smallpox virus has been returned to the CDC, and your names have been completely cleared and you two are being hailed as heroes."

"So it's over," he whispered. Jackie walked over and gripped his hand. "It's over."

"And Gus is complaining about your neglect," Ron said. "He's ready for you to get home and for things to get back to normal."

Ian was quiet for a moment. "I guess this means I'm unemployed." He glanced at Jackie. "How do you feel about being the breadwinner?"

She flushed and Ron coughed. David and Adam laughed as they backed toward the door.

"We'll just leave you two alone," David said. "He might want you to kiss his boo-boo."

Jackie picked up one of Ian's shoes and threw it at David's departing back. It bounced off the door. Adam picked it up and turned, mouth opened. Jackie held up the other shoe and lifted a brow. Adam shut his mouth, dropped the shoe he held, and slipped out the door.

Ron snickered. "I'll just keep my comments to myself too."

"Wise choice," Jackie muttered.

But that didn't stop him from laughing all the way out the door.

When everyone had left, Ian looked at Jackie.

She crossed her arms and narrowed her eyes. "The bread-winner?"

He flushed. "Sorry, it just came out. Don't throw any shoes at me, please, I'm wounded."

She tried to hold back the giggle but failed. A guffaw slipped out. Then they both laughed until tears ran down her cheeks. "How did they guess?"

"My love-struck expression probably gave me away," he whispered.

She leaned closer. "Love-struck?"

"Mmhm, yes. I've loved you forever, Jackie." He swallowed, his eyes unveiled, holding nothing back from her. "I know you might need some time, but—"

She sighed, then leaned over and kissed him, leaving no doubt in his mind that she didn't need a bit of time. Elation filled him and he wrapped his good arm around her. When she pulled back, he kissed her nose. "So does that mean you love me and you'll support me until I get a job?"

She gave a small laugh and straightened. "Yes, I love you, Ian. I love you very much. I always have, and even though I moved on and married someone I cared about very much, I never forgot about you. My first love."

"But?"

"But I need to tell you something. Something that might change the way you feel about me." Jackie pulled at the hem of her shirt and glanced around the room. Her eyes landed on the door, but leaving wasn't an option.

"Lucy's yours, isn't she?"

---

Jackie gasped and felt the blood drain from her face. She swallowed hard. "How did you know?"

"I simply took a second look. She has all of your features. The only thing different is her hair color."

Jackie covered her mouth with her hand and walked to the window. "She got that from her father."

"But her eyes, her nose, her bow-shaped mouth. All of that is you. Even some of her expressions are yours."

Jackie nodded. "Yes."

"Why did you give her to Holly?"

Jackie blew out a long sigh. "I was in such a low place back then, Ian. I had lost my husband and blamed myself for his death. If I had just kept quiet about my stupid ice cream craving, he wouldn't have been killed. It was just too simple. I mean, he wasn't on duty or anything, it was just some random *stupid, stupid* thing. I couldn't focus, couldn't function. Couldn't do anything but grieve. After my husband's funeral, I went to stay with my uncle Ron."

"Uncle?"

She smiled. "Yeah. I guess I haven't told you that, huh?"

"No, that's one fact you left out. No wonder he was so intent on helping us."

"Yes, that was one reason." She shrugged. "He made some pretty heavy-duty enemies during his years in the service with Special Ops that we keep our relationship secret. Just in case."

Ian shook his head and shifted on the bed. She could almost see his brain processing everything. "When did Holly come into the picture?"

"When I was about seven months pregnant, I made the decision to give the baby up for adoption. I just couldn't pull myself out of my depression. God didn't seem to care about me and I just saw no hope for my future. I didn't want my baby growing up in that kind of atmosphere," she whispered as a tear rolled down her cheek. She sniffed and brushed it away. She cleared her throat. "So, I called Holly and told her I wanted her to take the baby. At first she tried to talk me out of it, but I was adamant. She flew down to see me, and when she couldn't change my mind, she cried and said she and Brant would take her. We did it all legally, of course."

"Of course," he murmured.

"And she sent me pictures and videos of Lucy, posting them on Facebook and sending by email." She drew in a shuddering breath. "I've watched her grow up. I know it's not the same thing as being there and being her mom, but it was the next best thing."

"Did you ever regret it?"

"Second-guess myself? Yes. Regret that Holly and her husband loved my child like she was their own? No. Never. They gave her much more than I ever could have."

He pulled her down beside him. "Will you give me a chance, Jackie? I know it's fast, I know it's been crazy, and we probably need some time to decompress and get to know each other without worrying about looking over our shoulders because someone is trying to kill us, but I don't want to let you go again."

"I'll give you a chance, Ian, if you don't mind putting up with my crazy hours and all the traveling I do for my job."

"I'll put up with it. I may even go with you when I can." He kissed her again.

She smiled and stroked his cheek. "You did a fabulous job taking down some Russian terrorists. We may recruit you to work for Operation Refuge."

He grimaced and leaned back against the pillow. "I'll pass, thanks. I'm going to find me a nice, safe lab job and discover a cure for cancer."

"Or a vaccine for malaria."

"Or that."

"I love you, Ian."

She watched tears gather in his eyes and it was a few seconds before he could speak. He cleared his throat. "I love you too, Jackie."

She wrapped her arms around his neck and lay her head on his good shoulder. "Let's build a future together."

He kissed the top of her head and gave a contented sigh. "Yeah. Let's do that."

# 39

*SIX MONTHS LATER*
*SOUTH CAROLINA*
*SPRINGWOOD CEMETERY*

**Holly Marie Jacobson Kent**
*Beloved wife to Brant and loving mother to Lucy*
Gone too soon at thirty-two years of age.
–John 3:16–
"For God so loved the world
that he gave his one and only Son,
that whoever believes in him shall not perish
but have eternal life."

Jackie swiped a tear and sniffed. "I'm amazed she hung on this long."

Ian wrapped an arm around her shoulders and Lucy clung to her left hand. "She was finally ready and she wasn't afraid."

"I know. That's why I can have peace about it." She hugged Lucy to her side.

"You love me, don't you, Jackie?"

Jackie looked down at Lucy, a little startled by the question. "Of course I do. I love you more than anything. I tell you that every day, don't I?"

"Yes." Lucy looked up and squinted against the bright summer sun. "So why does God take away the people I love and who love me back?" she whispered. "Is he going to take you and Uncle Ian away from me too?"

Jackie dropped to her knees, her tears almost out of control once more. "God didn't take her away, honey. It was just her time to go. I don't really know why you had to lose both your dad and your mom at such a young age, but God loves you more than anything—even more than your uncle Ian and I do, even though I don't understand how that's possible."

Lucy shook her head. "I don't understand."

Jackie sighed. "I know. I used to blame God for letting my husband get killed, but that wasn't his fault either. It was the fault of the person who pulled the trigger."

"But no one killed my mom, so whose fault is it that she died?"

Goodness, this child thought a lot. Every day, Jackie saw more and more of herself in her daughter. It thrilled and scared her all at the same time. She was so scared she wouldn't have the right answers. Could she tell Lucy she just didn't know about some things and still have the child trust her?

She looked at Ian for help. He squatted next to them. "Lucy, Holly was a spectacular mom. She loved you and she loved God, which means we'll all see her again someday. And while sometimes God allows bad things to happen, it doesn't mean he doesn't love us."

"Then what does it mean?"

"I think it means he wants us to learn from those things and trust that he loves us enough to take care of us even when bad things happen."

"Then why doesn't he just make the bad things not happen?"

Ian cleared his throat and met Jackie's eyes. She shrugged and bit her lip. How did one explain free will, the fall of man, and the introduction of sin to a six-year-old in terms she would understand? Studying Lucy's inquisitive eyes, she knew she had to try. "You know the story of Adam and Eve from the Bible?"

"Of course. Mommy told it to me."

"And you know what sin is?"

"Uh huh. It's when you do something wrong and make God sad."

Sin makes God sad. Yes, it sure did. "Well, when Adam and Eve chose to sin, all kinds of bad stuff entered the world, including the disease that your mom died from. And as awful as that is, maybe we can look for God and still find him, find something good that's happening around us. Good that God allows in our lives in spite of the bad that sometimes happens."

Lucy fell silent and looked away from them. Jackie wondered what the little girl was thinking now. After several moments, she looked from the headstone to Jackie then to her uncle. "I know something good that he let happen."

"What?" Jackie asked.

A small smile played across Lucy's lips. "He let me have people who still love me more than anything and will take care of me. My mom and dad might not be able to be here, but God let me stay with you."

Jackie didn't bother to stop the tears. One day they'd tell Lucy the truth of her birth, but not now, not when the pain of losing Holly was still fresh. She heard Ian sniff and blow out a long breath. Jackie pulled Lucy into a hug and felt Ian wrap his strong arms around both of them. Together, they stayed there, buffeted by a gentle breeze. Then Lucy laughed.

Jackie pulled back. "What's so funny?"

"Mommy told me that when I felt the wind in my face, that was her way of giving me kisses from heaven. I think she just kissed me."

Ian hoisted the little girl onto his shoulders. Thankfully, his wounded one had healed up with no residual damage. "I think we need some ice cream. What do you two ladies think?"

"I think that's an excellent idea," Lucy said and patted his head. "Are you having ice cream at your reception?"

Ian's eyes met Jackie's and she grinned. "If you want ice cream there, we'll have ice cream."

Lucy threw her head back and giggled. "I want ice cream there. Lots and lots of ice cream with sprinkles and marshmallows and M&Ms and . . ."

Jackie sighed as Ian held on to Lucy's knee with one hand and slid an arm across Jackie's shoulders. She leaned into Ian as they strolled back to the car. *Thank you, God, for the blessings in my life. I would have worked things out a little differently with Holly, but I'm trying to accept that you know best. Tell her I said hi, please, and that she's missed.*

Ian helped Lucy into her booster seat and buckled the belt around her. Jackie opened the door on the passenger side and slid into the seat. She buckled up and waited for Ian to do the same. While he worked, she studied him.

He looked up and caught her watching. "What?"

"You're a good man, Ian Lockwood. I'm blessed."

He reached over and took her hand in his. "No, I'm the one who's blessed."

"No, really. I am."

"Are you going to start that *again*?" Lucy asked, exasperation ringing through her question. "We're *all* blessed. Now can we go get that ice cream, puleeze?"

Laughter ruptured from Jackie, and Ian leaned over to kiss her. She returned his kiss, then reached back to tickle Lucy's ribs. The child squealed with laughter, and as Ian drove away from the cemetery, Jackie decided Lucy's laughter was the sweetest sound God ever invented. And she was quite sure that somehow, some way, God let Holly hear it too.

# ACKNOWLEDGMENTS

A special thanks to Drucilla Wells and Wayne Smith, retired FBI agents. Thank you so much for the hours you spent reading and "fixing." I appreciate you two very much and wouldn't feel nearly as good about the story as I do if I didn't have your input. Thank you for your service to law enforcement. Thank you for all you've done to make the world a safer place, one day at a day, one criminal at a time.

Thank you, DiAnn Mills, my friend and critique partner extraordinaire. I cherish our friendship and consider myself blessed to have you in my life. Love you, friend!

To the Ironmancers: Ronie Kendig, Becky Wade, Susan May Warren, Rachel Hauck, Dani Pettrey, and Katie Ganshert. Thank you for your prayers, your encouragement, your tweets, your Facebook posts, but most of all, your friendship. I love you all!

To Lynn Blackburn, thank you for loaning me your equally devious mind to brainstorm and plot a lot of this story. I dedicate the bubble float to you! LOL. I've enjoyed getting to know you and thank God for our friendship. I also look forward to watching your writing career soar!

Thanks to my awesome editor, Andrea Doering; my fearless agent, Tamela Hancock Murray of the Steve Laube agency; copy editor extraordinaire, Barb Barnes; my amazing marketing manager, Michele Misiak; and Claudia Marsh, my fabulous publicist. These are only a few of the people I need to thank. The entire Revell team is amazing and I appreciate you all!

**Lynette Eason** is the award-winning, bestselling author of several romantic suspense series, including Women of Justice and Deadly Reunions. She is a member of American Christian Fiction Writers and Romance Writers of America. Lynette graduated from the University of South Carolina and went on to earn her master's degree in education from Converse College. She lives in South Carolina with her husband and two children.